Lion Fangs

Lewis Frobisher Tales, Book I

C.A. Fitzroy

Copyright © 2021 C.A. Fitzroy

Evenwood Press

All rights reserved.

Cover illustrations by Rafido.

'Lion Fangs' is a work of fiction. All incidents and dialogue, and all characters with the exception of some well-known historical figures, are products of the author's imagination and are not to be construed as real. Where real-life historical figures appear, the situations, incidents and dialogues concerning those persons are entirely fictional and are not intended to depict actual events or to change the entirely fictional nature of the work. In all other respects, any resemblance to actual persons, living or dead, events or locales is entirely coincidental. Historical research has been used to provide the overall context for the setting, while the narrative is the product of the author's own imagination.

For my family and their never-ending patience.

C.A. Fitzroy, 2021.

Prologue

Praça do Rossio, Lisbon, 1720 AD

Outside the small window of his dormitory cell the frost stuck to the masonry and signage of the various storefronts in the market yet again.

Being told to bundle up at dawn in order to pick up some highly sought-after supplies was not an ideal start to the morning. Unfortunately, by the time Lisbon's bells started to ring out in calls for Terce it would become difficult to track down some of the more exotic goods.

He had served the hospital faithfully for over three years without any major complaint, but this recent expectation that his patient receive specific wares from the market was becoming an issue. It would normally not have caused the monk any real concern—indeed, he tended to rise early without any encouragement from the abbot—but the daily task also happened to coincide with the coldest winter anyone could remember in living memory.

November was always a time of persistent rain in the Portuguese capital and to be expected. Bitter cold draughts of wind though, along with the veil of ice draped across the city's stonework which caused one to slip, were more difficult to endure.

Baltasar das Chagas, lay-brother of *Santa Casa da Misericórdia* and former shepherd of many years, resigned himself to the unfortunate circumstances and ducked out of the archway into the open plaza.

Within seconds the howling wind purged any

remaining sleep from his eyes and he awoke in full to the day ahead.

Immediately, he began to weigh the coin purse at his side and to consider the list of items the Englishman had given him the night before. Normally any beggars or urchins being cared for in the various quarters of the hospital would receive whatever daily fare was provided for them, and that was the end of it. Baltasar was not used to fetching expensive produce, spices nor any number of other special requests for a guest of the *Hospital Real de Todos-os-Santos*, let alone when prices tended to be more than double the usual rate given the current weather and time of year.

Eggs, coarse bread and honey were some of the usual staples and easy enough to come by. Saffron from the fields around Basel in the lands of the Swiss, or oil paints made from lapis lazuli imported directly from Venice were another matter entirely. There was a reason why Affonso Carneiro, the brother responsible for the wing Baltasar helped with since joining the brotherhood, had readily agreed to permit such unusual requests from the newly arrived guest: The *Inglês* was without question a man of significant wealth.

Despite being utterly mad, or perhaps merely rattled from his life-threatening experience, there could be no denying the man's status. So numbed by the cold and lost in thought was Baltasar that he didn't even realise he had crossed the *Praça do Rossio*, and was being hastened over to the shop's entryway by its owner. The glowing light promised warmth, and Baltasar quickened his step to cover the remaining distance of the large, snow-covered plaza.

'Irmão, come along quickly,' ushered the shopkeep with

a degree of urgency in his voice. 'You will catch your death outdoors in such weather, and wearing such modest attire. We really must get you to try on one of the newly arrived velvet basques, my friend. A nice pair of leather boots from *Toscana* would serve you better in such cold as well.'

'Good morning to you, Symao,' quipped a shivering Baltasar in response. 'I can tell you've started early with your usual attempts to dispose of these trinkets on some gullible soul.'

'Oh you wound me Baltasar,' chuckled the rotund middle-aged man, adorned in his usual outfit consisting of embroidered fabrics in at least three to four different colours. Today Symao was adorned in no less than five, and looked even more like a gaudy merchant than usual.

'You know all too well I sell only the finest provisions and articles to both the hospital and the *Palácio dos Estaus*. What have you brought me this morning then, hmmm?'

Symao rubbed his hands together in anticipation of seeing which foreign bauble or bit of cloth would be offered for barter this time.

'Well, that all depends on how many of the items you can manage from this list,' replied Baltasar as he handed over the piece of bandaging which the patient had used to quickly scribble down his desired goods.

Symao's eyes quickly scanned the list at first but then gradually slowed. Baltasar knew he was trying to decipher the last few requests, which had come out as little more than chicken scratches upon the linen wrap, before Louis had once again fallen into a deep slumber.

That was the Englishman's name insofar as the hospital could tell, although he said it with a strange drawl and had not revealed a surname of any kind. The man spoke Portuguese quite well, and as a result Baltasar was able to communicate with him.

However, Louis' manner of speaking was peculiar. It was almost as if the man had learned the language second-hand through an uneducated tutor, and one from *Brasil* rather than Portugal for that matter. Still, it allowed for them to discuss basic needs and to converse with one another.

Baltasar was not one to judge folk for their coarse language or lack of refinement either, having spent the majority of his life in the countryside. He remembered quite clearly the looks of derision and occasional barb thrown in his direction when he first moved to the capital.

'The only thing I don't have here currently is the gooseberry medicine from Macao, but I remember my friend Camillo from Génova saying he expected a shipment in sometime over the next few months,' said Symao as he gestured with the bandage to the copper bin next to his desk.

The shopkeep tossed it away then he continued, 'the foodstuffs, paints and luxuries he is after won't be cheap. The blue pigment itself is worth…'

Baltasar placed the finely stitched silk shirt down upon the desk. It was of the softest cream hue with what appeared to be gold lace at the cuffs and collars, and the neckline also sported numerous expensive-looking decorations hewn from what looked to be large, cut gems. He was no expert on fashion nor the latest trends at court, but even Baltasar could tell the shirt was the type of thing only royalty or the wealthiest lords might wear, and even then only when ceremony demanded it.

The trader's eyes practically bulged out of his head, and this was a man who was accustomed to trading in the finer luxuries of Lisbon. For all of his affected wealth and tendency to the extravagant, the shopkeep had not been idly boasting.

Symao de Briho was indeed one of the most reputable merchants in the entire city and member of the *Conselho da Fazenda,* or royal finance council, and could be trusted to find any manner of wares. If it was for sale in Portugal, this man knew where to find it along with the item's exact price.

'I forgot to mention, he also wants a ship of some kind constructed and to be seaworthy by the spring,' mused Baltasar with a wry smile on his face.

'I can certainly contact my colleagues in Belém and see what they think about the latest ship designs,' replied Symao.

'The vessel need not be overly-expensive, but I think a galleon would be reasonable considering the value of trade,' said the lay-brother while preparing to leave the shop.

It was unlike his friend to forgo a quibble over the authenticity of fine metals or fabrics. Baltasar had known him to often bite into gold coins or examine needlework closely prior to shaking on a trade.

Nonetheless, this time Symao simply nodded as if in a daze.

'I'll have young Martim gather the items and bring them along to your chamber this afternoon,' said the beaming shop owner.

'That would be a great help. My thanks, as always. Hopefully this will keep Louis satisfied for at least a few days,' replied Baltasar as he shook the man's hand and turned to leave.

The former shepherd couldn't help but laugh and shake his head, as he pulled up his hood to venture across the wide square yet again. Just before closing the door behind him, a voice shouted from behind the entrance to the shop:

'Tell that invalid he will be paying for any rigging or cannon out of his own purse.'

※

As Baltasar emerged into the area of Lisbon commonly referred to as the *Rossio* he took a moment to adjust his hood and look out over the various storefronts. The detailed stonework and intricate carving which constituted the entry into the *Palácio dos Estaus* never failed to make him pause for a moment. Despite being home to the Inquisition for almost two centuries, the architecture was somehow both elegant, delicate and powerful at the same time. The buildings of Lisbon radiated majesty and prosperity, and the winter storms blanketed them in a calming layer of frost.

Baltasar was no longer a young man as his sixtieth year approached, but he still had enough vigour to withstand a few strong gusts of wind. Thoughts of his youth spent in the hillside made the man smile in fond remembrance. His superior Affonso had been quite sure Baltasar must have been raised in the middle of nowhere due to his gawking upon first arriving into the city.

To be fair, that wasn't far from the truth.

It wasn't that he had never been to towns before, as the former-shepherd had often taken wool for sale to a number of larger settlements throughout Estremadura, but nothing quite compared to the scale of the capital.

Suddenly, a faint light became visible from across the plaza, flickering from a window above the colonnades and main gate leading into the *Hospital Real de Todos-os-*

Santos.

He finished preparing for the quick jaunt across the square, now that it was likely Louis had stirred from his fitful sleep. Either that, or one of the brothers was checking the dormitory and the comfort of its current residents due to the unusually cold weather. With a sigh, Baltasar das Chagas, brother and attendant to the unfortunate of Lisbon, began a brisk walk while keeping his head tucked into his chest.

'Where's my damned shirt, you useless little shit?'

Baltasar heard the cup smash against the wall to the cell before he even managed to finish climbing the small spiral staircase. He quickened his step in order to try and diffuse whatever nonsense was taking place in the small dorm.

'Queen Maria Francisca gave me that shirt nigh on sixty years ago when I was still a young man,' growled Louis towards a clearly uncomfortable young attendant by the name of Gaspar.

'That truly is an incredible honour and achievement, to have been granted such an exquisite gift by *Dona* Maria,' Baltasar piped up as he strode into the room.

'It was reward for my having safely escorted her majesty from the family home in Paris all the way here in order to be wed. I remember at one point having to shield her with my own body, as I fought off no less than twenty Basque bandits with my own bare hands,' Louis practically yelled, while shaking both hands out in front of him. 'Your fellow brother here has some quick and nimble fingers, I think. Now where is that shirt?'

Baltasar caught Gaspar glancing over at him with shoulders shrugged and a puzzled expression.

'Oh, you misunderstand me, *Launcelot,*' quipped

Baltasar with an amused twist at the edges of his mouth. 'I meant to say that there is no chance you are a day over forty, so for the queen to have bestowed such a gift on you two decades prior to your birth seems rather, how shall I put this… odd?'

'I told him I have no idea what he's on about,' Gaspar said in his usual painful-sounding voice.

The lad was on the cusp of manhood, and already his voice was beginning to break. Between his thin hair, unimpressive build and deep scars resulting from a childhood bout of red plague, Gaspar had enough to occupy his thoughts without this madness. Baltasar ushered him out of the room and began to wet a linen cloth to place over the Englishman's forehead.

'Did I tell you about the time old Sam Bellamy and myself fought off an entire Barbary squadron near Tripoli? The two of us, drunk on *Moselman* blood, kept the wolves at bay for days while the fleet regrouped,' Louis yawned as he stretched out his back in the small cot. 'Well, on that and the rum of our good Queen Anne as well. They say the leader of the corsairs was a relative of that Murat Reis who raided Ireland when my Da' was still on the seas.'

'I see you're more in the mood for tall tales than hearing about your list,' Baltasar replied while gently placing the cloth to the man's head and settling him back to rest. 'Louis, you were the one who sent me over to Symao at the crack of dawn with that shirt, in case you have forgotten. You were quite clear on the point and told me it was of no consequence. The look on the merchant's face told a different story though, he seemed to think it an item of very great value.'

'I've told you before, I'm not some bloody Frenchman prancing about in a powder top and painted up like a harlot,' Louis muttered as he ceased to resist the gentle compress.

'Yes, I know, but I can never seem to wrap my tongue around it properly,' Baltasar said gently as he finished folding the fabric and lowered himself into a stool at the side of the bed. '*Lyu-wees* is about as close as I seem to get.'

'That was a better one,' the wiry foreigner chuckled.

'Well, I know how it feels to constantly hear one's name spoken incorrectly,' retorted Baltasar.

'One of Symao's staff from Sicily called me *Bartolomeo* for about the first year after I moved here. Thankfully, he is away trading in Constantinople until next summer, so I am at peace for the time being.'

'It's spelled L-e-w-i-s back home, if that's any help,' said the thin and leathery-faced sailor, for there could be no doubt this was a man who had spent many a year at sea.

From the weather-beaten and cracked fingers, to the countless scars across the man's back, *Lewis* had the telltale look of someone who had lived through difficult times aboard ship. Baltasar had not known much of sailors before moving into the capital after his land and flocks were seized, but enough trips for provisions down to the docks had quickly opened his eyes.

Lewis had an easy smile, but there was a fire behind his eyes that promised danger as well.

If the Englishman had been slightly shorter and not quite so light of feature he would easily have been taken for a crew member returning from *Brasil*. This was what perplexed Baltasar since the man's arrival: Lewis showed all the typical manners of a lower crew member aboard a trade cog or galleon, but his expensive clothing and overall confidence suggested something altogether different and more menacing.

More sure of his own status and power, that was how Baltasar thought of it. The Englishman was quick to rage, but equally quick to laugh, and he had yet to show Baltasar any real hostility, other than an obvious bit of light-hearted mockery on occasion.

'Actually, that may help indeed. My letters are not exactly worthy of His Holiness, but brother Diogo was assigned as my tutor when I first entered service to the hospital. I will try to bear it in mind, now do you want to hear about your list or not?'

'Yes, yes of course,' cackled Lewis as he folded his hands across his stomach. 'Just be thankful I refuse to go by my mother's preferred way of saying my name. I thought that a fine enough trade in return for your tender care since those two louts dragged me up from the shore. Did you manage to procure everything as I requested? Your superior assured me there would be no problems considering my display of generosity yesterday.'

Baltasar recounted his discussion with Symao de Briho and said, 'the other matter you mentioned is also being looked into. He seemed to think an older galleon might serve, although he was adamant that you pay for any lines or sailcloth yourself.'

Lewis waved away the latter point as if it was no reason for concern. Suddenly, a cold and piercing look came over his face. He sat up slightly and turned to look Baltasar directly in the eye.

'Do I look like a fool to you?'

'I... no, you look like a man who has been through a very rough spell, and someone who could use God's mercy until you are recovered.'

'No, no, not that…' said Lewis tersely, 'I mean, do you think me mad, my friend? You of all people should be able to tell, having spent the most time with me since I washed up here.'

Baltasar looked at the man and carefully weighed his response.

'Well, you did tell me last night about how you once stole a sea nymph from Neptune and have her stored away in a cave outside of…where was it?'

'Up in St. Kilda,' Lewis replied, 'and so what?'

'Well, wouldn't you say that's a bit of a peculiar tale? Some would likely call it mad.'

Lewis visibly relaxed and grinned practically from ear-to-ear.

'Good. If it has been enough to convince you of my madness, then I am sure the likes of Gaspar have no doubt. I can assure you Baltasar, I am in my right mind. You have been a good friend to me these last few weeks, and it will not be forgotten.'

'Well, as much as running your errands every morning has become tedious, I do enjoy listening to your ramblings,' Baltasar replied, as he quickly poked his head out into the corridor to make sure no one was eavesdropping.

There had been a young lad by the name of Bruno being cared for in the cell across from the Englishman's; the boy had been skin and bones resulting from severe malnourishment, but Baltasar had not seen him since *Vespers* the night before last.

Lewis fidgeted on the bed so that his leg hung free off its side. The man could never seem to stay still for very long, and he would often scratch at the cot's frame or on the window sill.

'At any rate, I'd wager we have a bit of time before

your friends get in touch concerning our arrangement,' he sighed. 'Have I ever told you about the time I single-handedly defeated a French ship of the line? My fists were raw to the bone by the time I was finished.'

Baltasar rolled his eyes and poured himself a cup of wine from the flagon which was sitting on the bedside table.

'No, I can't say I've heard this one.'

'Well, maybe it didn't happen exactly like that, but we've got some time to pass so let me tell you. If any of the other brothers happen by you can just tell them you are attending to my needs,' Lewis grinned.

'Fair enough, it beats being out in that miserable weather,' replied Baltasar with a nod to the frost-covered window pane.

'Alright, but before I begin you really should be thanking me,' Lewis said.

'For the blessing of your esteemed company on such a cold evening?'

'No, for not demanding that you use the name my mother gave me,' Lewis chuckled.

The Portuguese brother of the Holy House of Misery raised an eyebrow.

'It's *Llewellyn*.'

Baltasar opened his mouth as if to speak, but after a moment's hesitation he decided to close it.

Even attempting to sound out the name would have felt embarrassing. Instead, he bowed deeply in a gesture of gratitude. Lewis, caught off guard by his friend's overly-dramatic gesture, slapped a hand against his knee and laughed.

'You're welcome. English father and a Welsh mother, you see. I imagine we have a few days before a half-decent crew can be assembled as well, even if your Symao comes through with the ship. That gives us plenty of time to drink and exchange tales of our youth.'

'Most likely only a few hours, as you forget one important thing,' Baltasar said with a grin. 'This is *Lisboa*, my friend. If I threw this cup out of the window I would probably hit a sailor on the head.'

He made as if to toss the cup out of the small dormitory window for added effect.

'Between Symao's connections and your generous offer of coin, you will likely have your crew turned out before the call to *Nones*.'

'Fair enough,' Lewis replied. 'Where shall I begin then?'

Baltasar gave the Englishman an exasperated sigh, then stood up and walked over to the cell's small entrance.

'Hold that thought, I'll be back in a moment.'

After about a minute passed Baltasar returned with an expensive-looking glass bottle.

'I'd been saving this, but now's as good a time as any,' he said. 'A friend gifted me this last year after I helped treat his burns from a fire at his tannery. It's Venetian glass, but what's inside is far more valuable.'

Following a slight struggle to open the bottle without breaking it, the Portuguese elder poured a dark liquid into their goblets.

'I hope you like good *vinho do Porto*.'

Lewis smiled and offered his cup.

After both men had sampled the sweet drink they returned to their relaxed positions. Baltasar leaned forward, and in a quiet, almost conspiratorial tone, he began to speak:

'I've heard all your tales of dragons or fleets of

Berbers. How about we start at the beginning?'

Chapter 1

Southwark, London, 1678 AD

My arse was on fire.

This was by far the worst thrashing I had received since being deposited at the workhouse several years earlier. I will admit the beating had been well-deserved, although at the time all I could do was run all the way to the Thames to avoid the other orphans seeing the tears well up in my eyes.

That would have ended with even more problems, particularly if that brute Will was involved.

It turns out refusing a chance to interview for an apprenticeship does not sit well with the men responsible for your care. Telling the alderman in charge of governing our employment 'I don't want to be a fucking apothecary's boy' to his face definitely didn't do me any favours.

I stopped to catch my breath by the rubble of the old Globe Theatre and looked out across the river lost in thought, trying to take my mind off the pulsing pain in my backside. These days there was not much rubble left, as lofts and new structures had gradually been built over its charred remains in the decades following its closure. I'd never been to any of the shows since it was torn down before I was born, not that Cripplegate and its staff would ever have taken us anyway.

Prayer, daily coarse bread and shelter for the nights were about as far as charity extended. The rest of

London may have been in a festive mood, with the recent war against the Dutch concluded in England's favour and King Charles gaining lands in the New World, but the men I answered to were of old puritan stock who had managed to avoid the purges a decade ago following the collapse of the Commonwealth.

Charles the Second, by the Grace of God, King of England, Scotland, France and Ireland, Defender of the Faith and so on, was by most accounts a fun-loving ruler with a sense of humour, even if my stone-faced carers felt differently. As far as they were concerned, the king was emptying England's coffers and more concerned with the latest fashions than the good of the people.

Still, as I gingerly sat down on the bank of the Thames I couldn't help but feel melancholy about my lot in life. The country was recovering from the plague which had carried off my father almost ten years ago, and London was in the process of being rebuilt following the Great Fire which swept the city shortly thereafter.

It was during the fire that I was rendered an orphan; my mother was caught underneath a collapsed roof whilst out visiting her friend Marjorie who worked in the Royal Exchange. So, while the rest of the city reveled along with its 'Merry Monarch' as Charles was affectionately titled, I just felt a profound sense of grief over the loss of my past life.

Here I was, a boy of fourteen without a farthing to his name and belt-lashes across his back from years of strict discipline. I picked up a shard of what must have been pottery at some point and tossed it into the rushing water.

Don't worry lad, someday we'll travel to see my suppliers in

Venice or Genoa, and after that we can visit the West Indies to see where your grandfather defeated the Papists.

I grimaced as the words from my father's letter echoed in my mind. His name had been Richard Frobisher, a fairly well-to-do trader of textiles and imports from the Italian cities, but his claims of descent from the great explorer Martin Frobisher of Good Queen Bess' court had always been mocked behind his back. My father held no written evidence of his connection to Sir Martin, and most of his initial wealth had come through marriage to my mother Gwen whose family owned extensive farmsteads in service to the March lords on the Welsh border.

Most in the community simply dismissed his claims as an attempt to puff himself up as an exotic merchant rather than a simple, everyday trader of linens and wool. I'd been too young to recall his words for myself—both my parents were killed in the blazing inferno when I was two years old—but reading over his various pieces of correspondence always conjured images of my parents in my mind.

One of my most valuable possessions was a small portrait of them painted years before I was born, but to my eyes they looked like any other man and woman portrayed in countless frames throughout the city. I tried not to grind my teeth as my head swam with a mixture of pain, anger at my father's empty promises, and at the fact no one on my mother's side of the family had accepted to take me in following their deaths.

It was a vicious cycle, as after every pang of loathing I felt towards my parents the guilt quickly followed.

That I had never really known them was not the point; it didn't change the fact my life had been stripped away from me before I had even learned to walk. But, such thoughts were always eventually replaced by ones of remorse. I would chide myself for blaming them, as if they somehow chose to die of the sickness or in the blaze a year later.

I stood up to take some of the pressure off my bruises and tried to ignore the hazy memories of my younger childhood which seemed especially relentless this afternoon. Tom and Michael would be expecting me in about an hour and I needed to make my way down to the docklands. Tom and his father had just finished building a small punt boat and we were desperately wanting him to take us out fishing.

My knowledge of boats was limited to having tagged along with my friends on the occasional day's work, but Tom and Michael had both grown up on the banks of the Thames. Well, Tom's family had moved up from Dorset when he was about three years old, due to his father's line of work. They both came from a long line of coastal fishermen and I would often sit wide-eyed at stories of close encounters with pirates out of Barbary.

Michael's father in particular often told his story of being taken prisoner by a corsair but later being freed in exchange for fresh water when the Moorish ship ran low on supplies and happened upon a French cog. His captors had underestimated the amount of water needed for their raid due to a series of storms delaying their return, and after a few days of thirst were unsure about attacking the vessel directly.

Instead, they pulled up alongside the much slower flat-bottomed cog and demanded water in exchange for Stephen, for that was his name, along with two other prisoners.

At first the French sailors were hesitant, but, between Stephen's promises of catching them a healthy supply of mullet or cod and the cutlasses of the corsairs, the Frenchmen finally agreed to terms. They were en route to the estuary of the Thames laden with fabrics and wines out of Burgundy, so Stephen was able to eventually make his way home to London.

Tom's father, Johnathan Coram, had been employed as a pilot for several years due to his knowledge as a mariner, but his stories tended to lack the flair and sense of detail. However, Stephen Bollard could always be relied upon to tell a good tale from his days at sea. Thoughts of their fathers' stories replaced my earlier melancholy mood with one of impatience as I rushed down to the Pool of London and its swaying mass of ships. Part of me always felt a mixture of nervousness and excitement when I thought about the Barbary corsairs, but the town criers had assured us there had been no major reports of raids against English towns nor vessels for years.

Even so, we would stick to fishing up and down the river rather than tempt fate. Well, that and punts were not exactly meant for coastal waters, let alone the high seas. The heat from my caning was starting to ease off and I remembered around this time my friends' shacks usually had a supply of fresh fish and whelks brought in. As hunger quickly took over my senses I raced towards the docks with a head filled with stories of far-off lands.

ఠ✤

'Look at the state of you, Lewis,' tutted Bethany Coram, as I tried to hide my awkward gait upon arriving at Tom's home on the river.

It was small and ramshackle with his father's fishing boat moored at the end of their small pier, but I loved the place. Tom and Michael were both fortunate in their families getting along well for the most part. There was always a warm and welcoming atmosphere as their mothers both doted on me. Michael, who was actually a French boy I met at Cripplegate named Michel, had been given a job assisting with mundane tasks for the fishermen three years ago.

He had connected with Tom's family through his service and they took a liking to the hard-working young Frenchman. Eventually, they proposed that one of the neighbouring families which had been unable to conceive a child take him in through adoption. Ever since the two families had become inseparable.

I stopped in the battered doorway and gave an extravagant bow one of the clerks had taught us back at the workhouse. Apparently it was expected in his work around Westminster when dealing with certain clients, but I always did it as a bit of a jest with Tom's family. It usually had the effect of making them roll their eyes or chuckle, although once it did end with me getting a playful boot up the backside from Tom's father when I was slightly too 'mature' in my manners.

That was the last time I took Bethany's hand and kissed it, even though I had just meant it as a joke to lift their spirits on a particularly wet and dreary afternoon.

'Good afternoon, Mother Coram,' I said.

'Welcome, *Sirrah* Lewis of the Golden Fleece,' Bethany returned with a mock courtesy of her own.

'I am here to obtain some pottage, preferably with some cod and onion.'

Bethany laughed at my formal language and the sound lifted my spirits even further. Alderman Samuel had never neglected my education, for all of his other faults. My earlier sadness was almost forgotten in the hope of a hot meal and a day spent on the river. I tried never to take advantage of their hospitality, but a couple of meals per week never seemed to bother the Corams.

In fact, more often than not they seemed eager to have me join them for supper. Tom's stepmother, she had married John shortly following the death of his first wife in 1671, was always unhappy with my weight and would ask about the meals at Cripplegate regularly.

His father might pipe up and mumble about another mouth to feed, but he never once begrudged me a place at their table and I got on well with the man. He could be stern and irritable, but John Coram also had a quick wit and often made us laugh with jokes which left his wife and daughters looking scandalised.

'Well, if you've brought some chocolate, coffee or fresh banana then I'm sure we can arrange something,' she replied with an amused twist at the corner of her mouth.

At that we both burst out laughing and I sat on one of the stools by the counter where she was busy peeling onions and boiling water on a hob.

'I'm afraid I'm fresh out, my Lady, prices at Leicester Fields' markets are still high from the war.'

Bethany chopped down on the end of an onion with a grin. She knew I had never set foot in that newly-built and wealthy neighbourhood in my life.

'How did the interview with the apothecary go?'

I shifted on my stool and looked down at the counter trying to look ashamed.

'That bad, was it?'

I rubbed my backside and grumbled, 'I never even had the bloody interview. Alderman Samuel gave me a walloping when I refused the chance at an apprenticeship.'

'For a lad who knows his letters and has a mind far beyond his years, you can be a fool Lewis Frobisher.'

'Well, you're probably right Mum. Still, I wasn't about to spend the rest of my days mixing *Venice treacle* and *oil of vitriol* for one of those dorbels who left my Da' to God's mercy.'

Bethany turned to me, her expression a mixture of sadness and reproach.

'That's unjust Lewis, and you know as much. There's no cure for the pestilence, no matter what the charlatans selling bottles of cold tea would have you think. Look, I'm not saying it was punishment for your father as I never knew the man, but sickness is just part of the world we live in. I miss Sarah every day, as does my John, but we have made our peace with God.'

I felt genuinely shameful upon hearing this. In my own moment of bitterness I had forgotten about Sarah Coram. She had passed away from the blood cough slightly before I got to know Tom through my friendship with Michael. By all accounts she had been a cheerful lass with a quick smile, and the thought I would never get to meet her brought back my earlier sense of regret.

'I… I'm sorry, Mum,' I said. 'Sometimes I get stuck in my own mind and forget other people suffered as well.'

Just as Mother Coram let out a sigh and was about to respond, a blur of colour and noise exploded into the doorway and leapt on to my pained back.

'Oi, that hurts,' I winced. 'Who's this imp?'

'She's a little changeling who's about to be sent back to her goblin kin, that's who she is,' chuckled Bethany with a wry smile. 'You should be out helping your sister with the braiding.'

'Lucy, have you been sloth in your duties? Well, it's off to the Tower with you,' I roared at the girl as I swung her off my back and over my shoulder.

At five years of age, Lucy Coram was the spitting image of her elder sister Jane. However, while Lucy was quick to laugh and possessed a cheeky smile, Jane, who was twelve years old and closer to Tom, was often cold and aloof. I sometimes wondered to myself if she resented the rest of her kin after Sarah's passing, in some way blaming them for the loss.

Tom had often told us how much Jane used to follow at the eldest Coram daughter's heels and try to copy her in every manner. Neither Tom nor his elder sister were unkind to their stepmother though, it was more that the elder daughter refused to show warmth to anyone else.

'Put me down!' Lucy giggled as she squirmed and beat against my back. 'Jane says we need more flax for the netting.'

I gently placed the grinning auburn-haired girl on the floor and she was swept up into a hug.

'Well, I will leave you in peace to the business of the day,' I quipped, as Bethany jokingly smacked at my hand with a wooden ladle. She was too slow, and I ran off to the doorway with the slice of cheese in hand.

'The lads are already down at the dock?'

Lucy flicked a clump of onion skin in my direction as her mother called after me with a reminder for Tom to have us back for before *Complines* and supper.

As I made my way down to the end of the old pier and passed by John Coram's trawler I briefly paused to take in the smells and view of the Thames. The pier itself was covered in lichen and barnacles with decades of salt markings covering the cracked wooden planks. Vessels of all shapes and sizes bobbed in the light breeze and at a first glance it looked like a complete mess.

After getting to know Tom and Michael I had begun to realise the fishing communities sprawled along the banks of the Thames had a very orderly and particular way of doing things. Ships' pilots knew how to avoid colliding into others for the most part, and some even used various flags to signal one another when it was too windy to communicate through the usual shouting.

While I looked up at the Coram fishing boat, which had belonged to Tom's grandfather and now his father John, I chuckled at the thought of their typical yells. The language was almost impossible to understand unless you were grew up with it, although I sometimes caught them asking about the weather or day's catch. Between the tang of salt and cooking fires in the air and the clear winds off the river it felt wonderful compared with the musty corridors back at Cripplegate.

I often wished I had been taken in by one of the families here the way Michael had, but my knowledge of the fishing trade was minimal. Once, I had read through a copy of 'The Compleat Angler' by Izaak Walton which had been collecting dust in the commons of the workhouse, but there is an enormous difference between reading about a man's love of fishing and actually knowing how to prepare a pole or haul in a catch.

Well, at least the governors of the orphanage and later the workhouse had never neglected my letters. Tom in particular was often quick to crack jokes at my expense, calling me the 'Bishop of London' or 'His Lordship', but it was usually in good humour. He was also grateful when I was able to read for him after receiving a written request from the markets. His father could read well enough for plying his trade, but if he was out fishing it was often left to Tom to handle the household tasks.

John Coram was quite pleased with my attempts at teaching Tom to read for himself, and I had earned more than one bowl of millet with herring for my efforts. Sadly, Tom did not make for an enthusiastic student and I was by no means an experienced mentor at fourteen. These thoughts all raced in my mind as I inhaled a large breath and continued to amble along to the end of the pier.

The three hulking shapes were huddled around the brand new punt resting in the river. I could tell by their hollering of delight they had just lowered her into the water.

'She actually floats, God be praised,' I teased as I came up to stand next to Tom.

'I was worried about the treads but they seem solid,' he replied.

'Aye, well the teak and spruce were well-seasoned,' his father added. 'I'd wager she will give you years of service if you treat her well.'

Tom beamed as he looked down at the small, narrow boat. Even though he was expected to contribute to the family trade with his catches, and to build the skills needed to someday take it over from his father, I could read Tom's impatience clearly. Having grown up in a two room fishing shack with his parents and two sisters, the opportunity the modest punt offered for privacy and his own space was almost too much for the boy to handle.

'I will make sure to take care of her, Father,' Tom said. 'She's beautiful.'

John simply nodded, but I could tell he was pleased with his son's earnest appreciation. Michael was bent over sorting out provisions and supplies for our first jaunt out on the river into a neat pile by the boat. After standing back up and cracking his back, he turned to the three of us.

'How did you get time to join us anyway, *Louis*? I thought you were interviewing for a job at the new medicinal gardens in Chelsea.'

'Ugh, not you as well,' I moaned. 'I refused the interview because I don't want to spend every waking hour covered in oils and mixing Aqua regia until my skin cracks. What's more, I've told you not to call me that, *Michel*.'

He put up his hands in a gesture of surrender, then turned to Tom and winked.

'It's not my fault you share a name with *le Roi Soleil* and are famous throughout the known world, not to mention—'

Tom jumped in to cut him off, 'hush, you jackanape. I've told you afore about spoutin' off in French. Have you forgotten the beatings already?'

Michael feigned a look of annoyance.

'First of all, my name is Michael Bollard, and I am a true son of England. Second, our kings are the best of friends and are once more at peace. As for the beatings, well… they helped with my English, no?'

I rolled my eyes as my two closest friends bickered back and forth while Tom's father busied himself loading the baskets of supplies aboard the punt. I've never known two people in my entire life who were so alike one another yet uniquely different in character.

Both boys were of a similar age having been born shortly after the Great Fire and about four years younger than myself. Tom was slightly taller than Michael but otherwise their builds were comparable enough, and they both shared the same colour of sandy-brown hair. Michael had a few marks on his face from some pox he had recovered from as an infant, but otherwise the lads were much alike. However, this was pretty much where the similarities ended.

'Are you two dolts going to help or not?' Tom interrupted my thoughts as if reading my mind. He was always impatient and tended towards being serious in his manner, whereas Michael took the opportunity to crack a joke whenever the opportunity presented itself. It wasn't that Tom lacked a sense of humour, he was as quick to guffaw at Michael's nonsense as anyone, but he was a bit more… stiff, is the word that usually came to mind.

Tom Coram had a raucous laugh, so long as he wasn't the target of the joke. Where Tom was rigid and easy to offend, Michael was perfectly content to roll his eyes and join in the merriment. My thoughts were interrupted as the small punt was finally ready to leave her small berth.

'Right, that's you then,' John said as he dropped a final wicker basket into the tiny vessel.

We all looked down into the punt, now filled with three fishing poles, several baskets for any catches and a few small linen sacks. I could tell by the size and shape of the bags they likely contained our lunches as prepared earlier by Bethany, as I was pretty sure I could make out the round bump of an apple in one of them.

'I trust you lads won't need me to come fetch you from the riverbank, you've been out with me a fair few times now and should know enough for a day's fishing on your own.'

Tom was already lowering himself into his punt and beckoning at the two of us to hurry up.

'Don't worry, Master Coram,' I replied while throwing my legs over the side of the small jetty.

'No going past Putney upriver and stay inside of Lymehurst if we head down the way.'

'Always say aloud when you're about to shift your weight and do it slowly,' piped up Michael, who had already taken a seat in front of where Tom stood ready with his long oar. Usually punts were not as deep as this and the pilot used a long, narrow pole better suited to the shallow rivers of the countryside. However, John had made some alterations in order for us to fish the Thames with less risk and with more space for storing our catches. The hull was about two hands deeper than usual for better balance, and a long paddle had been fitted to the stern.

'Half our catches go to the Corams for market,' I added, having finally dropped myself into the seat opposite Michael.

We were all beaming with excitement as Tom slowly pushed us free of the dock on to the river, as his father gave us a curt wave then turned back towards his shack.

At some point Tom's stepmother must have put together some small hay-filled cushions for the benches, and my backside, still slightly throbbing from a sound Cripplegate lashing, reminded me to thank her directly when we got back ashore.

'Freedom and liberty, lads,' Tom began to rotate the oar in a circular motion. 'I hope our fine lady here can hold all the carp and bream in store for her.'

With one last glance back at the pier, the three of us broke out laughing in giddy excitement, as the warm afternoon Sun cast its light across the gently flowing waters of the River Thames.

Chapter 2

Putney Ferry Crossing, River Thames, 1678 AD

Five hours…

Five hours of nothing but the pissing rain.

'It's because you keep dropping your line in too shallow they aren't going for it. *Bess* has nothing to do with your shite fishing,' Tom shouted from the bow of the punt. He had decided on the name after Queen Elizabeth who had driven off the Spaniards a hundred years earlier. The Virgin Queen had become something of a good luck omen to most sailors after sending Philip's armada back with its tail between its legs. Any pier in London boasted some version of Betty or Gloriana in the hope she would bring them safety through the violent winter squalls.

'Yes, well I don't see you with much to show for the day's work,' Michael snarled in obvious irritation. 'I told you to keep us steady Lewis, stop leaning to port.'

It had been my turn on the oar for the last twenty minutes and I was the least experienced pilot by a wide margin. That being said, Michael's tone, combined with the weather which had turned to heavy rain an hour earlier, caused me to fire back with some venom of my own:

'Shut up and focus on your own task, it's bad enough you forgot to put our satchels under the seats when the rains started.'

The apples and cheese slices were still fine if a little wet, but the rounds of bread had ended up feeding the nearby gulls. One of the greedy chancers sat perched on our bow, waiting for another morsel to be tossed its way.

'If Neptune here hadn't dumped the baskets over them when his fat arse finished rowing and needed a seat, I wouldn't have forgotten about them.'

At this Tom's eyes narrowed and I could tell we were in trouble as he rose. His fury was always quick to come and go, but it always arrived with a burning rage in the moment.

'It's my fault we can't catch so much as a perch then, is it?'

I couldn't make out Michael's reply through the pouring rain and sudden gust of wind. Then, I felt the entire world slip out from under me as something hard cracked into the side of my head.

'That's the last of them!' A husky voice boomed, cutting through the howling wind.

'Get us across quickly now, head for just up past Saint Mary's there Rob.'

A pair of rough hands dragged me over the side of a rough-hewn wooden railing and gently lowered me into the boat. As my wits slowly recovered I noticed the small cabin in the centre of the deck and slowly recognised the design. I was aboard one of the many ferryboats used to shuttle passengers across the north and south banks of the Thames.

'Don't fret lad, your mates are just in there with Goodman Robert,' said the figure looming over me.

'I…what…'

'Flipped yerselves right over, we saw it from The Swan and figured it was our Christian duty to help, ale or no ale. What, with Saint Mary next door to us and all. I'm no Catholic, mind, but all the same she's the English type of Mary, that one is…anyway, be thankful the current was movin' slow as you like.'

He looked up at the darkening sky and chuckled, 'an hour from now, and you three would be in God's hands.'

Between the man's cheery rambling and my sense of shock I was having trouble focusing on the conversation. He grinned and helped me to my feet.

'Simon Beecham, at your service. I don't suppose the three of you have the usual tuppence each for the crossing?'

'No, sir, I'm just… thank you, for helping us.'

The man grunted but didn't say anything as we went in to huddle away from the rain in the pilot's station. Tom and Michael both glanced up with their teeth chattering and looking thoroughly miserable.

'I'm Robert Smythe and this big lummox is Simon Beecham. If we're bein' exact, you lot owe him your lives, but don't let it go to his head,' the pilot winked at me.

Rob was a slender man with dark black hair and a scar over his lip who looked to be in his mid-thirties, while Simon was a red-haired giant of a man with the cracked hands earned through many years of hauling at oars.

'They've no coin Rob. Well, we've done well enough with all them noble-folk crossing lately, a bit of charity is good for the soul eh?'

Rob nodded in agreement and began to till the small ferry towards the shoreline as Simon returned to rowing. The boat had clearly seen many years of service judging by its cracked wooden beams and salt-faded decking, but it was otherwise clean and well-maintained.

'I really wish we had a few coins, or at least some

perch and eels to offer for saving us,' I said. 'We were just out fishing for the day and then it started to rain when—'

'My Da' is going to murder me when we arrive home without *Bess*,' Tom interrupted.

It was then I realised he wasn't just shaking from being soaked to the bone; Tom Coram was genuinely terrified about facing his father.

'What sort of fisherman comes back with nothing and loses his boat on his first day out?'

Tom buried his head in his hands, while Michael just looked utterly downcast.

'Good thing Millie's got 'er strapped alongside then I suppose,' Simon beamed from ear-to-ear.

All three of us leapt to our feet and scrambled over to the side of the ferry. There, in the water with cord sheets looped into her oar-holes and bumping gently along, was our little punt.

Tom burst into tears.

'Is Carolyn still running the kitchens? She was always one of the decent types,' Robert asked with a mouthful of fish pie.

'No, sorry sir, I can't say the name rings any bells,' I replied.

'Ah well, she was gettin' on in years and that was a long time ago, sure enough,' Simon said with a sigh.

'I imagine they probably got what's-her-face runnin' the meals now. What was her name again Rob? That tall one with the curls and the enorm –'

'Alice, I think you're meaning,' his friend quickly answered, with a nod towards Tom and Michael. However, my two young friends were paying precisely zero attention to the conversation, and were entirely focused on demolishing the hot meals and flagons of ale in front of them.

The two ferryman had initially been planning to drop us at the church next to the coaching tavern where they had been having lunch. After a casual remark I had made to Tom about him running off to Cripplegate with me to escape his father's wrath at our having lost the baskets and satchels, not to mention arriving home with a distinct lack of fish, all of that had changed. Both Simon and Rob had grown up in the almshouse and later workhouses of Cripplegate as well.

They had insisted we join them for a couple of drinks and a hot meal to warm ourselves, and, despite our feelings of guilt at being unable to pay them so much as a farthing for all their help, we readily agreed. Simon in particular seemed eager to hear about life back at the workhouse, while Rob preferred to tell his own childhood tales from two decades past.

Simon bit off whatever he had been about to say and took a pull from his own mug instead. After a moment he said with an amused expression, 'That's the one, sure enough. Cornish if I remember. Rob here knew her much better than me though.'

'I'm pretty sure I know who you mean,' I said while rubbing the side of my sore head where our punt had left her mark after colliding with my temple.

'If it's Alice Dunholm, I know her fairly well. She's usually complaining about having to serve pottage and not having enough meat, but she's well-liked and always sorts me out with extra tuck if I pop by the kitchens.'

At this Simon suddenly had to stop himself from choking on his ale and let out a loud, bellowing laugh. Robert scowled at him and put his own pewter flagon down on the table before speaking.

'Well, give her my best when you see her lad, tell her Robert Smythe was asking after her. Anyway, we've prattled on about Cripplegate for long enough. The three of us know we'd often rather forget the bastard place than dwell on it. What were you lads doing that caused such a scene? The rain and wind weren't all that bad.'

Both Tom and Michael looked embarrassed at this, and as their elder by a few years I answered to try and prevent tempers from rising again.

'Well, we were out fishing and testing Tom's new boat when the rains started up. I guess we were angry between getting soaked and not catching anything. To be honest sirs, we never even had so much as a bite on the lines. I'm not much use at it myself, but I think my friends were out of patience as they're both proper fishers.'

'Aye, my Da's got a full pier up at the Pool,' Tom said, having finished his pie. 'Michael here knows his way around the boats as well, even if he did nearly drown us.'

Michael snubbed his nose at the remark then returned to his meal. We spent the next few minutes in comfortable silence, with full attention directed towards the generous helpings of food on our trenchers. As Tom continued to finish his meal I could tell it was restoring his usual good humour. After we were finishing up the platters the earlier discussion picked up again.

'Well then, you're a fisherman so why the anger on a day out? You must be used to the weather, don't look much like a Saracen to me,' replied Rob.

Tom just looked confused and said, 'well, like I said we didn't even have so much as a bite and –'

At that Simon and Rob exchanged a knowing-grin and chuckled.

'You expect bites to be guaranteed, as you grew up

around the docks,' Simon said. 'Let me ask you this Tom, or you Michael for that matter, how often do your fathers come back empty handed from a trip?'

This time it was Michael who answered first. He had been quiet since we were helped to shore, but, as was the case with the rest of us, the warmth of the tavern was working its miracle.

'I'd say maybe once every week or two, Pater comes back with only a few bream or a couple of salmon. When that happens we don't even bother preparing for market and keep the lot for our own stores.'

Tom nodded along in agreement as Rob cut in, 'and how often would you say they miss out when they go angling on the Thames for a few hours in a punt?'

'They usually go out from before first light through to evening. Tom's father uses an old trawler and my own sails a corvette- er, sloop, rather- but they never head out in punts.'

Simon and Rob both flashed wide grins as the realisation dawned on us.

Even experience mariners who fished the coastlines and seas for their livelihood could come back with a meagre haul now and then. And, they went out with full rigging and crews, sometimes for days at a time.

All of a sudden, three young men on a punt coming back empty-handed after a few hours trolling on the river didn't seem quite as shameful as it had moments ago. We still had *Bess*, and all but one of the baskets had been gathered from the river by Simon using his long mooring hook shortly after he had pulled me aboard the ferry. Considering how much worse things could have gone during our mishap, the three of us were incredibly fortunate the two older ferrymen had been sitting with a view of the Thames at the time.

With a look to my friends I could see from their own expressions they had come to the same conclusion. Tom's father would likely give him an extra task and a smack upside the head for having lost one of the baskets, but that was only fair given the effort his wife had put into weaving it for us.

There was never any doubt Bethany would accept her son's apology, nor that it would be a sincere one. The Corams kept a warm household. If anything, his mother would see it as an opportunity to make another basket for the next trip and improve upon it. With improved spirits the three of us finished our meals as the ferrymen relaxed into their own various conversations.

ɛ❥

An hour later the five of us were easing *Bess* back into the water from a natural slope a short distance from the ferry crossing. It was the middle of July so there were still a good few hours of daylight left, so at least we didn't need to worry about rowing back to the Pool of London under dark. I had been insisting we would return with some form of payment for the ferrymen in the days ahead, however unlikely given the three of us rarely had any coin, but the two good-natured men waved away such promises as they finished lowering our punt into the brackish riverbank.

'That's you then,' Simon said, as he raised his arms above his head to stretch.

'Thanks again for the help, Goodman Beecham,' I replied while my two young friends gingerly got aboard. This time Michael was careful to secure the baskets and sopping wet satchels under his feet. It didn't go unnoticed by Tom who flashed him a grin. The boys' spirits were largely restored after the hours spent at the Swan. However, I was still a bit shaken from the experience but feeling better by the minute.

Sometimes I forgot the four years' difference in our ages due to the close friendship we shared, and at times like these my friends always seemed to bounce back from trouble more quickly than myself.

'Just mind your oar heading back up to the Pool, the flow's with you so let the river do the work,' Simon said.

'Take care of yourselves, when you're next down by Putney you can usually find us either working the stations or propped up with a mug at the Swan,' added Rob.

'You lot owe us a few rounds of ale there anyway. Take care not to flip again, you had God's own luck today and I wouldn't chance it twice. Well then, it's back to work for the two of us.'

The two men gave us one last push out from the shoreline. After a quick wave, they turned back towards the path leading to the ferry station on the southbank. I've met all manner of horrible folk in the years since, but Robert Smythe and Simon Beecham were two of the good ones.

As Tom started to guide us into the middle of the Thames, I let out a deep breath and began scratching a finger against the side of the small boat. For some reason, whenever I was lost in thought or in a state of relaxation I couldn't help but pick or scratch at something. The same could be said for any time I found myself in danger or under severe stress; the action of picking, scratching or tapping the nearest item to my person helped me to think. Thankfully, at the moment I was feeling relaxed and fully absorbed in looking out across the wide river.

Various waterfowl bobbed along the riverbanks searching for all manner of small beasts to eat, including three of the local swans which gave the nearby coaching inn its name, and the mass of greenery reflected off the surface of the water. Oaks, spruce, beech, birch and a number of trees I didn't know the names of lined the banks, with their branches often drooping down right into the river.

It was hard to see the Swan or any of the nearby stables through the cover of the trees, but Saint Mary's tower was clearly visible. Built over two hundred years earlier, the old stonework of the church's tower stood in stark contrast to the surrounding nature.

Putney had a few buildings catering to the nobility who often traveled back and forth from London to the countryside and made use of the ferry services, but for the most part the area was lush with foliage and unsullied. As I watched a white fisher of some kind swoop and pick up its meal, Michael spoke for the first time in a while. Tom had been more shaken by our accident due to his sense of leadership over our day's fishing in his new punt, but Michael had been slower to regain his composure.

'I dug up a few worms while Master Beecham was going on about the time his Da' ferried King James across the river,' Michael said. 'We still have the poles and hooks thanks to him and Master Smythe.'

'Imagine angling our fishing poles out from the water,' Tom joined in. 'We must have looked a right bunch of tits to them, floundering about like it was our first time on a fuckin' boat.'

Simon's comments from earlier at the pub came

flooding back to me, but after quickly refocusing my attention towards my friend I said, 'to be fair, he's a good hand with that hook and I wager it was no trouble. Did you see how easily he got us alongside the pier? Even on a good day your Da's mate Edward would be hard pushed to do that.'

I didn't know the man well, but Edward was one of the crew who worked under Tom's father whenever they went out. Without another word, we quickly baited the lines and gently dropped them into the water to trawl. We had learned our lesson the hard way, and all three of us were taking great care not to rock the small punt more than necessary.

Oh, don't give me that look Baltasar… I'm not adding tales of dragons, winged sirens nor fleets of corsairs assailing us from all sides. Now, do you want to hear about the rest of the day's events, or not? You said you wanted to hear everything from the start, and this was the beginning of my life as a sailor. I'm aware the Thames is not the bloody sea, you arse. Pour me a flagon of that, will you? Now, where was I?

'Eh, not a bad day's work for three young idlers,' John Coram said.

Tom and Michael beamed at the praise, even as they tried to hide their face-splitting smiles. I suppose I felt smug as well, but then I did not come from a family of anglers and was not as caught up in the trade as my two friends.

'Them chubs and bream were the hardest to bring in,' Tom gestured at the large pile of fish we had unloaded on to the dock for gutting and cleaning. I could tell by the wry smile on his father's face that he was biting back a comment about how small the individual catches were.

This was a man who was used to pulling in trout, pike, salmon or occasionally sturgeon.

Still, for all his gruff manner he had the good grace not to belittle our day's haul. And, to be fair, although the fish themselves were not particularly large, we had brought back eight of them. That in itself was a respectable figure and I could tell John agreed.

From the moment we hit the stretch of water above Battersea they were practically throwing themselves into our baskets. Michael proudly claimed this was due to his worms being fresh from the mud, while Tom was sure the light rain was to thank for our good fortune.

'Well, I can use at least five of these at market. The other three we will gut and dress for supper,' John said. 'Where's that last basket Tom?'

Tom's elation at his father's words quickly turned to dismay. 'Da' I was just –'

'I knocked it off *Bess* when I was standing up to shift the pole, sir,' I interrupted. 'How much do I owe you?'

John looked between the three of us and I could immediately tell he was not convinced by my attempt at shouldering the blame. The man stroked his thick, wiry beard and raised an eyebrow.

'Well, were any of these your own catches?' John asked.

'That middling bream is one of mine, the rest were off Tom or Michael's lines.'

'Aye, well that'll do then. A fish that size will fetch about half the basket's worth at market, the rest will cover the remaining half. You would have pocketed a shilling or two from the sales, a shame that.' Tom's father said with a tone of finality to his voice.

'Yes sir, if that covers my clumsiness then the fish is yours.'

'That suits me well enough. Tom, why don't you start cleaning this lot with Michael? I want a quick word with Lewis before the girls get started on supper.'

Tom and Michael scrambled to get started, and as I turned to head up the pier with John I noticed Tom give me a nod of thanks over his father's shoulder. The man brought my attention back to him when he said, 'I wanted to talk with you about Cripplegate and your plans there, away from the lads.'

'I don't really have any plans, sir. It's a meal and lodging... I mean, it can be a bit rough at times with Big Will and his cronies, but at least I learned most of my letters.'

'Yes, I was hoping that would rub off on Tom, but he is too often with his head in the clouds. Either that, or he is still too young and can't see any value in it.' John sighed.

'He's got a sharp enough mind for it, Master Coram. I'd say he just needs time to grow into it, after he sees its worth for ledgers and selling at market.'

'True, that was how I came to learn years ago from my own father,' he said. 'You know I can't take you on, with Tom and the girls to look after, nor can Stephen and Agnes with their hard times lately. It's not that we don't like your company Lewis, it's just a matter of the family trade. I could ask around and see if anyone wants a deckhand, but there's no promise you will be treated or paid well.'

'I appreciate the consideration, but to be honest I just don't have any idea what I will do when Alderman Samuel throws me out on my backside.'

As soon as the words left my mouth their blunt truth caused me to start scratching violently at the hem of my shirt behind my back, although I tried to clasp my hands to hide the tick from John.

After a long moment he looked at me and said, 'well, I suppose working as an apothecary's apprentice at that new herbal garden is out. Bethany told me about your decision while you were away fishing. I've seen the way you look out on the water though, so I can't say I blame you… shuttered up with brews and potions all day long in a dark cell, that's no way to live.'

I felt slightly better about the morning's events back at the poorhouse after hearing this.

'I mean, they do help people with the sickness and are paid well for their remedies,' I replied.

'Even so, I just can't see myself tailing behind a puffed up apothecary walking through London with his nose raised. I know my parents were fairly well-to-do before they passed, but I never really knew that life.'

Suddenly, the older fisherman stopped and gave me a serious look up and down, as if weighing me up for market like some prize catch.

'Have you ever thought about joining the Navy Ro… erm, Royal Navy?'

I paused and looked down at myself. With a slim build and average height the thought had never really crossed my mind.

'You don't need to be Hercules reborn to join the navy, Lewis,' John said as if reading my thoughts. 'The pay's not bad, since King Charles is trying to strengthen its numbers even further since our latest war with the French. I've seen the way you look to the Thames, with your eyes wide and full o' spirit.' John stopped at the entry to his home, with a look back towards his son who was busy filleting the day's catch. 'Word is there is a serious recruitment drive happening in Plymouth. You could likely find a spot through London as well, but I've heard if you want a better shot at a good berth it's worth making the trip down the coast to the shipyards in Devon and asking directly.'

'What about Tom and Michael?' I asked.

'They are needed here to take up our trade in the years ahead. I know it sounds hard Lewis, being away from them and all you know, but it mayhaps be the best thing for you. A decent wage, life at sea aboard a proper ship an' a chance to travel the world.'

The man cast his arm out to the Pool of London and chuckled, 'if you think yon trawler is a mighty vessel, or any of these old ladies for that matter, wait until you see some of the new man o' wars being built.'

He paused to roll his arm around and loosen the muscles in his neck.

'That new girl just finished in Portsmouth has two decks full of cannon, she's to sail for Plymouth after her livery is done from what I hear. Anyway, it's just something to think about. I'm sure we can manage supper tonight, and even should you choose to leave you're welcome here to help the boys with their own work whenever you're back in London. All I meant to say is I can't afford to take you on as crew, but the king's pockets run much deeper than my own.'

'Thank you for the advice, sir. I will give what you said some thought. God knows I don't want to spend the rest of my days idling around Cripplegate or Aldersgate for a pittance.' As we made our way up the rest of the path from the pier, my head was filled with thoughts of rolling waves, howling wind and a life at sea. It was a mixture of dread at being cut off from my only friends alongside a feeling of desire for a new life, away from the muck and squalor of the almshouses.

The two of us ducked into the shack and I made myself useful to the rest of the Coram family in preparation for the evening's meal. After what felt like a couple of hours Michael and I joined them at table. Following a quick prayer given by Lucy, we enjoyed a meal of stewed fish with a good round of crusty bread Bethany had picked up at the market, followed by a sweet board of apples and various cheeses.

We even had a spoonful of tamarind chutney to dab on to the cheese. John had insisted we open the small jar in celebration of Tom and his small punt *Bess* after their first day of unsupervised work. It had come all the way from the Punjab and would normally have cost a small fortune, but John had acquired it in trade with one of the merchants from the East India Company. Apparently it had been purchased at a very reasonable price as the man had owed John Coram a favour.

Tom earned a playful smack to the back of his head when he wished we had caught a few salmon instead of bream, but the stew had made the otherwise tougher fish nice and tender. After a bit of amiable conversation with the Corams following supper, Michael and I bade them goodnight and took our leave. I walked Michael back to his own shack which was about five minutes away from Tom's home, but my mind was elsewhere as he joked about the day's events.

Finally, once I was on my own the dread of returning to Cripplegate and having to deal with Big Will or Alderman Samuel took hold. As I made my way back across London Bridge in the direction of my workhouse my mind raced between such thoughts. I also thought about the day's accident, meeting Simon and Rob, of remembering to speak to Alice Dunholm and about

John Coram's suggestion.

Joining the Royal Navy in service to the king. Now there was a thought.

Chapter 3

Cripplegate, London, 1678 AD

The return to Cripplegate was largely uneventful and without any major disturbance or incident. My head was filled with the notion of a life at sea, freed from the dull and dreary life of an impoverished urchin-turned-scrounger surrounded by all manner of filth.

London may have been getting back on its feet following the fire, but my lot in life was not exactly one of honey-dipped pears nor white cotton linens. One moment I was Jason leading Heracles and Atalanta across rolling waves in search of the Golden Fleece. Then, within seconds I was our very own *Draco* exploring unknown lands under a burning Sun aboard the Golden Hind.

The only thing worth mentioning during my walk back to the poorhouse happened while I was ambling along distracted by such thoughts. I was almost across London Bridge after weaving through the sprawling construction yards setup in recent years to rebuild many of the burned houses on its northern side, when a voice rang out from one of the workers. He was around 30 years of age, built like a bull, and had just lowered a heavy-looking stone block into place with his bare hands. I was instantly shaken out of my daydreaming with a sense of foreboding.

'Oi were you just passin' by with not so much as a hello then?'

It took me a moment to gather my composure and pull myself together. After a moment I replied.

'Apologies good mason, I was lost in my thoughts I'm afraid. A very good day to you and yours.'

After raising my hand in a wave I turned to continue on my way, but the man was not finished.

'It's been more than a year but I still know a useless arsling when I see one.'

At that I turned back and looked more carefully at the man. There had only been one person I could recall in my entire life using that old insult, and even then it was usually good-spirited and in jest.

'Charles Mason, well look at the state of you.'

The man grinned and stretched out his arms before saying, 'I always told you they didn't feed us properly. All I needed was some good mutton or beef to put the weight back on, and for all its faults the guild always gives us plenty to eat.'

My tension at the thought of a fight disappeared and I let out a sigh of relief. A woman suddenly tutted at me as she shambled past in a hurry, and upon realising I was not making any friends standing in the middle of the walkway I walked over to stand next to Charles.

'You're not kidding, those things look like they could punch the head clean off one of these statues,' I said while gesturing at a nearby sculpture no doubt meant to adorn one of the stone facades.

Charles chuckled at the obvious flattery and made the most of it. He picked up another perfectly hewn granite square without any obvious effort and then gently placed it into the intended position along the wall.

'Of course no amount of tuck in the world will fill you out. I've never known a lad so thin, at least not one who has been getting fed at all.' He made a waving gesture at the stones and went on, 'we could use you as mortar between these and it would make no difference.'

I grinned because Charles had always been full of bluster and bravado, even when he had arrived thin as a rake to the almshouse years ago from Maidstone. However, for all his insults and mockery anyone who knew Charles quickly learned he was a kind-hearted man, with a love of fine ale and discussions about his trade.

He came from a long line of quarrymen out of Kent and often claimed his father had been one of the major suppliers of ragstone to the churches of southwest England, although Charles claimed to have fallen on hard times after an inheritance feud left him and his younger brother destitute. The latter had died on the way to London and the man never went into detail about the matter, although I knew his brother's name had been Brendan.

Charles was one of those craftsman whose surname was directly attached to his line of work, and the city was filled with any number of Builders, Farriers or Weavers. It was a trend that had been in decline for some time according to Alderman Samuel, and was now largely maintained by the yeomen in the countryside. It was true that neither myself, Tom nor Michael were named after our families' trades. Even so, the workhouse back at Cripplegate was filled with the like; we had no less than three John Smiths at any given time.

I gave one of the stone slabs a firm pat.

'Well, at least then I'd have a flat bed to lay on for once.'

Charles threw his head back and guffawed loudly. 'It's bloody good to see you Lewis, how are things?'

'A lot quieter since you up and left,' I retorted.

'Congratulations on the guild taking you on though, I'm always glad to see one of our own make it out of the shithole. I ran into Robert Smythe and Simon Beecham earlier as well, they're working the ferry out in Putney these days.'

Charles nodded and I could tell he was thinking back to our times spent together at Cripplegate, eating coarse gruel and receiving lectures about idleness from presbyters or Alderman Samuel during one of his monthly visits.

'It's a decent life, to be fair,' he said with a sweeping motion across the bridge. 'Plenty to eat and apprenticed to Master William thanks to the guild. They couldn't do anything about the will, but thanks to my family's supply of ragstone over the years they took enough pity to at least offer me a steady job. Glad to hear Rob and Sym are away from the place as well, they were two of the good ones.'

I saw Charles' eyes shift to the half-finished masonry, and, after realising I was picking and scratching at the stone, I quickly put my hand into the side pocket of my britches. He raised an eyebrow and I could tell he wanted to comment on my old tick, but he decided against it. Instead, the dust-coated mason shifted the conversation away from his own stroke of good fortune and inquired after my own situation.

'How have things been on your end? You were wanting to sell potions or something like that if I remember, any luck?'

I rolled my eyes at hearing apothecaries described in such a way, but I was in no mood to be difficult.

'Well, Samuel came all the way down from his townhouse to give me a caning for failing to show up for the chance at an apprenticeship. It doesn't matter though, I am just on my way back now to gather my things and head off for Portsmouth to try and get work aboard a ship.'

'What, as a trawler or labourer for the Company ships?' Charles was referring to the Company of Merchant Adventurers of London, who were known to always be on the lookout for young workers to help with loading or offloading their trade cogs.

'Actually, I was thinking of enlisting into the navy if there is anything available,' I replied while trying not to look unsure as I braced for one of his ribald comments.

At first Charles looked ready to give me one of his typical jibes, but after opening and closing his mouth he then gave me a more serious response. 'To be honest Lewis, that's not the worst idea you've ever had. I often help Master William with deliveries taking stock at the port and we see the navy lads coming ashore.

They're usually not short of money and off to the taverns or knocking shops, more often than not already half-drunk and in good spirits. Keeps 'em safe from muggings or the like as well, since only a madman would try his luck with a group of sailors. That goes double for men wearing the king's colours and known for being good in a fight.'

He paused and nodded thoughtfully then continued with his explanation. 'They coin is pretty good from what I hear, and the king is known to make sure his boys are looked after and paid when they're supposed to be. You see all sorts in the gangs leaving ship for their leave, but a lot of them are slim and wiry like you. No offence mate, just God's honest truth.'

I felt hope burst within me at hearing Charles' encouraging words, and I suddenly felt anxious to be on my way as quickly as possible.

'None taken, I will leave you to your work and stop wasting your time,' I said. 'It was good to see you keeping well Charles, I'll be sure to pass it on to the rest of the lads back home, they could do with a bit of hope these days.'

The big mason reached into a satchel by the side of his workspace in the yard and pulled out a link of sausage along with half of a cheese wedge. He handed them to me and then sat himself down on a wicker chair which was propped up in the corner. 'You're welcome to these, I know all too well how it is. One bit of advice though Lewis: Don't get your hopes up. It's a good idea, but they're hardly going to see the name Frobisher and give you a new Man O' War to command, all while you stuff your face with fruit straight from Hispaniola and fondle beautiful maidens on each arm.'

He cracked his back and took a swig of ale from the gourd flask before placing it back into his bag.

'More likely you'll be put to some awful job cleaning latrines aboard ship or scrubbing the woodwork. Look at me, a mason who can read plans and knows how to design in stone, but here I am building the most basic wall in all of London. Meanwhile, Stephen over there is in charge of the sculpting and detailing.'

I felt my spirits sink somewhat at the thought of scrubbing excrement from latrines; it was a task I was not unfamiliar with at Cripplegate over the years. Charles noticed my deflated expression and decided to try and undo the damage.

'Don't get me wrong Lewis, I am not complaining and my life is much better since landing this apprenticeship. I get to work everyday on a full belly with people who are mostly a good laugh. All I'm saying is to try to not get carried away. There's no reason twenty years from now you couldn't be in command of the entire fleet and supping with the king, eh?'

At this genuine attempt at encouragement I smiled and wished Charles well with his day's work. After promising to come back and see the houses once they were all finished, I shook his hand and made my way to Cripplegate without any further interruption.

It was after dark by the time I gradually made my way back to the almshouse. The bells were already tolling for *Compline* at Saint Giles which meant I had missed the evening meal of pickled onions, pease pottage and carrots, but I was going to the kitchens to see Alice Dunholm anyway so I was not overly bothered. Thankfully there was no sign of Will Baker or his usual thugs as I made my way through the outer court to the dormitories. There was an old guard of sorts by the name of Adrian Thorpe, but he was dozing off at his bench against the inner wall of the entrance.

It was more of a token gesture having the guard post; it had been insisted upon by the almshouse's benefactors, but for the most part we stayed away unless it was time for a meal or to sleep. The only exceptions were the invalids or the sick, but they were never in any position to cause Adrian any trouble.

In any case, the guard was there to protect the possessions of the almshouse and its material goods from theft rather than to prevent any violence or problems between the residents. The building itself was one of the few in the area to escape the Great Fire alongside Saint Giles, and this was even more surprising given its wooden construction. Apart from the dormitories there was also a kitchen, hen house, latrines and a number of smaller rooms suited to cleaning beddings or weaving fabrics. There was also a small stable with a groom suitable for three horses for when patrons or Alderman Samuel required its services.

Other than the sounds of people trying to sleep the halls were mostly quiet as I made my way downstairs to the kitchens. One of the staff responsible for changing linen wraps in the West ward passed by with a nod, no doubt on his way to the infirmary for supplies judging by the dour look on his face. I asked if Alice was still working or if she had finished, to which he said she was just taking stock for the next day and nearly done. Upon hearing I was on my way to see her he raised and eyebrow with a bemused expression and then went about his own tasks.

δ♥

Alice was in her usual cloth apron with her hair pulled back underneath a headwrap in order to keep it away from any open flames. Two of the kitchen slaves were piling fresh rushes on the floor and wiping down the chopping block while she was hastily checking over a list of what was likely provisions for the next day. I could tell from her countenance that Alice was exhausted and ready to wind down for the night, but that didn't stop her from giving me a quick smile when she noticed me in the doorway.

At the age of nineteen Alice should have been married with several children by now, but she had proved headstrong regarding any suitors and her father was completely under her thumb. She had always treated me with kindness and slipped me an extra bread roll or morsel of food when I was around, to the point that I had gradually become conditioned towards a level of respect for Alice which boys my age generally lacked.

While they would oggle and instantly break out chattering about her figure or make obscene gestures as soon as she was out of earshot, I was never quite able to bring myself to feel that way about her. It wasn't the result of any lack of attraction towards her, rather, I was too terrified of betraying her in some way and jeopardising our friendship. However, even taking into account my bashfulness towards Alice, there was no question that she was considered a great beauty throughout the entire city.

At one point she had even refused a suitor who traveled all the way from Oxford to shower her with poetry after hearing about her from one of his fellow pupils, Alderman Samuel's son Oliver no less. At the perfect height to stand alongside most men, and with long golden curls and flawless light skin, Alice would have easily looked at home in any Lady's entourage throughout Christendom.

What was really striking was her figure though, on that point Simon had not been exaggerating. Alice was somehow both very delicate and slender, yet also incredibly well-endowed in those areas men tend to notice. Women visibly seethed with jealousy at any social events around Cripplegate whilst feigning indifference, and their menfolk pretended not to stare. She had received a number of offers to take her out of the kitchens and into a life of comfort, but for some reason she rejected them utterly.

'Not you too then,' Alice said as I stood halfway through the small entrance from the hall. 'Are you going to just stand there making faces or come and sit?'

I had been so distracted thinking about my future

plans that she had mistaken it for staring. Thankfully I knew she was just playing coy though and was not actually offended. We had never actually discussed our friendship in any way, but I assumed she liked me well enough from all the small gifts of food over the years.

'Sorry, my mind has been all over the place and I just walked back from the bridge, how was your day Alice?' I asked after taking one of the small oak stools out from under the table. 'I ran into Rob and Simon earlier in Putney, they were asking after you. They saved my arse from drowning, so I figured I would at least pass on their well wishes.

A look of worry passed across her face as Alice put down her grocer's list and folder her arms. 'What do you mean, drowning? If you've been getting into trouble with Will I'll drown you in that tub myself.'

She pointed over the corner of the room where one of the slaves was vigorously scrubbing one of the cutting boards in a large pewter basin.

'You know me better than that,' I replied. 'Why, what's any of this got to do with that arsehole?'

'The stupid boy fell into the new drainage canal for the Thames down in Vintry and had to be hauled out by one of the local coopers who saw him flailing around in the water,' said Alice with the hints of a smirk forming at the corners of her mouth. 'He had been trying to impress that Bess girl from the street by leaping the ditch, but he accidentally tumbled into her and she went in. Then, he jumped in to save her only to get stuck floundering, unable to swim.' At this point Alice began to openly laugh out loud. 'All the while Bess was already halfway out, and when he called to her for help she told him exactly what he could do.'

As Alice finished telling me about Will's shameful

display I couldn't help but return her grin. Then, out of nowhere I began to laugh so hard I doubled over on top of the stool. At first Alice just laughed along, but after a moment when I didn't stop she asked what the matter was with me. Between gulps of air I quickly recounted the day's events with Tom and Michael.

'So you see,' I said after regaining my composure enough to speak, 'that's the second Bess that's gone tits-up in the Thames today.'

At this we both burst out laughing as the two slaves fully dedicated themselves to chores in an attempt to mask their overhearing the conversation.

Theirs was a miserable lot Baltasar. I can say that even now, after having traveled and seen so many things, few compare with the abject misery I have seen on the faces of those kept in slavery. As you'll hear later, my ownership and then freeing of these people became important parts of my life for many years. At the very least, Alice was a kind lass and not disposed to cruelty so the domestic slaves at Cripplegate were lucky if they were assigned to the kitchens.

Even so, she would not hesitate to severely discipline any theft or lack of work if she felt it justified. This brutal treatment from even the most kind-hearted of masters was something that greatly influenced my decisions in my later life. For now though let us return to the day I left Cripplegate. It would be some time before I ever returned.

After our outburst of laughter eventually calmed Alice dismissed her two slaves to their quarters and finished setting up the kitchen for use the following morning. At that point I brought up the fact I was just back to get my meagre belongings before going down to the port to the try and enlist with the Royal Navy. I found it hard to understand Alice's reaction to the news; her face was drawn up into a mixture of anger, sadness and sympathy.

She asked how I intended to get to Portsmouth if there was no ship taking on crew in the capital, and when I told her I would likely just walk she offered to pay for a shared carriage if I needed one. My first instinct was to reject the offer out of pride, but then the thought of my blistered feet and aching body after such a long journey got the better of me and I gratefully accepted.

It was not a particularly large amount to Alice, who was well looked after in her role as head cook for the entire building, but to me it was a Godsend. In her kindness she went a step further and offered to keep the few valuables and mementos of my parents safe in her own home, rather than me taking them to sea and risk losing them overboard during an inevitable storm.

I agreed to her offer and returned after a few minutes with a small box containing my various books and trinkets. More importantly, it also contained my father's various claims to titles or lands, even though they had been largely discredited in the years before my birth. After placing it upon the counter Alice promised she would keep it safe alongside her own valuables at home, and not to worry about any burglars since she was clever in choosing her hiding space.

It was clear she was ready to get home from a long day of work, so I decided to wish her well and be on my way. Suddenly, I felt myself choking up at the thought of not knowing when I would next see one of the genuinely kind-hearted people in my life.

As I was readying to leave Alice threw her arms around me and hugged me tightly, to the point that it would have been indecent outside of an empty kitchen, particularly to any puritans in the vicinity. For all of her jilted suitors and spurned marriage proposals, Alice was by no means prudish nor someone who ever came across as cold or distant. She was not meant for a nunnery or any form of convent; Alice was just a woman who insisted on doing things her own way.

I remember one Oak Apple Day, when we celebrate the glorious return of the king after Cromwell's joyless decade, heading back to the festivities from the latrines and seeing her in an alley behind the White Stag with the local dyer's husband, who thankfully didn't notice me as he had his face completely buried between Alice's chest as she was unlacing the top of her dress. It was also well-known that she had been intimate with Robert Smythe after Michaelmas on at least one occasion, after the two of them had been seen coming back to Cripplegate in the early morning and retiring together to her nearby home.

However, Alice was shrewd and usually engaged in such dalliances or discreet affairs during major holidays, when the Church was typically more willing to cast a blind eye towards such behaviour. I simply think she rejected the authority of a husband and being tied to someone else's whims, whereas in the kitchen she was the master of her own demesne.

I think this boldness and self-assurance only enhanced her level of attraction in the eyes of most men, although there were quite a few who became bitter and resentful of her constant rejections. There was more than one furious goodwife to refer to Alice as a strumpet or harlot after a night of revelry, but they were never able to make any accusations stick due to the sheriff being one of her most ardent admirers.

Whatever the case, there was no denying the genuine

affection and care she had shown me during my time at the almshouse. I was quick to look past her faults and focus upon her many acts of kindness since my arrival at Cripplegate following the deaths of my parents.

'Right, it won't do for me to start weeping here over my own counter,' Alice finally said as she slowly broke our embrace, although I confess to holding her longer than was strictly necessary in the thought I might never see her again.

'I will miss you though Lewis, you're a gentle soul. Don't you worry about your things while you're away, I'll be sure to keep them safe for when you come back home.'

I gave her hand a squeeze and smiled, hoping to convey my gratitude for her many small acts of compassion.

'I'll be sure to bring you something back as a gift to repay you, thanks Alice. Take care of yourself.'

Without knowing it at the time, my fate would lead me to cross paths with this woman in the strangest of circumstances over the coming years.

Chapter 4

Deptford Dockyard, River Thames, 1678 AD

I was glad to finally stretch my legs upon arriving into Deptford. After a restless night's sleep at the almshouse, with my mind torn between visions of distant lands filled with one-legged creatures and the bright hazel eyes of one of the local washer girls, Sally, I think her name was, I rose to a chill morning.

After grabbing a bowl of porridge and mug of ale I began my search for someone going to Portsmouth who wouldn't mind sharing the cost of a stage coach. There was no sign of Alice and I presumed she must have been away on an errand or somewhere other than the kitchens, but I decided not to wait. The parting last night had felt like a good way to leave things between us until my eventual return to London.

It was the middle of Summer and likely to be a warm day, so at least I didn't need to worry about my humble clothing or the weather turning foul during the trip. Then again, the day before I'd spent hours soaked to the bone under a dark sky, so there was never really any guarantee. London weather, it's the one thing you can be sure to hear people moaning about in the taverns for being too hot, too cold, or somehow both. After my simple breakfast I tapped the small linen purse underneath my britches for good measure and made my way out of the halls to the outer court.

I honestly had no idea where to even begin, other than possibly asking a stage coach driver for the best course of action. They were known for being expensive though and it was common for drivers to fleece new travelers. John Coram had once been red in the face when he was expected in Wrexham all the way out in Wales for a distant family funeral, and the coach was expected to cost a thruppence to the mile. That wasn't even for a comfortable seat, but for sitting up front with the driver or in the rear of the carriage.

Suffice it to say, poor John did not pay his respects to his second cousin's departed wife. Thankfully, a stroke of good fortune came my way as I was leaving Cripplegate. I was in the process of taking one last look around the outer court and its masonry, one of the few areas of the almshouse not made from timber, when Adrian Thorpe came up to wish me well on my travels. He'd heard through Alice I was leaving today, and the two of us had always been on cordial terms.

'If you come back with chests filled with gold dubloons remember old Adrian eh?'

'Will do, you've never given me any hassle or reason for grief. I take it you heard I'm off to become the next Sir Walter then,' I replied.

Adrian smiled and gave me a firm pat on the back. 'Just be sure you don't end up like him. Would have figured you more the Sir Martin type, being a Frobisher and all.'

'That feels a bit too close to home these days, my father's incessant demands we be recognised as Sir Martin's rightful heirs left a sour taste in my mouth for years.'

At this Adrian chuckled, as he removed his hand and

followed my eyes up to the unadorned yet well-made stone columns lining the perimeter of the court. 'You've always had a way with words. Penniless or not, you have the tongue of a cavalier, right enough.'

I knew this was a joke and did not take it to heart. Adrian was known for being frugal and not concerned much with wealth, so long as he had his meals and could sit at his guard booth in peace throughout the days. That's what had made the comment about returning laden with Spanish treasure so amusing. There were even rumours Adrian had been a puritan in the service of Cromwell, but he was not an outwardly devout man so it was hard to credit.

Either way, after a few more light-hearted remarks he suggested talking to one of his friends down at the gunpowder stores near the Tower. One of the third rates, the *Lion*, had just been refurbished and outfitted with a new armament of sixty guns over the last year and was expected to set sail in the coming days. He told me to ask for Douglas, as the man was due to leave under escort with a stock of her gunpowder and munitions. When I looked confused he quickly went on to explain that ships were always addressed in the female way out of tradition.

As I nodded along I was secretly kicking myself inside for my ignorance, as I'd heard this one more than one occasion previously in my time spent with the Corams and Bollards.

'You'll know Douglas soon as you see him,' Adrian went on. 'Thick Scotch accent and a face with more holes in it than a beehive.'

With a final farewell, the man left to return to his post and I made my way out of the almshouse on to the sprawling streets of London.

The trip to Deptford took most of the morning after I met up with Douglas. It was only about seven miles according to the driver, but, since we were transporting gunpowder kegs and raw saltpeter along with other dangerous items, we progressed more slowly than the average stage coach. At least it only cost me a tanner for the entire trip rather than the near two shillings it would have otherwise. Douglas had owed Adrian some unknown favour from their time together in the military and agreed to take me along for a token payment.

I couldn't help feeling troubled throughout the entire journey, despite my good luck in finding an affordable means of transport; every bump in the road or jolt made me worry I would be blown to Kingdom Come. Douglas told me to relax and explained that's not how it works. He said something about open flame and sparks being needed, or at least I think that's what he told me. The man's English was very difficult to understand to my young ears. Despite being the most well-read orphan at Cripplegate, my experience with languages was still mostly limited to the other residents, most of whom were Englishmen.

This would change in the years ahead, as I became familiar with people from all over the World, Scots included, but for the time being I had to struggle to keep up with the man. I did manage to gather that he came from somewhere in Scotland named Edzell and had moved to London as a child due to his father's work. Douglas Fergusson was everything you would expect a soldier to be: He was stocky and well-built with taught muscles from years of heavy lifting, and there was a natural swagger of confidence visible in his every movement. Although these days he helped with shipments for the Royal Navy, he was an army man at his core due to having spent years in King Charles' restructured English Army following his restoration to the throne. His face was pockmarked as the result of an illness during his youth which had sadly carried off his older sister. Such sights were hardly uncommon, but his was one of the worse cases I've seen, with deep, harsh dimples and scars covering his entire visage.

After our initial discussions about home and family we gradually ran out of things to say, and sat in amicable silence for most of the journey. I wished there had been time to see Tom and Michael one last time before leaving London, but I knew they would both be overwhelmed with preparing for market this morning. I made a mental note to write them both letters as soon as possible. They were both competent enough by now to understand my handwriting so long as I kept things simple. Douglas was not one for lengthy conversations and was a man of few words. In my current mood of apprehension about getting a position with the navy this suited me just fine, and I was content to watch the banks of the Thames as we rode southeast towards the dockyards.

'Thir's nae mony yards lik' this yin 'ere, eh laddie?'

I got the gist of what Douglas was saying and was in full agreement. Deptford Dockyard was a sprawling mass of dry docks, rows of accommodations for workers, warehouses for victuals and foodstuffs, launching basins and a number of structures which were of unknown purpose to me. Along with Portsmouth, Plymouth and the newly created Jamaica Dockyard in Port Royal, this was one of England's major centres for the production of new or experimental ships for the

Royal Navy.

There were also dockyards at Sheerness, Woolwich and Chatham, but I was less familiar with these by way of reputation. Indeed, I was only recently made aware of events in Jamaica because one of my fellow residents at Cripplegate, an older man by the name of Jacob Willard, received a letter from his brother who worked as a carpenter in Port Royal and asked me to read it aloud for him.

'It's the first proper naval yard I've seen, before this I mostly just helped out around my friend's fishing trawler out by the Pool,' I said.

'Weel that's th' lion ower thare wi' th' stowed oot riggin,' Douglas pointed at a two-decker resting in the wet basin with freshly painted livery and polished cannon. The ship had obviously been moved out of dry dock quite recently judging by her condition and lack of any barnacles nor scuffing to the hull along the waterline. I had expected Douglas to accompany me down to the wharf, but he was to take the munitions to one of the warehouses from where it would be distributed to the handful of ships ready to set sail in the port.

After he went about his business I had a moment of near-panic, as I was left standing utterly alone in the middle of a bustling shipyard. Then, my experience gained through years spent milling about the Pool of London with Tom and Michael helped steady my nerves, and I made my way down to the docks. I might not be a sailor yet, but I could tell the difference between port and starboard, bow and stern. Hopefully my knowledge, however basic, would prove to be some sort of advantage in landing a job.

๖๏

'Sorry lad, we're already running a full compliment.'

The *Lion*, which I learned was still often referred to as the *Golden Lion* or *Red Lion* by its crew, was a beautiful third-rate ship of the line. There was every sign that she was a force to be reckoned with in any competition at sea. With a long gundeck of over one hundred feet and armed with twenty-four heavy guns on the lower deck, the *Lion* would be able to hold her own in most confrontations.

This main battery was supported by twenty-four demi-culverins on the upper deck alongside ten sakers and two three-pounders. These were smaller cannons which could be used to rake an enemy deck and target its crew, while the twenty-fours below fired a broadside. When added together, the potential to cause devastation was overwhelming in the vast majority of engagements.

There were around eighteen first-rate or second-rate ships currently in service which would be able to outperform her if it came to trading blows in a line of battle, but the smaller third rate had the advantage of being more maneuverable, and it was not a foregone conclusion. I knew none of this at the time, but even her size was enough to inspire a mixed sense of awe and dread. Unfortunately for me, I had just been told there weren't any openings for a wastrel from London begging for work.

'I don't mind whatever it is, I'll scrub decks and help the cook if need be,' I replied, trying to mask the desperation in my voice.

The man had introduced himself as one Stuart Effingham and he was the quartermaster for the *Lion* in charge of its supply and provisions. He gave me a look up and down as if sizing up cattle before answering.

'We just took on the last cabin's boy we'll be needing,' he said. 'You're about an hour late, the lad's already away to fetch the captain's personal requisitions.'

'Is there anything left? I'll kill bloody mice up and down the hold. Hang me overboard from a sheet and I'll scrape the hull as we're under sail.' My feeling of urgency was starting to show itself despite my best efforts.

'Fuckin' Hell, you really do want out of London eh?' Stuart chortled. 'Orphan or thief? Meanin' no offence mind, I've been both in my day.'

I saw an opportunity here and leapt on it. 'Orphan out of Cripplegate, but I've grown up around the Pool.'

'I was at Penrose's down in Barnstaple,' the man replied with a hint of sympathy in his voice. At my blank expression he added, 'down in Devon, that is.'

Just as I was about to press Stuart to do me a good turn from one orphan to another, a loud voice bellowed out from behind us along the wharf: 'I wish I'd had her riding under me at Solebay or Texel. The Dutch wouldn't have stood a chance.'

The man was quite tall with a head of messy black hair, but it was hard to tell his age since his face was flush with cracked skin. This was one of the surest ways to tell an experienced sailor, as the years of sea amidst salt water and heavy winds caused a distinctive ruddy complexion. His bulbous, red nose also spoke of a man who was happiest with a mug of ale or bottle of spirits at hand. However, he was not particularly overweight nor staggering. If anything, the man seemed fully composed and full of vigour.

'What do you think of our fair Lady here, eh boy?' Before I could answer he walked halfway up one of the boarding planks which had been setup for loading cargo and rested a hand against one of the gunports.

'Well, Sir, she's –'

'She's a whore, is what she is. A beautiful, powdered-up, expensive and wonderful strumpet.' The man was now bellowing this loudly, and I noticed the nearby men look up from their tasks with growing smiles.

'Built at Chatham, rebuilt at Woolwich and refitted twice now in different yards,' he went on, 'and with balls in her from all over the world, this lioness has been around more than half my men.' With that he jumped down from the wooden planks to the dock and landed squarely without the slightest hesitation.

After throwing an arm around me, the man came in close and whispered: 'But don't let her know we think that about her eh? It's our little secret, saucy trollop that she is, I also happen to be madly in love with her.'

'This little agger wants to join our crew, Sir,' Stuart finally interrupted.

'What, this wiry sprat thinks he deserves to sail aboard my lover? Does he know how to make her hum with joy, crashing through fifty foot waves with a French cuckold chasing at her heels?'

I opened my mouth but was totally spellbound and unable to say anything. The power of this man's charisma was overwhelming. I noticed a small crowd had gathered to watch us, so it was likely a common enough reaction around the dockyard.

'Well, boy, do you? Answer quickly, we are all busy men.'

Out of nowhere and without thinking I sputtered, 'well, I don't know about that, I reckon she's had enough lovers chasing her over the years.' I paused to point directly at one of the gunports and continued, 'to be honest, I'd much rather listen to her sing.'

There was a moment's pause while everyone digested what had been said. Then, there was an explosion of raucous laughter around the entire pier. At first I was unsure of myself, but one look at the men's faces told me I had said the right thing. The laughter became mixed with cheers and hurrahs as the man extended his hand in my direction.

'Captain Henry Williams, at your service,' he said. 'I'd love for you to come along and hear her roar, but Mister Effingham will no doubt have told you we are full. If anything, we're needing to cycle out one or two lads for the coming voyage.'

My face must have visibly dropped after hearing the captain reaffirm what the quartermaster had already declared.

'I'didn't catch your name, boy?'

I regained my composure and said, 'Lewis Frobisher, Sir.'

'Oh-ho, Frobisher, you say? Well, be that as it may, I will do you a favour for that clever reply of yours, rather than for your namesake. There's a ship heading out from Woolw –'

Just then a boy of about seventeen came running up the wharf, with a small leather-bound chest under each arm.

'Here they are, Sir,' the boy gasped between breaths. 'Both the chests for the captain's quarters as you ordered, Sir.'

The captain raised his eyebrow, and it was then I noticed to my dismay that I knew the cabin boy all too well: It was Will Baker, my very own tormenting demon.

'What's this little shit doing here?'

I eyed Will with my usual feeling of terror, enhanced

by the fact there was no way I could run in front of three dozen sailors and ever hope to get a spot on the *Lion*. Just then something out of the corner of my eye caught my attention rustling on the pier below my feet. I reached down and picked up a small piece of linen wrap, which had the following written on it in a clear text:

-One small portrait of my wife Charlotte
-Four ink wells
-Eight writing quills
-Two lengths woolen fabric
-Three small chests for general storage
-Cat

The rest of my quarters has already been brought on board.
H.W.

'You may be bigger, but clearly there's not much going on between your ears,' I mocked, feeling a sudden surge of confidence after reading the note. 'You're one chest short if I'm not mistaken.' I had no idea if Will had already been back and forth to unload the captain's belongings, but thankfully my gamble paid off.

'He's right, there should be a third chest,' put in Captain Williams. 'We needed to trim down a bit before heading to Barbados again, so this is good enough a reason as any. Mister Effingham, if you could be sure to strike Mister Baker from the crew listing.' With that he turned to head back in the direction of the mast yard, no doubt going over final preparations and checks prior to departure.

Suddenly, I felt a crashing pain to the side of my temple and my vision swam before my eyes.

Before I knew what was happening, Will was on top of me and pummeling me about the head with both fists.

I brought my arms up in order to try and fend off the blows, but his reach and strength made sure the majority of his swings connected.

After a moment Will started to slow his punches then stopped altogether and shouted: 'I know how to throw shit like this overboard, that has to count for something.'

As the captain had turned to watch along with the rest of the men, I lay on my back and looked around desperately for anything that would help. Just as Will was finishing his boast I noticed a heavy iron bollard near my right arm which was on the verge of coming loose from its fittings. It was just out of reach, but if I could get a few inches over…

My thoughts were interrupted by another brutal punch to the face, this time connecting with my cheekbone and no doubt leaving an awful bruise. I made a point of trying to cover most of my right side, which in turn made Will lash out more with his right fist. This caused us to slowly shuffle sideways away from the *Lion*. On the verge of passing out from the pain and unable to fully focus my eyes, I reached out and felt the rough metal post in my right hand. With all of my remaining strength I pulled upwards and the bollard came crashing into the left side of Will's head. There was a sickening crunch and I felt his weight fall on top of me. After that, my eyes rolled up in my head as everything faded from existence.

I gasped as I awoke to the feeling of ice cold water pouring across my face.

'There he is, you had us worried.'

Captain Williams and Mister Effingham were kneeling over me, the former with a wide grin on his face and the latter looking seriously concerned. I slowly rose up from where I had been sprawled out and the world burst into pain. Suddenly, I felt the cool, smooth surface of a clay pot in my hand.

'Take a swig or two of that, it'll see you through,' said one of the crew who briefly knelt next to me. I uncorked the jar and was instantly hit with the pungent aroma of strong rum. Without a second thought I greedily poured a large mouthful of the burning liquid down my throat. It was enough to steady me for sitting upright rather than laying on the wooden dock.

'I feel like I've been run over by a brewer on his cart,' I muttered.

'That's nothing, you should see the other boy,' the captain said. He seemed amused, but there was something about the tone of his voice that seemed off, as if he regretted making the remark.

I slowly go to my feet, with two of the crew steadying me from the sides. My face felt like it was going to explode from pressure, and I could barely see anything out of the narrow slits my eyes had become through the swelling. I've been through worse since, but at the time it was by far the most viscious beating anyone had ever given me.

'Well, you can read a list and hold you're own in a fight against a bigger man,' said Captain Williams.

'Those are always things we can be doing with when we're hunting marks or in port. Have you any belongings then?'

I was slow to respond, but the captain was patient given the circumstances. 'No... Sir, just the clothes on my back.'

'Good, that keeps things simple. You'll be answering to me directly as cabin boy, but a quick word of caution: Every other lad comes from a respectable background and their families sent them to me with careers in mind. Just be prepared for any nonsense and keep your wits about you. The pay is four shillings per month with the chance of future promotion through commendable service.'

As my mind started to slowly process the turn of events, I nodded and instantly regretted doing so.

'Well then, what are you waiting for?' Captain Williams asked. 'Get aboard with my chests. Don't worry about the third one, I already sent one of the other lads to bring it here.'

I gingerly gathered up the chests into my arms and made to walk aboard the *Lion*. As I was passing Stuart Effingham he gave me an odd look then said, 'having a killer in the crew is no bad thing, so long as he follows the captain's orders.'

It was only then I fully grasped the outcome of the fight and looked back to a ghastly sight. Will Baker was flat on his stomach surrounded by a pool of blood, the bollard firmly embedded in the left side of his skull.

He was stone dead.

Chapter 5

The Narrow Sea, 1679 AD

It turns out killing a man isn't the end of the world when you're in the navy.

The soldiers of the Admiral's Regiment, those men picked from the Trained Bands of London to serve aboard each ship, were accustomed to seeing such violence between shipmates. These *Marines*, as most of us had taken to calling them, were hard men hand-picked for their ability to fight on deck at close quarters. Even though they largely kept to themselves and would sometimes jeer at the general crew, I came to realise there was a strong enough bond between us that, in the event some sheriff's man from the Old Bailey came asking after Will Baker, I could rely on them to turn such glorified-clerks away.

It never happened, probably due to the fact Will was unknown outside of the almshouse. If he had been the son of a wealthy merchant or minor noble, I wager it would have been a different matter entirely. I also learned the men of the *Lion* had loathed him during his brief stint aboard ship.

He had resented being given the tasks of a ship's boy due to his age, and made his contempt for the menial tasks well-known; it had been a test by Captain Williams to check the bull-headed newcomer and his ability to follow orders. It goes without saying that Will failed miserably. He had been slow to understand the first and most vital rule when you become a sailor of any kind:

Aboard ship, the captain is king.

My time with the Corams had definitely helped condition me to following orders without question, and I had a keen grasp of this relationship before even setting foot on the large third rate. Old John was not someone to be argued with. However, even I was arguably too old for the role of cabin boy at sixteen, but my wiry frame and inability to keep my nerves from showing made me appear a few years younger. Mister Effingham had commented on my nervous scratchings a few times once we were underway. It was a habit which tended to irritate others, and I made an effort to at least hide it while at sea with the two hundred other men who were now my brothers.

Actually, that's bollocks.

They treated me like shit for the first several months, but we'll come to that.

Before I get into my first experiences of life aboard sea, I really haven't done the *Lion* justice. Make no mistake, Captain Williams had not been making idle boasts about her beauty. With pristine woodwork polished through many hours of careful labour, mostly a mixture of oak and elm, even the most casual observer could tell she had undergone a brand new refit. Her hull had been painted a jet-black to mask the expensive Swedish tar used for waterproofing.

Two large bands of pale orange paint were then added in stark contrast along the sides of the hull, stretching from the captain's quarters at the stern to the foremast near the bow. King Charles and the admiralty were keen for England's ships to form some semblance of uniformity to avoid any accidental engagements, but ultimately the captains still had the final word. The most they had been able to agree on was this hooped design of either one, two or three thick lines of lighter paint against black.

They were most commonly painted in ochre, what Captain Williams always referred to as 'baby puke' yellow, but orange, green, blue and red were not uncommon either. Indeed, the *Lion* had been painted this way prior to her latest refitting, when the captain opted for the new orange-black scheme. In theory, it was enough to distinguish our own from the French, Dutch or Spanish fleets which tended towards a simpler use of colour. However, unless you were within range for boarding it was not reliable, and identifying a ship's flags, pennants or sail was the usual method for telling friend from foe. The man o' war had three main masts and a bowsprit painted and varnished to match her hull, with white square-rigged sails made from strong storm canvas.

A number of studding and spanker sails were on board as well, but more often stowed away below deck. Our sailmakers, led by a fellow Londoner by the name of Benjamin Bridgeman, were always kept busy patching and repairing the inevitable wear-and-tear. One of his mates, Henry Every, would become one of my closest friends in the years ahead. I didn't know it at the time, but Henry, this cocksure twenty-something who helped keep the *Lion* looking her best, would play a central role in shaping my own future as a sailor, for better or worse.

It was aboard this striking vessel that I got my first true taste of life at sea. No amount of time spent fishing on the Thames could have prepared me for the harsh, brutal reality of life as a whipping boy at the bottom of the pecking order in the seemingly endless chain of command. When I was not running back and forth between the kitchen and the forecastle I was either standing watch for hours on end, or forcing myself up the rigging to help trim the sails. If any member of the crew needed so much as a button sewn or his boots mended, that fell on me to sort out, no matter my current orders. Here was the main problem and source of my frequent beatings:

I was usually running errands for the captain, but one of his direct commands was to assist any member of the crew at their request. If I neglected getting a new whistle for the bosun because I was fetching tobacco for Captain Williams, that was a boot up the arse. And, if I didn't arrive promptly with the captain's tobacco due to helping the cook peel carrots for the evening meal, that was likewise a swift kick to the backside. There was simply no way to avoid someone's ire.

Even the men I was on decent enough terms with like Stuart Effingham or the Ship's Cook, Daniel Evatt, would give me a smack to the back of my head at times. I could tell from the lack of force this was usually just to keep up appearances in front of the nearly three hundred men aboard when we were running a full compliment, but it made me fume all the same.

Unfortunately for me, others were much more severe. James Whitworth, a rotund and red-faced older prick who served as the Ship's Chaplain, was particularly fond of walloping me with his cane. I was used to beatings during my time in Cripplegate from Alderman Samuel or his staff, but there was something about being lashed in front of laughing marines while having to listen to a never-ending sermon which felt more shameful.

For all of Samuel's faults he did care for me in his

own way ever since my parents' deaths, and I can't honestly say he ever gave me a thrashing out of pure malice without reason. Part of me felt guilty for not saying goodbye to him properly when I left the almshouse, but it certainly didn't keep me up at night.

Anyway, so much for dreams of exotic vistas and shaking hands with Sir Henry Morgan at a banquet in Port Royal. Instead, my life ebbed and flowed to the daily rhythm of exhaustion and pain.

Thankfully, this miserable existence did not last forever. After about six months serving under Captain Williams as his cabin boy something happened to finally lift me out of this wretched position. It was the middle of January, and we were about to have a few days' leave during the *Lion's* monthly resupply of provisions. As I was in the middle of fetching new sheet for the midshipman there was a sudden shout from above deck.

'The stupid fuck's gone over.'

It was the voice of one of our marines, I couldn't even begin to try and remember his name.

'What you reckon?' Answered the man standing next to him as I came running up to see what the commotion was about. 'Tuppence says he goes under as well.'

As I turned my attention from the intimidating presence of the two marines leaning over the ship's side next to the rear swing guns, my eyes snapped to a writhing shape in the water. One of the crew had fallen overboard. This wasn't the first time it had happened, but in the darkness of a Winter morning before most of the crew were at their stations it became much more dangerous. I recognised the man's sputtering voice as that of Bill Pritchard, one of the Carpenter's mates. He was well-liked by the crew and known for telling lewd stories or jokes to keep spirits up. Without pausing to think, I got to my knees and shouted through one of the wooden grates: 'All hands, man overboard!'

I knew the ventilation grill was positioned roughly above the men stuck working overnight on bilge pump duty two decks below. I was hoping that someone would get the message and pass it along. After a few long seconds, there was grumbling from the hammocks immediately below. I repeated my call and then heard the sound of the alarm bell ringing out from the aft of the ship; one of the helmsmen had reached a similar conclusion and was vigorously rattling it to rouse the crew. Within moments, the *Lion* went from quietly swaying at anchor to a cacophony of noise.

'Get a line out to him,' bellowed Captain Williams as he took swift control over the situation. He was in his dark blue coat as always, while the men were in their usual mishmash of clothing, but I could tell they had all been fast asleep moments earlier. Now that the captain and entire crew were coming alive, the marines who had moments ago been placing a wager on Bill's situation snapped to attention and joined the rescue effort.

To his credit, the man who had suggested the bet hoisted one of the spare sheets from behind the swivel cannon, tied it to the nearby timberhead, and then cast it out with remarkable accuracy in the direction of the drowning woodworker. There was an audible groan from the crew as we quickly realised it fell short due to a wave rolling him away from the line. Then, I did something that to this day I've never been able to fully comprehend. Bill Pritchard had never been especially kind and had booted me a few times for good measure, but I knew him to be popular with the men. It's the only reason I can think of to explain why I threw myself overboard in one swift leap. The distance to the water would have normally given any man pause, let alone under the cover of darkness lit only by the faint half-moon.

With no concussion unlike my prior time overboard, I was able to start swimming out in Bill's general direction as the crew shouted at him to keep calling out. With my wiry frame and lean physique, I had never felt uncomfortable in the water and was a comfortable swimmer. It still makes me shake my head when I think of how many sailors I have known over the years who would drown in a puddle if they happened to trip. Bill was one of these men, who despite years at sea was completely incapable of keeping himself afloat.

'I've got you…' I spattered between gulps of air. 'Just hold the line and breathe.'

Above I could hear one of the lieutenants shouting the usual rhythm of 'yo-heave-ho' as the crew hauled in the spare jigger line. The final minutes of the rescue passed in a blur. I remember reaching the beam end with Bill and being jostled aboard, but then my exposure to the freezing waters took hold of my senses.

꙳

My next recollection was sitting in the sickbay next to Bill draped in a coarse flax blanket with a pewter mug of rum in my hands. I looked up and saw Captain Williams, Benjamin Bridgeman and James Whitworth huddled nearby in discussion. The Ship's Surgeon, one Walter Crouch, must have just left to give them some privacy after tending to Bill and myself. Our chaplain had likely been told to remain at-hand in case either of us required the sacraments. After a moment he turned to leave, but gave me an appreciative nod before exiting through the small doorway.

'How are you feeling?' Captain Williams sat at the surgeon's desk to address us.

'A bit groggy, sir,' replied Bill wearily, likely in anticipation of his punishment. 'If it weren't for the lads I'd be… well,' he tapered off.

He made no mention of what I had done whatsoever. I remember feeling betrayed at the time, but eventually I came to realise the whole event had been a severe blow to the man's pride. A competent sailor of many years needing to be rescued by a cabin boy of six months was not easily forgotten by the rest of the crew. Still, everyone had seen what happened, so there was no real need to bring it up.

'You wouldn't be sitting here drinking my rum, I'll tell you that much,' said the captain with a barely contained grin. 'What in God's name happened, man?'

Bill then explained to us how he had been fitting a new timberhead, one of those smaller wooden bollards for securing sheet, but had dropped his hammer and it got wedged under the marine's walk. After trying to lean himself underneath his grip had failed and he had plunged into the water, thankfully far enough alongside as to avoid getting sucked under the keel.

'Well, so far as I can see it you owe one hammer out of your wages,' the captain cracked his back. 'But, I reason you've had enough torment for one night. Finish your mug then see yourself to Mister Adams. I imagine he will have a few choice words for you about losing one of his valuable tools.'

Bill nodded into his mug but did not reply.

Captain Williams then turned his attention towards me. 'As for you, Mister Frobisher,' he went on. 'I have need of a new undergarment Mister Bridgeman here fashioned for me from some of that fine Dutch cotton he keeps in reserve. Fetch it and bring it back here.' With that he gave me a curt dismissal of the hand, and Ben indicated for me to follow him out of the sickbay. While I was thinking about how ungrateful both Bill and Captain Williams had been given that I had just thrown myself in harm's way to save a member of the crew, Benjamin Bridgeman, who I learned preferred to go by Ben, led me to the sailmaker's workshop. The galley and lower gun deck were quiet as we made our way towards the sailroom, as the crew were only now slowly returning to their stations or hammocks, but the few men we passed gave me a quick hurrah or clap on the back.

'Well, here it is,' Ben handed me a bundle of soft fabric. 'See to it the captain gets it right away.'

'Yes, sir.' I replied and turned to leave.

'Oh, one other thing,' the sailmaker went on, 'after doing so you're to report back to me for your first duties as Sailmaker's Mate.'

I turned to look at him, no doubt with a perplexed countenance. He was smiling broadly and added, 'We thought about making you a landsman, but I'm in over my head keeping this Lady properly dressed and could use another mate or two, so the captain agreed to wave the usual order for promotion.'

'For the bigwigs at the admiralty there's still only the captains, lieutenants and masters anyway as official ranks, so it's an easy enough thing for him to decide on his own ship,' Ben continued. 'That is, unless you'd rather work with the bilge boys?'

'No, that's perfectly alright Mister Bridgeman,' I replied. 'I'll happily work for you and try to perform my duties with the utmost dedication.'

He laughed aloud at this overly verbose and flowery response; it was well-known that bilge duty was the most despised job anywhere on the ship.

'Good, then join my mate Henry in sorting that backup jib after you see the captain,' he said. 'The one we have up is starting to show signs of fraying at the seams.' With that he turned to get back to his endless checklist of tasks.

I was still numb from my midwinter swim, but could barely keep the spring out of my step as I made my way astern with the captain's new chemise.

It turns out I was pretty popular.

For six months I had endured the mockery and abuse as part of life, having resigned myself to the role. Not once had it ever occurred to me that it was a rite of passage for every ship's boy throughout the entire fleet. It explained why quite a few men only smacked me upside the head or put barely any effort into their swings. Also, if I had been less preoccupied with my own Hellish duties I would have noticed the two other ship's boys having an even worse time of it.

I have long forgotten their names, as we rarely had time to talk, but I recall one of them would often throw unfriendly glances in my direction between errands. I had always just figured he disliked me for one reason or another, but after a while I came to understand the root of such hostile glares: The boy was jealous.

Sure enough, Captain Williams was beaming when I returned to the sickbay with his new attire slung over my shoulder. He must have finished talking with Bill and dismissed him to his work, for he was nowhere to be seen. The captain shook my hand with relish and congratulated me on showing such bravery and courage in the face of danger. The clever bastard had been masking his emotions behind a mask of indifference ever since I dragged Bill back from Neptune's cold, wet fingers. Now, the jovial and energetic man I recalled from first arriving in Deptford returned in full force.

'That's more like it,' he barked between swigs of ale. 'A man of my crew, not some piss poor excuse for a lowly cabin boy, eh?'

He passed me the flagon of ale and motioned for me to take a seat. After doing so and taking a long pull I remarked, 'I'd be lying if I said it didn't feel damned good, sir. The last six months have been shit.'

'Oh I have no doubt,' he chuckled with a mischievous look. 'I can't say I know how it feels, but our esteemed surgeon Mister Crouch certainly does.'

The knowledge that a man as well-respected and influential as Walter Crouch had his start as a ship's boy raised my spirits significantly. Captain Williams must have noticed the effect his comment had on me.

'I've commanded six ships before this lovely lass, and of all the boys I've seen you handled the humiliation with the most grace.' The captain narrowed his eyes and said, 'given that you killed a man within your first ten minutes on my dock, that is doubly worthy of praise.'

As I was about to protest, he threw up his hands in mock acquiescence, 'I know, I know… you were wholly within your rights to defend yourself, a poor jest on my part. I was standing right there as a keen member of the audience, if you'll recall.'

At this I couldn't help but let out a laugh myself, despite feelings of guilt over the death of Will Baker creeping into the back of my mind. It took every bit of concentration to stop scratching the sides of the chair's smooth velvet cushion. Still, the good-humoured encouragement from the captain assuaged my feelings of bitterness or regret. I listened as he went on to tell me about how the crew had appreciated my quick banter upon arriving at the dockyards.

Apparently my bit about hearing the ship 'sing' had gotten jumbled around into hearing the 'Lion's roar' through word of mouth, but I was more than happy to take the credit. As for my fight with Will, the crew was divided on whether or not I took things too far by grabbing the iron bollard, but they were all in agreement that I was ultimately in the right of the dispute. Hearing such things directly from this storm of a man I couldn't help but believe them; Captain Williams was one of those people who you just knew was not the type to lie.

There was something about his frank openness and lust for life that made him come across as completely and utterly earnest. It's likely that all the world's best tricksters seem that way, but in all the years I kept in touch with the man he never gave me reason to doubt his sincerity. Finally, after about twenty minutes the captain wished me well and gave my conduct one last note of praise, then he dismissed me to my new station as one of Ben Bridgeman's mates.

The *Lion* was unusually deserted as I left the sickbay. It was eerily quiet for some reason, and I could not hear nor see anyone on the entire lower gun deck. The only sound apart from the usual creaking of the oak beams and tinkling of the masts was a soft stomping sound coming from above. Even the bilge below was strangely quiet, and the hammocks were all empty which was something I had never seen before. My initial thoughts were that I must have somehow missed our arrival into port while talking with the captain, and had in turn missed going on shore leave with the majority of the crew.

Ships generally left a minimal skeleton crew behind, serving on rotation at crucial stations while moored. However, that didn't explain the hammocks; there are always a handful of sailors sleeping while off-duty, no matter the circumstances. My mind then turned to feelings of irrational panic: What if the ship was sinking and I had missed the long-boats to get ashore?

Suddenly, I saw Captain Williams rush past on the opposite side of the deck in a mad dash. This did nothing to steady my nerves, and only served to increase my growing sense of dread. At the same time, I couldn't help but wonder what on Earth was going on. In my six months at sea there had been nothing like this. It couldn't be an attack by the French, because if that were the case the gun decks would be a mass of activity and noise. Granted, I had yet to witness a full broadside in action, but I had seen the gun crews discharge test shots often enough to imagine the scale of smoke and chaos on some level.

The only thing for it was to go above deck and see if any of the marines were at watch who could explain what was going on. I increased my pace and, after popping my head into the powder stores and galley to no avail, eventually made my away above into the typically overcast and dull January weather.

It was with these mixed feelings of cautious apprehension and curiosity that I emerged on to the main deck, only to see all two hundred and sixty men erupt into a mass of cheers, cat-calls and whistles. Even the marines, who could be stone-faced and reserved at the best of times, were hollering and pumping their muskets above their heads.

It turns out diving into the water to save Bill Pritchard was a damned fine decision after all.

Chapter 6

Moorfields, London, 1679 AD

I woke up with someone's foot in my face.

Within moments every one of my senses recoiled in horror, as I scrambled to lean my head over the side of the makeshift bed and void my stomach's contents from the night before. It was with great relief that I realised there had been a clay basin positioned next to the bedpost, likely for this very reason. Slowly, I wiped the foul aftertaste from my mouth and managed to sit upright as a torrent of pain washed over my entire body.

The room was dimly lit, with the remains of two tallow candles burning upon a poorly-built wooden table in the middle of the room. Sunlight was coming in through cracks in the equally shoddy wall and only added to my confused sense of dread. It was already morning, if not later in the day, and I had no idea as to my whereabouts. My stomach was queasy beyond measure and my head was pounding as I squinted to survey my surroundings. I tried to speak, only to find my mouth was completely parched with the taste of stale drink and my own sick. Ah.

Well, that would explain quite a few things.

My first impulse had been to try and wake the person laying next to me upon the straw bed, but after a moment's hesitation I thought better of it. Then, an overwhelming desire to escape and flee the premises took hold. There was a mass of brown curls half-covered by a woolen blanket hanging off the end of the bedframe, and as I looked around the room I saw my britches and coarse linen shirt laying on the floor next to an old armchair.

A slender ankle poking out from the blanket, where my head had been resting seconds earlier, showed clearly feminine qualities, and the reality of what had happened began to dawn on me. Or, at the very least, I was beginning to realise in what type of establishment I had passed the night.

There was an empty flagon resting on the table next to the candles, and between the rank smell of body odour and cheap wine I quietly stumbled to my feet. I tried to gingerly gather up my meagre belongings without waking the woman, in order to avoid the inevitably awkward conversation which would follow, but quickly discovered it was not necessary; I could have made all the noise of a tavern during Christmastide and it would not have mattered.

The woman was in the thrall of a deep, drink-induced sleep, and would not wake until it passed of its own accord. After quickly dressing myself I crept out of the doorway into the small hallway lined with doors no doubt leading to bedrooms very similar to this one, and I made my way downstairs.

My hopes of leaving the brothel unnoticed were crushed when I descended the rickety stairs into the common room below. It consisted of a small entryway from the street, two wooden benches propped up against the walls and a small counter behind which rested two large casks. I remember they looked ancient, with splintered wood in several spots, and thinking they must have been strictly decorative. A short man who looked to be perhaps ten years my senior stood behind the counter, while two broad-shouldered men sat opposite one another on the benches.

They had that look of menace to them which was all too common down on the docks around port. One was slightly taller and wore a shirt with slightly fewer sweat markings around its collar, but both were adorned in dull brown coats made of coarse wool and had large oak clubs strapped to their belts. At one glance I knew them to be the local bully boys hired by the shop for keeping patrons in their place, and to ensure they didn't try and pull a runner without coughing up for the night's entertainment.

The three men all looked in my direction as I paused at the bottom of the stairs. In a moment of panic I patted at my coat but felt the reassuring weight of my coin purse. Whatever happened the night before, at least I had not been robbed nor blown my entire month's pay in a night of drunken debauchery. I raised my hand in a quick gesture of greeting to the men and they returned my wave with friendly smiles. Actually, that's not entirely true—the man on the nearest bench made a terrifying grimace through a scarred face covered with painful-looking sores—but the reception was nonetheless a courteous one.

'You had a nice evening then, yes?' The small, thickly-jowled man said in a thick French accent.

'Bonjour, pour être honnête, je ne me souviens pas beaucoup,' I replied. *Good morning, to be honest I don't remember much.* My attempt at French, using a combination of the words my Father had taught me and a few bits and pieces I had picked up from Michael over the years, paid off and the brothel's proprietor beamed.

'A man of culture, see Jean?' The man made an

elaborate bow towards one of the hired goons. 'I told you I know a man's station by his noble bearing, non?'

I guessed the man's name to be John through the accent, but he just grunted an acknowledgment without comment.

'Henri Allard, at your service,' the Frenchman continued. 'Make sure to tell your many friends they should stay the night as well when next you visit,' he trailed off with an odd glint in his eye. What was it? Lust? Greed? Before I could reply, Henri quickly regained his composure and with a flourish beckoned me to take a seat. I made my way over and took one of the tall white stools out from underneath the counter.

Then, with my aching body groaning in protest, I lowered myself into a more comfortable position.

'How much do I owe you for the night, Mister Allard?'

'Oh, call me Henri, please,' he said. 'Only Madame Cresswell calls me *Monsieur* Allard, and she has not come for her collections in a while.'

Despite the man's insistence against formalities he was clad in expensive-looking clothing, likely to try and mask his unfortunate looks . Henri's greasy black hair was combed over to mask a vicious burn mark which covered the entire left side of his scalp, and his poor attempt at a beard only highlighted the sickly yellow hue of both his skin and eyes. As the man took a deep pull from a flagon before placing it back upon the counter, I tried not to stare and directed my gaze towards his attire.

He reminded me of those peafowl painted in one of the displays at Saint Giles, as cloth dyed in every colour imaginable was visible in his multiple layers of fabric. It was still midwinter, and although a small brazier was lit in the corner of the room it was nevertheless a cold morning. His coat itself was finely stitched and dyed in a deep blue colour which must have cost him a substantial amount of coin.

Henri patted my hand and assured me that no payment was required other than a smile, and I had the uncomfortable sensation of being studied like a prize bull. Still, considering my head was still swimming and I felt ready to throw up at any moment, I was in no mood for any type of confrontation so I sat there no doubt looking confused.

'Your shipmates paid your meal and board before heading off for the Anchor,' he explained. 'They insisted, even though I charged double rates because of the…' Henri paused, as if looking for the proper words in English, 'condition you were in.'

I groaned as the hazy memories came flooding back to me. After my raucous reception on the deck of the *Lion*, I had gone ashore for leave with about fifty of the crew as the rest dispersed in smaller groups of their own. I remember seeing the captain in the crowd, along with Mister Effingham and several other familiar faces, but I had been rat-arsed by the time our longboat even reached the piers. The rest was a blur of laughter, shouting and bawdy jokes. I'd had one too many cups a few times before during one holiday or another, but this was the first time I'd gone completely overboard, swept up in the moment and basking in the frenzied attention from my mates.

'Yes, I apologise for any trouble I may have caused you last night, Mist–um, Henri,' I said.

'*Non, non* you were a perfect gentleman,' he replied. 'I'm sure Dorothea will say the same when she awakes.'

Just then my stomach let out a rumble easily heard by

everyone present, which led to a round of laughter. I joined in despite myself, since the knowledge that my evening had been paid for in advance, which in turn meant I was under no immediate threat from Henri or his staff, had helped to calm my mood.

However, I was still feeling very ill and weary of my surroundings and I wanted to leave as quickly as possible. After a mug of tepid water offered by Henri, along with a half-round of cheese and a pork sausage which I swiftly devoured, I bid them a good day and staggered out into the street.

After a few disoriented minutes walking past grocer's stalls, taverns and other knocking shops I came out to a wet marshland surrounded by rows of trees. As I looked to my right I saw in the distance the new buildings for the Bethlem Hospital and knew exactly where I was: The Finsbury Fields just up from the Moorgate. With a great sigh of relief, I walked over to sit underneath one of the oak trees lining the walkway through the green. No longer feeling the overwhelming sense of worry which comes with being lost, I sat and closed my eyes for a few minutes.

Taking deep breaths and scratching frantically at the thick bark behind my back, I allowed my mind to wander aimlessly. I was just north of the Moorfields, which gave its name to the Moorgate entrance through the London Wall. Cripplegate was not far to the west, easily within walking distance. I'd been up this way many times looking for work and running errands for Alderman Samuel, but this was my first taste of its well-known nighttime attractions.

I briefly considered going to see Alice at the almshouse, but the bells of the nearby churches had started clanging for Terce and I knew Alice would be run off her feet with work. I remembered drinking several mugs of brandy with Henry Every in a cheers from one Sailmaker's Mate to another, and he had told me we didn't need to be back aboard until the following Tuesday afternoon. That gave me an entire day and night to fill before returning to work.

Work.

I remember smiling to myself, sitting there beneath a gnarled, old Oak tree in the soaking wet grass. I was in service to the king and a member of his fleet, however humble my station. After deductions for the widows' and invalids' funds my pay came in at around nine shillings each month, although from now on it would be closer to seventeen shillings with my promotion.

By no means a life of luxury, but enough to keep me fed and free from Cripplegate or the streets of London. Besides, there was always the chance of Captain Williams spying a nice, plump Dutch cog laden with spoils for us to seize. Even with our modest pay, a good prize could set up every crewman in comfort for years to come.

As if on command my stomach gurgled in protest, clearly reminding me that many sailors would piss their spoils away on drink and women within a year of attaining such good fortune. The rain began to pour more steadily as I sat there daydreaming and getting soaked through.

At first it had felt refreshing after emerging from the whorehouse and its cloying stench, but now I was starting to feel the January chill underneath my thin shirt and undyed woolen coat. I cursed under my breath as I got to my feet and decided to drop in unannounced on the Corams and Bollards. The fair walk would keep the cold away from my bones, and if the rain turned into a downpour I knew of several sheltered spots between Moorfields and London Bridge where I could take refuge. With thoughts of seeing my friends for the first time in months I started out for the banks of the Thames.

&⬥

About halfway through the walk I stopped off to treat myself. This was the first shore leave I had been able to take advantage of since enlisting with the *Lion*, and I fully intended to make the most of it. After having a bowl of mutton soup washed down with a mug of ale at a tavern on Cheapside I purchased a good round of Wensleydale and a couple of small mince pies from a nearby cheesemonger and bakery.

Feeling content at having bought a good meal out of my own earnings, I lazily made my way towards the river. It had stopped raining and the skies were now the usual dreary grey for this time of year in London. Every step farther away from the morning's events helped to improve my mood. Indeed, by the time I was passing through Walbrook my thoughts had shifted to telling Tom and Michael all about the night's escapades.

I'd just have to be sure to do so well out of earshot of John or Bethany Coram, unless I wanted a God-fearing thrashing to put Alderman Samuel to shame. With a spring to my step thanks to the hot meal, enhanced by a growing sense of excitement at seeing my closest friends, I was starting to feel like a new man by the time I came up to the north bank of the Thames not far upriver from the old bridge.

My thoughts turned to the girl who had been fast asleep back at the brothel. Dorothea had been what Henri called her, but whether or not that was her working name I would likely never find out. I wasn't completely inexperienced when it came to making 'the beast with two backs', as Adrian Thorpe was fond of calling it, but this felt completely different.

The few times I had enjoyed someone else's company for the evening had been with local girls living around Cripplegate, since I could usually charm them enough with a few poems or stories for a quick turn. One of these days I would have to thank Samuel for ensuring I learned how to read. Waking up half-drunk from a night on the town next to one of the Devil's own succubi felt significantly more dangerous and wanton. A more devout man would likely have felt appalled and run for the nearest church seeking absolution or some form of guidance.

As a lad of sixteen who had just said goodbye to the lowly position of Cabin Boy and become a man in the eyes of his fellow crew, I felt much more inclined towards arrogant bravado. The matter of Will Baker and some of the less admirable parts of my life aboard the *Lion* I had resolved to keep to myself as best I could.

Lost in my own thoughts, I didn't even remember crossing over the bridge. Usually I took my time to look along the water or underneath to the stone foundations, and I was always curious to observe the progress of the construction yards. I hoped I had not passed by Charles Mason without so much as a hello, but I was already coming up to the southern end of the bridge. It was still quite early in the afternoon by the time I walked the winding paths down to the ramshackle fishermen's huts and moorings comprising the Pool of London. The familiar scenery where I had spent so many days of my youth brought a smile to my face as I made my way down to the tightly-packed cluster of homes.

'You'll be fine with that lot aboard,' said Stephen. 'You just be sure to stay below deck Lewis, don't get any notions of bravery or you'll end up stuck like a pig on the end of some heathen's cutlass… or worse.'

The image flashed before my eyes and I shuddered.

'No sir, I have no desire to end my days as a slave in the markets of Algiers,' I replied with more confidence than I felt.

I'd found Michael helping his father restock the winter stores of salted eel and Tom had come bounding up to join us from the wharf when he heard my voice. After a few minutes of slaps on the back and excitable banter the discussion had taken a more serious tone; Stephen Bollard had heard talk of Berber corsairs. A few years ago Sir John Narborough had beaten the pirates of Tunis and Tripoli into submission, but there were still tales of raids along the coast and France was becoming increasingly frustrated with *Dey* Mohammed. The threat of the corsairs had been greater in the time of Cromwell for most of the English coastline, but Algiers was still taking slaves throughout Christendom.

'I don't know the man well, you know what marines are like,' I went on.

'True enough, they might seem puffed up and God knows they love to lord it over the men,' Stephen said. 'But, you can trust them to do their duty when you've got Musulmen clambering up your hull, with their curved blades between their teeth, eh? For all their ways, the king's marines are hard as they come, to a man.'

Unfortunately for Stephen, his brief service in the

merchant fleet had ended in a brief period of captivity aboard a Tunisian galley. Even so, he was always quick to praise the four men who had laid down their lives trying to protect the ship against overwhelming odds. He didn't like to talk about the details of his time as prisoner and tended to keep the story vague, but one point he never left out was the self-sacrifice of the small contingent of marines who he had come to know over months at sea.

Our own Lieutenant George Selby often told tales of his experiences fighting the Ottoman corsairs out of Barbary. I've no doubt many of his stories were exaggerated, as it's hard to believe a single man fending off a dozen heathens with one of his arms in a sling, but the cadence of his voice made it clear he was experienced in the ways of man-to-man combat.

The pot calling the pot black, you say? Oh Baltasar, hush. Have I not kept my tale free of serpents and fantastical beasts thus far? What? Don't worry my friend, we have time yet and I promised you the honest truth. It's not my fault sea serpents are all too real! Anyway, we will come to them, so stop interrupting and let me finish.

We finished helping Stephen fillet the eel and rub salt deeply into the flesh for about another hour in relative silence, with each man focused upon his task. My mind was preoccupied with thoughts of men barking an unfamiliar tongue pouring over the sides of the *Lion* with murderous intent. I'd never seen a Berber galley before, but I'd seen the occasional trader out of the Maghreb around the city. Adorned with knee-high boots and layers of finely-stitched fabric, often dyed in a striking red or light blue, they tended to stand out amongst the drab browns and dark greens common to the London docks.

Every one I had ever seen also covered his head with a form of wrap, although the shape and design of these varied considerably. For some reason they seemed more menacing to me at the time, whereas our own marines in their duller reds and blues had become an everyday sight since joining the navy. I suppose familiarity breeds contempt, while the unknown breeds fear. I was deep in thought about such things when Stephen arched his back and thanked us for the help.

With that I quickly ran off to see *Bess* alongside Tom and Michael, eager to avoid any further requests for assistance; the three of us knew all too well you could end up working from sunrise to sunset in one way or another around the wharves.

'Well, what do you think?'

I looked down to where Tom was pointing and saw they had given *Bess* a new coat of paint since I'd last been to visit. Her tiny body lay low on the waterline, and it was now a bright white with the name 'Good Queen Bess' written in black at the prow.

'Who wrote her name?' I asked. 'It's not half-bad mate. Good to see my lessons weren't a total waste of time.'

Tom rolled his eyes and was about to reply, but, after closing his mouth for a moment, he said something that caught me completely off guard.

'Actually Lewis, I reckon I could write my letters even better than you,' he said.

Tom picked up one of the fishing poles from within *Bess*, and out of curiosity I followed him down to the brackish waterline since it was at low tide. Michael followed along and I could tell he knew what was coming, but the grin on his face told me to let Tom have his moment. Sure enough, within a couple of minutes Tom had scratched each letter of the alphabet with passing skill into the thick mud.

'How's that then?'

The impulse to write my own version and show how paltry Tom's letters were crossed my mind. Thankfully, I was in good spirits since my hangover had passed, and I had no desire to mock one of my two closest friends. Instead, I nodded and complimented his progress. It was not simply a gesture of empty praise. The letters etched into the bank of the Thames were perfectly legible, whereas months earlier he had barely been able to write out his name.

'It's Katheryn Wooler you've to thank for that,' piped up Michael.

'Oh that's how it is, is it?' I leered at Tom. 'My ample backside not plump enough for your liking? I thought we were friends. Kat, eh? You could definitely do worse.'

'I wouldn't fuck your scrawny arse if it shat out all the riches of Cathay,' he retorted with a wide grin. 'She's been teaching me how to read, what of it? You know her pater spoils her rotten with every fancy.'

'He's also one of the most prosperous wool merchants in the south of England,' I said. 'If he finds his daughter has taken to a fishmonger's son there will be Hell to pay.'

Before Tom could reply I quickly added, 'no offence Tom, I spent the last six months as a ship's boy so I'm not exactly the Duke of Monmouth. Christ, I'm not even one of the king's many bastards.'

'He pays you well enough though,' Michael said through a mouthful of mince pie. I'd given one to each of them and we sat with our feet dangling off the end of the pier above *Bess*. I told them about the daily life aboard the *Lion*. Mostly, I talked about Captain Williams and how I'd saved Bill Pritchard from going overboard. I made no mention of Will Baker as I had no idea how my two friends would treat me if they knew I had killed a man, even if I tried to argue he started the fight.

Deep down I think they would have understood, if anything they probably would have wanted more details, but I felt it best to keep it to myself. I left out my time at the brothel as well even as I told them about the tavern hopping and merriment with the crew. It wasn't so much that I didn't want to boast about having set foot in one, but I couldn't even remember what the girl looked like so there wasn't all that much of a story to tell. The fact I had no idea whether or not we had even done anything didn't help. For all I knew my night had consisted of laying passed out between bouts of throwing up, unable to even get it up. Not exactly a tale for the ages.

'Does she have those new swivels or do you still need to move the light gonne manually at the stern?'

Michael still referred to the cannons with a French accent, and when was excited or in a rush it tended to come out more strongly than usual.

'We have swivels for the rearmost guns,' I answered. 'The *Lion* is top of the line when it comes to third rates.'

Questions about the fleet were by far the main topics of conversation as we spent the afternoon catching up. We must have sat for a couple of hours as they drilled me about every conceivable point concerning the various warships I had seen during my six months in the Channel. I saw out of the corner of my eye John and Bethany Coram looking out from their shack, and after she said something they both went back inside. I'm sure he had a list of tasks for Tom to help with, but knowing his mother she had told him to 'let them be, you old goat.' That was one of her preferred reprimands, but it was almost always said with a smile. That is, unless it was one of the rare occasions when John had seriously fucked up. Then, not even Saint George himself would have put up much of a contest.

Eventually I'd exhausted my knowledge of life at sea and things turned to more mundane topics. Tom was hoping his robust strength and inheritance of a successful fishing trawler would be enough for Katheryn's family to accept him. She had been helping her mother with a shipment of wool at market and noticed him carrying two large wicker baskets filled with various fish to one of the stalls.

After that, the girl had been rather bold and figured out for herself where Tom was likely to live. She checked any docks within walking distance of the market near Billingsgate until she found him at the end of the jetty in the process of painting *Bess*. When he had told Katheryn his intent to write the punt's name she offered to help, and they continued to meet regularly.

Kat, as he and Michael had taken to calling her, had a great deal more liberty than most girls her age, since she came from a wealthy merchant's family. Not only was she doted upon by her parents and given every possible luxury, but she didn't have the usual concerns for modesty which ladies of the gentry were forced to endure.

Her entourage consisted of two slaves for helping to carry her wares and a guardsman who had moved to London from Swansea. All were quick to obey Kat's orders which allowed for some privacy, although her group would never be out of earshot in case of danger. When I learned her man's name was *Llewellyn* I couldn't resist the easy joke:

'Well, whenever she's back home be sure I'll keep my eyes all over her,' I mocked.

Tom just scowled but then barked out a laugh. It was never in his nature to brood on things for long.

'I've actually been thinking of joining the navy myself,' he said out of nowhere. Tom must have been thinking how to broach the subject for a while, and hadn't really been listening. 'I might go look into signing up with one of the merchants. Figure they can always do with a strong back and able fisherman.'

'This wouldn't have anything to do with Kat coming from a long line of successful merchants?' I said.

'Fuck off,' Tom fired back. 'Why should you get to fight the French or Spaniards while I wear my fingers to the bone for nothing? I meant the arsehole French mate, you're an Englishman.'

Michael just grunted at this. It was true enough, despite the accent he was the first to declare himself as English whenever the matter came up.

'Well, I hear there's an opening for a cabin boy on the *Lion*,' I winked.

'What, and have you lording it over me all day long? No thanks, I'll take my chances with the blackamoors,' Tom drawled as he stood up to stretch. 'Anyway, it's about time we were getting back. You're staying for supper and the night I take it? Jane and Lucy will be dying to see you, as will Mum. Da' will act like he isn't interested, now that you're too good for us fisher folk, but that's bollocks. He never stops asking after you.'

'Well, I've never been one to turn down a free meal,' I

jingled my coin purse. 'Even though I can afford real tuck these days.'

They both knew Bethany's cooking, her stews and pottages in particular, were my favourite dishes. I felt ready for a bowl of fish stew after such a trying day. We slowly got to our feet and in amicable silence made our way up the pier towards the Coram's small home. The smell of baking bread was already reaching my nose along with a range of other mouth-watering aromas. I remember thinking that for all its humble appearance, this small fisherman's hut was still the best place in my world.

Chapter 7

The Narrow Sea, 1679 AD

'That's it lads, keep it steady now.'

I heaved with all my strength at the benchhook as my back screamed. Using such tools to keep the sail pulled taut while Ben mended its damage was brutal work, and the wooden handle bit deeply into my palms. I had felt cocky the first few times working alongside Henry Every to stretch the material across the sailmaker's workshop. Now, after the fifth such task my muscles were beginning to feel as though they had been put upon the rack.

'Don't worry boyos, this is the last big bastard for the day, then we can take to our benches and finish up the reefbands.'

Ben spoke without looking up at the two of us, his face a visage of utter focus. I chuckled under my breath and wondered if Ben had any Irish or Welsh blood in him. It's true, compared with the daily misery of a cabin boy most of my new jobs were far less physically strenuous. More often than not I would be perched at my sailmaker's bench sewing those repairs which Ben deemed beneath him, or I would be raveling the seemingly endless lines of heavy cord into organised piles in the corners of the shop. We were often called idlers by the other crew since we didn't need to stand watch, but you never heard Henry nor myself ever complaining about this privilege.

Today was not the typical day though, and we had a

lot to gain once we came out on the other side of such grueling work.

'Come on Every, put your back into it man,' I said. 'I can feel the slack on your end.'

Henry shot me an evil grin, but I saw the muscles in his arms bulge as the sail tightened.

'I'm the one doing all the fucking work here, never mind your womanly grip.' Henry then quickly added, 'present company excepted, Mister Bridgeman.'

Ben didn't even acknowledge the remarks. He had been the navy long enough to filter out such typical banter. The three of us got on well and tended to take our meals together. There had been another sailmaker's mate by the name of Anthony, but he had been shuffled over to the Pearl before my promotion. He'd be off somewhere in the Mediterranean by now aboard his new posting, meanwhile the three of us had endured a week of solid squalls with the needed repairs to show for it.

Rather than working at our individual benches as was normally the case, we combined our efforts to patch up the largest of the *Lion's* sails. The Narrow Sea, our sliver of water separating England from France which the Dutch called *Engelse Kanaal*, was usually placid enough for the most part. However, the last week had been absolutely horrid, with a constant downpour of sleet and heavy February westerlies. Captain Williams had promised us a double ration of beef, rum and good ale from his own stocks tonight if we managed to get the mainsails, topsails and shrouds patched up before the call for supper. So, despite the growing aches and pains in our joints, we applied ourselves to the checklist with fervour. One of the first things you learn in the fleet is to never turn down the chance at a good meal. That, and to eat it away from the usual mess to avoid any trouble.

The captain had said we were welcome to join him at table, which only further compelled us to get everything finished by sundown. The man's stories were worth looking forward to on their own. As if sharing the exact same thought, we clamped our jaws shut and redoubled our efforts.

Captain Williams did not disappoint.

As the four of us came up to the captain's quarters at the stern of the ship we were joined by Martin Campbell, who was the *Lion's* Master and second in the chain of command. We were waiting on a new ship's lieutenant to be sent over, and for the meantime Lieutenant Selby of the marines was filling the role alongside his own duties in exchange for a monthly stipend. Master Campbell was responsible for the day-to-day piloting and running of the ship, so it was no surprise to see him arrive to take his meal with the captain.

'Evening, sir,' I said as the man approached. 'I presume you will be joining us for the evening?'

'Indeed I will,' Martin replied. 'The captain promised a good slab of salmon and a mug of brandy if I got the main and mizzen fully rigged.'

He winked at us and broke out in a broad smile. 'Good thing you lot had my sheets ready in due time, eh?'

As we returned his grin the door swung open and we heard Captain Williams bellow:

'Come, come gentlemen, all this sitting around has left me ravenous.'

As we ascended the small set of steps and entered the captain's quarters one of the new ship's boys closed the small door behind us.

'How can you be hungry when you've done fuck all since getting out of bed, sir?' Martin chided with mock exasperation.

Captain Williams waved his hand dismissively and beckoned for us to take a seat around the fine redwood dining table he had purchased from a Swedish trader the year before. It was laden with a mixture of silverware and pewter dishes and cutlery of various types. I confess, I was not familiar with every piece on display before me. I recall seeing a small, blunt tool in the vague shape of a spoon, which I learned many years later was used for spreading fish roe upon dishes. As we took our seats the captain slumped down into his own.

'I know, I know...' he replied. 'There's shit for a captain to do, sitting in port or waiting off the coast. We just have to wait and see what the king decides to do. Maybe we'll give the Dutch another go.'

The rest of us nodded along at his words. A captain ruled over his ship with a high degree of authority, but given a competent crew during a time of peace there was little requiring his direct intervention. The *Lion* possessed such men in abundance. Despite newcomers such as myself and a handful of others, the majority of her crew were veterans from the Dutch wars and had seen years of service.

They knew their duties and went about their business with the clear confidence which follows from experience. The most Captain Williams had done over the last few weeks was cane one of the lads for blaspheming. Even then it was half-hearted and more to remind us all who was in charge. Personally I think it was to spare poor Patrick Byrne from the much heavier lashings he would have received from Chaplain Whitworth.

'Jesus Christ,' the captain said as if reading my

thoughts. 'You should have been at Texel, now there was a fight.'

My ears pricked up at this, and I noticed similar reactions around the table. The captain often spoke of his command during the Battle of Solebay seven years earlier, but he almost never went into any detail about what happened during the Battle of Texel in the subsequent summer.

'The cavaliers in Parliament can say what they want about King Charles going behind their backs to join the war alongside the French, but by God the Hollanders know how to run a ship.'

At this Captain Williams motioned for one of the attending cabin boys to fill our various goblets with brandy. Once we each had a generous amount of drink in our hands he began his tale.

Fireships are just like the old brigs or sloops we see used for ferrying supplies out from Portsmouth. Next to our beautiful girl here they look paltry and insignificant. Well, be that as it may, I had developed strong feelings for my own. My first command had been a pathetic thing no bigger than a fishing boat, but the Supply was my first true love. Yes, her name was Supply... you can blame the blow-hards at the admiralty for that one. Walking on to her deck was the first time I ever thought to myself, 'by God, Henry, you're one of the king's own bloody captains.' She only carried about forty men but had sleek lines low to the water. Not long after taking command she saw us through Solebay without any losses, and my fondness for her only continued to grow. But, like any love for the ages, it was a story destined for tragedy and loss. I know you all love our lioness with every bit of your souls. If you didn't, either big George or myself would have thrown you overboard by now, make no mistake. But, we have it easy these days. There's no need to fret about our current mistress, she can hold her own in any fight.

Boys, the trouble with fireships lies in the name.
They're made to burn.

We had been slugging it out with De Ruyter's line for hours when the command came through to light her up and send her in. The Supply had run through most of her munitions by this point anyway, so I imagine the late Sir Edward Spragge, God keep his soul, decided it was time she performed her final duty. I had been ordered back to His Majesty's Ship the Saint George aboard one of the Supply's two longboats. Instead, I stayed with the men responsible for setting her alight and saw her through to the end. I remember the feeling of wet tears quickly drying against my face from the blazing heat, and I am not ashamed to say they were not all from the resulting smoke. I watched as my first love's rigging and deck became engulfed in swirling flames, as we boarded the remaining boat to push her off in the direction of the Dutch line. I sat staring at the billowing tower of fire the Supply had become, feeling an overwhelming sense of despair and loss. I buried my head into my hands and wept openly without holding back, and many of the crew nestled in the small craft did the same.

After what felt like an eternity I raised my head to the sound of cheers from somewhere high above. As my small company of men looked up, we saw men lined along the starboard deck of Saint George towering above us pointing. As I lifted my gaze to take in the sight, my sense of loss was replaced by one of utmost pride. I looked up just in time to see the Supply crash into the Dutch line of ships, setting no less than four of them aflame. Over the next few minutes as we reached the side of our own man-o'-war three Dutch sloops were completely swallowed in the inferno, and the port of one large three-decker was taking serious damage. My love had not gone to her end meekly, she had lashed out in a furious rage and left untold damage to the enemy in her wake. With a feeling which brewed from my innermost depths I leapt to my feet and screamed in triumph as my companions did likewise.

Such was the Battle of Texel for me. I don't speak of it often to the men, not because of any feelings of loss or pride, but because that moment of glory belongs to myself and the ten other men who sat beside me in that small lifeboat. Well, and to the twenty men already aboard the Saint George. It would be churlish to exclude the rest of her crew simply because I ordered them to abandon ship ahead of us.

I rarely speak of that day, and even then only to those I feel have shown me the call of the sea in their blood. To men who could even begin to understand such things.

'What the Hell is Frobisher doing here then?' Henry Every interrupted. 'He's never even seen a full broadside or left the Narrow Sea, and he is built like a street post.'

He gave me a wink to let me know it was in jest, and everyone else in the room was accustomed to his sense of humour, but to be honest I did feel out of place sitting there listening to such deeply personal tales of battle. Henry was of average height but stocky with large arms and a thick beard of coarse brown hair. The young man was definitely the largest of the five men sat around the table, but Ben, Martin and the captain were of a similar physique.

Captain Williams looked older with his sea-battered skin and mop of thick black hair, but they all had what we call 'the look' of the sea. With my wiry hair, tall and lanky limbs and pathetic attempt at a beard, I instantly began to scratch at the underside of my chair, my nerves rattled.

'That may be,' the captain said, as if carefully choosing his words. 'But, I can think of three good reasons.'

He lifted one finger and began to list off his points.

'First, Lewis is a Frobisher.' Before Henry could interject the captain silenced him with a wave and continued. 'Whether or not he comes from Sir Martin is not important, there's power in a name.' Captain Williams leaned forward and raised another finger.

'Second, he has given good service since joining us, even going so far as to save Bill from drowning.' Ben and Martin nodded in approval, as did Henry with both hands raised in a gesture of mock surrender. The captain then lowered his voice to barely more than a whisper and took on a clearly menacing posture.

'The third point is the most important though. Of the five men sitting in my quarters,' the captain swung his arms out indicating the small room, 'you are the only one who has yet to kill a man, Mister Every.'

I watched Henry slowly swallow as the colour drained from his face.

After a moment with his eyes locked on my unfortunate friend, Captain Williams threw his head back and shook with laughter. He was one of those people who could make a funeral procession burst into hysterics, and within seconds we were all laughing aloud, Henry included. After a long pull of brandy something in the back of my mind pushed me to say something. I'd never really talked about Will Baker, not even with Tom Coram nor Michael Bollard.

The atmosphere in the small room with these men I had come to trust implicitly just pulled the words out of me, although the strong spirits certainly helped to loosen my tongue.

'I sometimes feel like I should regret what happened,' I said. 'Or, like I should be in fear for my soul through the teachings of our Saviour, but the honest truth is I looked back at him sprawled out on the pier and all I could think of was good riddance.'

'That's because he was a fucking prick.'

I looked up to see Martin taking a swig before he went on. 'He made no friends in his short stint with us, I can tell you that much for certain. What's more, he would have killed you without a moment's hesitation if you hadn't done him in first. I'm no minister, so for all I know you should look to your soul, but I wager God would rather you over William Baker.'

'I've never been as devout as I should,' I replied. 'Perhaps a visit to Chaplain Whitworth wouldn't be the worst idea, even if just to clear my own conscience.'

At this Ben decided to have his say. 'All Mister Campbell means is that it's not as if you pulled some good husband and father from his bed in the middle of the night to kill him in cold blood. Will Baker brought it on himself when he went at you, there's no shame to be had on your end. The captain knows it, I know it, and the men of the *Lion* know it.'

'Too right we do,' added Martin with a widening grin. 'Besides, I'm half-Scottish so we're practically brothers. If we could only find a way to suppress your wild, murderous Welsh tendencies we'd be set.'

At this I had to laugh, and the joke helped to restore my confidence which had been ebbing for the last few minutes.

'Shouldn't there be a few noises in there sounding like you're clearing your throat? Martin, it sounds to me like you've gone full-English.'

The large Master of the Ship ran a hand through his

brown hair and guffawed, then raised his goblet in my direction. 'You know I've never even set foot anywhere farther north than Norfolk, I really should visit someday. Cheers lads, last one has to help James Adams fix the foremast tomorrow.'

I've never seen five men empty their cups so quickly. There was no risk of the captain getting stuck on such arduous duty, but he joined in for the sheer joy of a drinking contest. Ben came in last, and both Henry and I held nothing back in gloating over our headman. He swiftly reminded us that about three hundred reefholes were still needing patched into the recently repaired canvas, at which we both audibly groaned. Still, I resolved to pay our good chaplain a visit sometime soon and the conversation lifted my spirits. These were rough men by anyone's standards, but they were also earnest and quick to friendship. So long as you did your duty and stood by the captain, they were the type who would think nothing of throwing in their lot with you when one of the inevitable brawls broke out during leave.

'You were definitely right about one thing though, Henry,' the captain said through his fourth cup of brandy. 'We need to put some meat on Mister Frobisher's bones, so it's fortunate we're about enjoy a feast worthy of Prince Rupert himself.'

The smell of roast beef washed over the table as the two servants for the evening entered with wooden trays piled high with various cuts of meat, fish, carrots and loaves of bread. One major perk of being stuck with nothing to do in the Narrow Sea was that victuals were never an issue, being so close to our home ports and resupply. Mister Effingham was an excellent quartermaster by all accounts, and we never lacked for basic kit nor our beer or hardtack.

Of course the captain and our company of marines enjoyed certain benefits befitting their ranks and social backgrounds, but the crew received sausages, rashers of bacon or other such comforts often enough to prevent their grumbling. I later discovered this was not the case throughout the entire Royal Navy, particularly when serving aboard ships in the Americas or Indies. To my dismay, I realised one general rule in the years to come: The farther you were from England the worse your treatment tended to become at sea. Nonetheless, on that cold night dining in the captain's quarters I made the most of my good fortune and stuffed myself until I could barely move.

※

Captain Williams was shrewd when it came to handling the men under his command. He was a master of juggling grand gestures of generosity with ruthless punishments. The thing is, whenever he gave you a thrashing you always came away feeling you deserved it. He had only given me a proper caning once since I joined the *Lion*, and it was because I knocked over one of the Surgeon's mates while running errands as a cabin boy. As a result the man had sliced himself across the palm with a rather vicious cut.

Hard to argue with that. Stern, but fair.

Even the members of the crew who had been pressed into service decided to stay in service after the end of the wars, and the captain had insisted on retaining the crews from his recent commands of the *Holmes* and *Stavoreen*.

We kept a contingent of slaves back in Deptford and another in Woolwich to take care of bringing on provisions when in port. This was common enough, despite keeping slaves while under sail being generally shunned in favour of trained sailors, but what made Henry Williams different from most men was that he referred to the slaves by name whenever we were moored.

The man had an uncanny memory for people, and would be able to recall everyone he seemed to meet, from the lowest slave or cabin boy to any number of the gentry who all looked alike to my eyes. When I was younger and serving on the *Lion* I struggled to distinguish between any two Blackamoors or the traders from Cathay, and I could never quite understand how he managed it.

As I got older and saw more of the world this began to change.

I learned to notice subtle differences or individual traits which I failed to observe in my youth. By the time I was in charge of my own crew out of Nassau I had learned a few words in over a dozen languages. My three closest friends consisted of an outcast from the tribes of the Five Nations, which the French commonly refer to as the *Erocoise*, a Barbary corsair who I saved from being hanged and a fellow Englishman by the name of Edward Teach.

Yes, that Edward Teach, or *Thatch*, whichever you prefer. He generally preferred to go by the name which made grown-men piss themselves anyway.

For the time being, it suffices to say that I was still in awe of Captain Williams and his ability to form bonds with people from all walks of life. After several hours of drinking we bade the captain goodnight and made our way staggering to our berths. The men on watch were all in good spirits as well, and they gave us no mind despite our drunken staggering being worthy of Bacchus himself. The crew had received good white bread tonight and a hefty double ration of bacon alongside much better rum than usual, another example of the captain's ability to predict trouble and assuage it ahead of time.

If they'd been on hardtack with watered-down grog and seen us coming back from an evening of roast beef and peppered lamb shanks things could have become ugly very quickly.

He had not tried put a spin on it either, which was another testament to his strength of character as a leader. The captain simply told the men he was entertaining a few guests this evening after their having completed a particularly difficult job, but that it was only right the rest of the crew should get to join in the celebrations.

Keeping the morale of the crew high is an incredibly difficult thing to balance, and requires careful consideration. On the one hand, if the crew become too accustomed to luxury and the choicest cuts of meat, things get all the more brutal in times of hardship. On the other hand, if the men are constantly forced to eat the leather from their own boots, well… you can imagine how that situation resolves itself.

I made my way to my hammock with my head swimming, thankful that sailors were no longer expected to sleep on the decks as had been the case a few years ago. After a muffled grumble from our cook Daniel Evatt who was bunked below me I lay back in a mixture of exhaustion and drink. I'd finally become used to the nightly cacophony of human noises which were truly prodigious amidst two hundred drunken sailors, and quickly fell asleep. I was in the middle of a dream involving several women I'd noticed back in Deptford during leave when I awoke to loud shouts and utter chaos from all directions.

Chapter 8

The Narrow Sea, 1679 AD

An eerie quiet had descended upon the deck of the *Lion*.

We made our way upstairs to see what the commotion was about, and I recall staggering alongside one of the Master's mates who was still wiping the sleep from his eyes. I want to say his name was George, but all I clearly remember was the violent scar across his face. It tore up from underneath his chin and across the bridge of his nose to his temple.

As we muttered about getting dragged out of our berths we jostled up to the gangway leading to the quarterdeck to join the rest of the crew. I was still feeling more than a little bit drunk, and being dragged from my sleep left me feeling sick to my stomach and more irritable than usual.

'They're not whales,' quipped one of the men in a hushed tone. 'How many times we seen them fishers comin' back from up north hauling their kills in eh?'

'Joseph's right, remember that boat of Danes headin' for home?' came another barely audible voice. 'Fuckin' thing was massive.'

I spied an opening next to the ratline from which long shrouds connected the main yards to the deck and took a look for myself.

After a week of awful storms we finally enjoyed a respite as the evening was clear and calm across the horizon. The waters of the Narrow Sea were gently rolling under the pale light of the crescent moon and endless stars up above. Our lioness gently lolled in the waves, and her rigging was making that chorus of peaceful tinkling which all men of the sea come to love.

The only thing to disturb the silence, other than the occasional stifled whispers of the crew, was a soft churning in the sea running parallel to the lower keel of the ship. My eyes widened as I noticed scores of dark, red shapes moving just below the surface. At first sight I took them for a type of mullet I'd seen often enough around the piers of London, but their movement was just somehow… wrong. The shapes didn't glide through the water in the way of fish, but seemed to somehow pulse along in short bursts.

I heard Captain Williams' loud voice from farther astern.

'Right, lieutenant, if you would.'

'Marines on me, we need men on the sakers and three-pounders and the rest of you get our hooks along starboard starting from the forecastle.' Lieutenant Selby barked out his orders as a man used to being obeyed. 'Actually, let's get one of you up on the bow sprit as well in case the monsters go for the jib boom.'

'Mister Frobisher is just the nimble and long-legged man for the job,' the captain put in. 'See to your stations and get ready. The last time I fought these devils off the Assurance lost six of her crew.'

My knees almost buckled beneath me. Here I was, barely able to stand up straight from a night of heavy drink and a lack of sleep, and I was being told to lean over the water at our bow. Oh, and never mind that I was expected to fend off any horrors from the deep with nothing more than a boat hook. There haven't been many times in my life when I felt compelled to prayer, but this was one of them.

As I made my way along the deck with a sense of dread I felt someone to my side pass a coarse and heavy wooden shaft into my right hand. A few of the landsmen and seamen had taken up positions on the swivel guns or stood with their own hooks at the ready. I continued along past the two marines who stood readying their weaponry near the foremast and carefully lowered myself flat against the head.

After making sure my balance was secure I shuffled forward to where our bow sprit connected with the jib boom. Together the two wooden poles jut out from the bow and secure our jib sails' rigging. They are slender by design, and don't offer much protection for anyone unfortunate enough to clamber along them. I lay in wait for what felt like hours, but was likely no more than a few minutes. Something had felt off as I made my way to the station, but I couldn't quite put my finger on it. As I was mulling over such thoughts the beasts came into view underneath me.

I felt waves of terror course through me, but I did my best to swallow the nausea building in my stomach. If I were to be sick now it would not stop until morning, and I was not about to spend the rest of the month as the ship's laughing stock. I began to salivate and heave as the dark shapes roiled about in the water below. Still, there was no way I could reach them with my meagre boat hook unless…

Visions flooded my mind of the creatures leaping out of the depths across the bow of the ship, pulling me down in a frenzy of violence. I felt my hands shake and I had to clasp the shaft tightly against the bow sprit to prevent it from dropping.

Still, nothing happened.

'SHIT YOURSELF YET?'

I almost fell overboard but had thankfully kept enough sense to hook my knees and feet into the rigging.

'What the fuck is hap—'

I turned and saw Henry Every with an enormous ear-to-ear grin across his face. Behind him, with the exception of the landsmen and seamen on the guns the entire deck was roaring with laughter.

Bastards.

That's what had felt so odd during the call to stations. The crew of the *Lion* had a reputation throughout the fleet for their efficiency and speed. No hangover nor any such trivial thing would ever prevent the men from rushing to their duties, as it was a point of pride and something we would often boast about while ashore. This morning though, in the hours before sunrise, the majority of the men had stood around, thumbs up their arses, while myself and a handful of others rushed to take on the serpents. I'd been unable to fully comprehend this facade since I had been facing away from the deck.

It was all a bloody prank on the new boys.

'I could count on one hand the times I've seen these,' the captain said as he walked up to join Henry. 'They're no trouble. Mister Crouch figures they're some type of squirt like the ones the Spaniards eat.'

As if on command, our good surgeon sauntered over to join us at the bow.

'I think it's most likely,' he said. 'In parts of Spain it's not uncommon to see such *calamar* at table, and I've seen them writhing in a similar manner while out fishing with an acquaintance of mine from Biscay years ago.'

I lowered myself to the deck as Henry passed a cup of

rum into my hands. My stomach was still very sour, but it was not yet light out so I didn't feel overly guilty about draining it to soothe my nerves.

Big mistake.

In one swift motion, I leaned over the port side and upended the contents of my stomach into the black waters of the Narrow Sea. This brought out a chorus of hurrahs and shouts of 'you owe me a thruppence,' or 'knew he would, if you'd seen the state of that lot after supper.' Clearly, the men had been placing wagers.

I wiped the sick from my face and thanked the angels above that Walter Crouch had the common sense to offer me another mug, this time filled with water. My stomach was still heaving, but I managed to keep it down and turned to the three of them.

'Fair enough, but I've seen the like back in London as well. They're nowhere near the size of whatever these are.'

'Agreed,' Walter nodded. 'These must be some different creature, but look at all the shapes and sizes fish come in. It stands to reason that squirts would be the same.'

'My friend calls them squid and one of his neighbours sometimes has them hanging up to dry.' I paused to take a drink of the tepid but life-saving water. 'I've never eaten one but he makes decent coin selling them, so someone must be buying.'

'I know a few folk down around the coast in Kent who eat them,' added Captain Williams. 'Still, these were near big as one of the ship's boys. I've come across them a handful of times and they were never any danger, but never in such numbers.'

'I take it you were all in on it then?' I asked. 'Secretly plotting my demise for a few pennies?'

'Oh, Big George and most of the marines planned it when the creatures first came into sight,' Henry said. 'Apparently it's a tradition whenever there are whales or such to wager on scaring the landsmen. Don't forget, depsite your promotion you've still been with us less than a year.'

'Aye, felt only right you got a front row seat,' the captain chuckled.

'Fuckin' Hell,' I muttered. 'You couldn't have just covered a night at the Cardinal's Hat?'

Captain Williams howled with delight and gave me a firm pat on the shoulder.

'I'll do you one better,' he replied. 'You can sleep it off and see to Mister Bridgeman when summoned. He's already agreed the lot of you deserve a rest after yesterday's double shift anyway, said something about reefholes and sheet for later.'

I visibly shuddered at the thought of work and noticed a similar reaction from Henry, who up until that point had been in much better spirits than myself.

Our conversation was interrupted by one of the seamen back on the poop deck who shouted at everyone to come take a look. When we finally joined the rest of the men to look over the stern castle, I heard Bill Pritchard say, 'now that's a first, now two ways about it.'

One of the creatures had attached a long snake-like limb to the rudder. We stood unsure what to do and just watched for a moment. After a minute, with a strange sucking sound the appendage came away and vanished below the surface. After we let out a collective sigh of relief, I arched to try and soothe my aching shoulders. With a scowl I curtly wished the captain and the men nearby a goodnight, and went straight for my berth, head down and ignoring any possible chance of distraction. I was asleep before my head hit the small, straw-filled pillow.

For a man who has lived in Lisbon for years you still don't understand sailors very well, my friend. I told you we had enough time for me to speak of what brought me to this sickbed, and I promised it would be the truth. So, I told no lie. The monsters did look like snakes, after a fashion. What's more, they did attack our steering. You'll recall I never said it was much of an attack though. How long do you suspect we have until news of the galleon arrives? Right, pour me another cup of wine and I'll continue the tale. Where were we? Ah yes, the sea serpents. I guess the next thing worth mentioning would be our fight with the French then.

For the remainder of the winter and spring life aboard the *Lion* went through its usual rhythms: Patrol, anchor, resupply. I applied myself to improving my skills as a sailmaker along with the hundreds of other random tasks which made up life at sea. Every now and then I would have to pitch in and help with the carpenter's mates or other stations, but thankfully sailmakers were never required to keep watch.

Shortly after our episode with the 'serpents' we received the command to lift anchor and head for the island of Guernsey.

It was one of a cluster of small islands still belonging to our own king as leftovers from earlier wars with the French. Henry II had also become the Duke of Normandy, Duke of Aquitaine and Count of Anjou early in his reign. About thirty years into his reign he added the County of Nantes to his demesne and ended up ruling over the western half of the French mainland. His youngest son John had lost most of our continental possessions during his infamous reign, but a number of their descendants waged a series of wars to try and reclaim England's former glory. The attempts ultimately resulted in failure, thanks in no small part to a certain peasant girl from Domrémy who rallied the Kingdom of France to her cause.

Then, we burned her at the stake.

I'm only telling you all of this to make one thing clear: When we disembarked for Guernsey, an island commonly visited by Englishmen and Frenchmen alike, there was centuries' worth of bad blood between us. Our king having annulled the alliance with France in order to support the Dutch in the last years of the recent war had certainly not improved relations either. The centuries' long history of conflict between our nations would impact our stay in the royal bailiwick, but, as you will see, not necessarily in a negative manner. For now it suffices to say the English and French have a long-standing tradition of battering one another at their king's behest.

※

I sat scratching at a barnacle which had fused itself to the side of the longboat while one of the recent additions to the crew sat in front of me and heaved at his oars. The thought of having to haul at them myself on the return trip was not a pleasant one, but for the time being I just relaxed my aching shoulders as we approached Saint Peter Port. There were the ruins of the nearby waterfront castle which had been devastated by lightning several years earlier and beyond that lay an enclosed port town with steep hillsides and closely-packed buildings. It was late into the month of May and at midday the Sun added a welcome feeling of warmth as I took in the view.

Several gulls called out and circled the dry stone pier, no doubt looking to swipe some of the fishermen's scraps. As we came in closer to the jetty I could see them in more detail. Every bird I saw was plump and full of feather, and I knew from my time with the Corams this was always a good sign of the nearby waters being bountiful.

As we tied up to the jetty and stepped on to the well-made stone pier people moved about in their daily business, bringing their catches ashore or getting ready to head out. One thing I quickly noticed was the more relaxed pace of life compared with the various ports around London. Saint Peter Port was clearly prospering, judging by the upkeep of the nearby structures, but there was more of a slow and steady atmosphere.

While six of the crew readied themselves for the return trip to the *Lion* in order to ferry over the next group, I made my way up the pier with Henry Every, Bill Pritchard and Patrick Byrne, the latter having managed to avoid further canings for blasphemy in recent weeks. We briefly discussed how to spend the day and if we should go see the castle or walk around town, but naturally we decided to head for the nearest tavern.

As we made our way along the port we ran into the captain heading in the opposite direction. He was on his way to meet with the Baron Hatton who was governor of the island and responsible for the summons. We had been given leave for the day and evening with the usual instructions about protocol and behaviour. The first longboat would make several returns in the evening for any crew who felt inclined to sleep off their drink aboard ship, while the second would ferry any remaining crew the following afternoon in the same manner.

One tried and tested method of incurring the full weight of the captain's wrath was to miss all of the departures because you were either snuggled up with some local girl or unconscious beneath a table. Captain Williams had no issue with whoring nor drink, and he could best most of us at both pursuits. However, he absolutely despised having his time wasted. Still, he was happy to point us in the direction of the best inn and gave us all a warm smile as he continued on.

It was clear why the captain had recommended *La Belle Fleur* as we approached its frontage. Charming is the only word that begins to do the place justice. Located just far enough off the main thoroughfare without being cumbersome to reach, it consisted of two levels built in smooth stonework. Ivy climbed up the sides of the main entrance and flowers of every colour were carefully arranged in plots leading along the sides of the inn. Several local people sat at small tables and seats of polished wood a few paces down from the entrance amidst the vibrant display. We were approached by the owner who introduced himself as Guillaume Le Cras, although it was clear from his accent that he more often spoke either French or some form of the local Norman tongues which were common in the islands.

At first he seemed unsure about welcoming our patronage, but we were all turned out in the best attire we owned—it wasn't every day we had a chance to impress the local girls—and the thought of reliable coin likely won him over. We took a table in the yard behind the inn. There were several other parties eating and drinking at nearby benches, and the yard displayed the same mixture of ivy lattices and floral arrangements as we had seen upon arriving. As our meals of whitefish, sharp cheese, eggs, bread and mugs of dark beer were brought over the four of us attacked them with relish.

Going on leave isn't like going to the local publican when you live and work in town. For men of the Royal Navy, shore leave is an event. Every one of us tries to patch up his clothing and clean it as best possible, while even the most rank-smelling member of the crew somehow gets his hands on rose water or some other concoction from the apothecaries. The opportunity to meet women with dry land under your feet, away from the constant stink and noise of the hammocks is a powerful motivator.

You can always tell which men have been granted leave in contrast with those who are remaining behind, you just have to follow your nose. The nights always begin with a feeling of good-natured fraternity between crew, after having enjoyed a day free from work and a proper meal. But, there is always one inevitable problem: The only thing sailors like more than unfamiliar women is ten flagons of unfamiliar ale.

'Keep your eyes to yourselves, lads,' Bill said, as he drained the pewter tankard half-filled with the dark local ale. 'This lot has trouble written all over them, and we don't be needin' that.'

I risked a glance over his shoulder at the small portico leading from the inn to the yard where we were sitting, the festivities of the evening in full swing.

'Eh, they just look like any other drunk sods to me,' I replied.

'You're still new to this Lewis,' Henry bluntly stated. 'Look at their clothing and belts.'

I tried not to look conspicuous as I looked at the group of six men out of the corners of my eyes. They were fellow sailors, that much was clear from their swarthy builds and salt-encrusted jerkins. They wore red leggings with white garters and coarse blue britches above them, with a mixture of plain brown coats and blue caps. I took them to be merchantmen at first, until I looked at their hands as Henry had instructed. They stood with their fists clenched at their sides as if ready to lash out, and clear on the front clasp of two of the men's black leather belts gleamed small, ornate iron buckles.

They were cut in the shape of the lily which the French kings use on their banners.

'Fuck,' I said. 'This could get ugly, they look ready to get stuck in.'

Patrick Byrne sat with his eyes on them, making no attempt at subtlety. He wasn't a particularly big man by navy standards, but he had the gleam in his eye of a man anticipating what steps he will take once the carnage begins. Unlike Katheryn Wooler back in London he was always adamant people called him Patrick, and became hot-tempered when one of us shortened it to Pat.

He was the type to push people too far and cause trouble when deep into his cups, despite otherwise being a friendly-enough sort. Unfortunately for both us and the French sailors, Patrick was on his ninth large tankard of heady, dark beer. All it took was a couple of the Frenchmen turning their heads and whispering to one another then laughing for him to see red.

'If there's a joke, speak up and tell it to the rest of us,' he said. 'So far the only good laugh we've had is you fussocks comin' in like you're a bunch of hard cu–'

Henry swiftly cut him off with a boot to the shins and a glare to chill the blood, but the damage had been done.

'*Oh regardez, un autre petit cochon anglais vêtu de chiffons de la latrines,*' the man who looked to be the leader of the group said between glances at his fellows.

The man closest to the door with sandy-brown hair and a clean shave barked a reply:

'*Je peux les sentir d'ici, même les fleurs n'aident pas.*'

The six men burst out into laughter and I turned my head to see Patrick's face turning the same shade of red as one of the roses propped up along the wooden fence behind us.

He muttered to me, 'what did they say?'

I tried to think of a way to avoid setting him off, so I made some weak response about my French not being good enough to understand their accents.

'They said you stink like a pig and the flowers don't help,' said Henry with a grin. 'Or, something along those lines anyway.'

The next few moments were a frenzied blur of noise and motion. Patrick didn't even say anything, he simply jumped up from our comfortable bench and launched himself across the yard. With a groan, Henry and Bill got to their feet and turned around. I sighed and finished my mug in one quick pull then threw myself into the brawl.

They beat the shit out of us.

It wasn't even much of a contest. There were six of them to our four, and whereas we were all well-underway in our revelries, the French crewmen had just come ashore within the hour. I remember landing a weak left on the tall one, but then feeling something hard connect with the right side of my head. The next thing I knew, I was propped up alongside Henry with a fresh mug of dark port being placed into my hands.

My head was throbbing, but I was drunk enough that it was more of a distant ache in the background rather than a sharp or immediate pain. I'd never taken a liking to port the same way as to rum or brandy during my early years at sea, but over the last decade or so it has become one of my favourite drinks. I suppose all of my time spent fighting alongside Portuguese rogues is to blame. Even so, I was in no position to refuse and I quickly downed it to further dull my senses.

Henry was shaking his head with his own mug propped up on top of his knee, and he pointed over at the table where we had been sitting minutes earlier. Patrick was bellowing out in laughter, engaged in a drinking contest with Bill and the six French sailors. Just as I looked up he beckoned for us to come over.

'Lads, stop sitting there like a couple of peddlars and come meet my brother.'

Chapter 9

Saint Peter Port, Guernsey, 1679 AD

I'd met Patrick's wife once before.

She lived in a small but well-maintained home not far from the docks at Deptford and had come strutting into the dockyards one afternoon with a bolt of linens for her husband. Douglas Fergusson had recently returned from London and was regaling me with stories of fishing off the wind-swept coasts of Scotland when she swept past. Her accent had been unmistakably French, and I learned through Patrick that her family came from somewhere outside of Soissons.

The leader of the Frenchmen with whom we had just brawled bore a clear resemblance to Jeanne, but in the heat of moment the connection had never occurred to me. Now that we were all rat-arsed and had mollified the proprietor with a generous sum of extra coin I was able to pay more attention to Patrick's brother-in-law.

Etienne Beaumont was, for lack of better words, the spitting image of our own good captain. From his mannerisms to his waves of black hair and cracked skin, the man was eerily similar to Henry Williams. To say he had a similar wicked sense of humour would be putting it mildly. In fact, when Bill voiced what we were all thinking, Etienne's reply was a sardonic joke about his father having taken any number of English peasant girls as his right, so of course he had brothers across the Narrow Sea.

It was exactly the type of barb the captain would have thrown back. Even the way Etienne's eyes lit up and the tone of his voice were right, if you ignored the mild accent. He spoke our tongue much more clearly than his sister, despite her living in England. Whereas Jeanne mostly stayed at home with her young daughter, Etienne had been a liaison between the mixed flotillas during our wars against the Dutch. As a result of this experience, he had quickly developed an impressively authentic-sounding Devonshire accent to match those of his English counterparts.

Once King Charles had decided to throw his lot in with the Zealanders things obviously changed, and the French sailor had returned to more mundane duties aboard ship. Still, I couldn't help but find the similarities with Captain Williams overwhelming, and I could tell from looking around the table it was a feeling shared by my fellow crew.

As if in answer to me thoughts, none other should come bursting out from the doorway than our very loud, and very drunk captain of the *Lion*. He was in good spirits as he made his way over to our table in the pleasant garden, which was now back in full swing and filled with a mixture of men laughing and tavern wenches squealing, no doubt at some pinch from a wandering hand. A shorter man with thick grey hair and an enormous beard strode alongside the captain, and I could tell from his expensive-looking attire the wizened elder was a man of some importance in Guernsey.

'What's this I hear about a fight, eh?'

I winced but before I could reply Etienne stood and bowed in response.

'My apologies, captain. It has become something of a

tradition with my newfound brother to test our—mettle, is the right word, yes?—against each other whenever we meet.'

At this Patrick chuckled and dabbed a wet cloth at the growing lump over his eye where Etienne had clocked him with a good left.

'No harm done cap'n,' he said. 'Only beat us 'cause they were sober with two extra sets of fists anyway.' The captain and the elder man both grabbed a tankard of dark beer and downed them in one quick pull. 'Well, you lot are on carrots for the week,' Captain Williams belched out. 'Dan always needs capable peelers.'

We groaned as one, but he wasn't finished.

'Mind you, it's not for the fight, but for getting beaten by a bunch of French bedswervers.'

He called out to one of the tavern wenches to bring a barrel over to the table, and after grabbing the mug right out of Bill's hands to gulp it down, we noticed the raised eyebrow on the greybeard's face.

'Are you quite certain your parents were faithful to the Lord and didn't dabble in the black arts, Henry?'

The captain gave him a grin as if he knew what was coming.

'This man could be your fetch or some golem made from clay in your image. It's uncanny to the point of feeling unnatural.'

Etienne mirrored the captain's grin, which only served to put extra weight behind the man's words.

Before anyone could respond the proprietor came out to our table with a large cask of dark ale carried behind him by a broad-shouldered man who we learned was his son Jacques.

'Gentlemen, I take it everything is to your satisfaction? My boy has brought a barrel of our finest local ale as requested. I am particularly fond of this batch, there's an earthier taste than usual.'

'Yes, we are quite merry from what I can see. You run a splendid establishment as always, dear Guillaume.'

The owner of *La Belle Fleur* made a quick response upon receiving the compliment.

'Oh, I did not recognise you with the heavy beard, my lord. I am grateful for your kind words of praise, and you have my condolences on this anniversary of the tragedy. Should you require anything further you have only to ask, my lord.'

After making sure we all had our mugs topped off Guillaume made a deep bow and returned to tending his other customers' needs. Once everyone was settled, Captain Williams began to speak.

'Where are my manners? I was so focused on quenching my thirst I forgot all decency. These rogues are Lewis Frobisher, William Pritchard, Henry Every and Patrick Byrne, all good men from my own ship.'

Upon hearing the man being addressed as a member of the nobility we all gave deep nods, although Patrick stumbled in the middle of his due to the drink. The corners of the baron's mouth twisted into a smile as the captain continued.

'These six French sailors are Etienne Beaumont, Richard Moreau, Gaston Cartier, Jérémie Orenbuc, Raymond LaSalle and…'

The captain paused for a moment whilst looking at the stout sailor sitting at the end of the table.

'I want to say, Jean de Chartres, or was it Francois?'

The man raised his tankard in a friendly gesture and said, 'you had it right the first time, monsieur. Jean de Chartres, at your service.'

As always, we were taken aback by the captain's ability to seemingly know every man in Christendom by name.

'Well then, I have the privilege of introducing you all to his lordship the second Baron Hatton and Governor of Guernsey. He is a good friend of mine, and I trust you will all show him the due deference and respect his station commands.'

For all his common touch and bawdy jokes, the captain was still used to the company of admirals and the nobility. He was just as comfortable putting on formal displays of etiquette as he was drinking himself under the table with landsmen.

The rifts between the officers and seamen wasn't as formal during the reign of Charles II as it has become over the last few decades, but even so we were keenly aware of the difference in class between ourselves and men like Captain Williams or our quartermaster Stuart Effingham, the latter being the third son of a lord somewhere in Northumbria. I could pose as a member of the lesser nobility through my father's claims of descent from Sir Martin Frobisher, but I rarely did so. I often saw self-proclaimed lordlings on the receiving end of jeers and guffaws at Cripplegate, and I had learned it was generally better to come across as a man of modest means.

The truly powerful don't need to stomp nor shout their status to the four winds; everyone can tell a true member of the nobility from their bearing and cut of cloth.

'It's an honour, my lord,' Jean quickly replied with a bow. The man clearly had experience with such courtly gestures, as it was elaborate and yet came across as perfectly sincere rather than mocking. Baron Hatton gave an approving nod and to our surprise decided to join our frivolity alongside the captain. After the rest of us gave the baron similar courtesies he piled some of the various meats and cheeses on to the freshly-cleaned trenchers brought by Guillaume and sat down opposite Captain Williams at the end of our table.

Christopher Hatton, Peer of England and the man in charge of Guernsey's governance, was an easy fellow to like. It was a refreshing change from the jumped-up types one usually encountered back in the capital, who were constantly trying to earn favour with the king. Baron Hatton didn't even insist on the men clearing space so that he could sit in the centre of the table, nor did he demand a seat brought to its head; he simply sat down at the end of the table like he was one of the crew and thought nothing of it. Unfortunately, despite the affable introductions I could tell both men were concerned about something, as they continually exchanged worrisome glances with eyebrows drawn.

'Your captain was just regaling me with tales of a life at sea during our walk here,' the baron said as he crumbled a piece of the local cheese on to a slice of ham. 'It has always brought me comfort knowing he is out there aboard ship, somewhere close at hand to avoid his causing any mischief.'

'Come now,' replied the captain. 'I'm an upstanding officer of the Admiralty and clean as you like.'

This brought grins from around the table, but none of us contradicted the man.

'Curious, then, why they should feel it worthy to pack you off to some frozen shore in the north in the coming year, no?'

I noted the hint of resentment in the baron's voice at this last remark, and turned my puzzled expression towards Captain Williams.

'Aye it's the truth our lordship speaks,' he said. 'Word arrived several weeks past that I may indeed be off for the Danish territories to the northwest of our own isles.'

With a glance at Bill and Patrick I could tell they had not failed to pick up on the same point: The captain had been referring solely to himself traveling, whereas he always spoke of the crew as a whole in such matters.

'I take it from these bulging eyes the lads don't know yet, Henry?' said Baron Hatton. 'My apologies, I suppose it really was not my place to bring up the topic. But, you understand my friend, it has been some time, so I naturally presumed…'

The captain brushed off the baron's apology with a wave. 'It's fine, now's as good a time as any. I will address the crew after we leave Guernsey, but what Baron Hatton says is true. I received notice from the Admiralty about my commission when we were last at home.'

After a moment's silence from around the table I decided to venture a question, hoping the captain would elaborate further.

'So, I take it by the Danish islands you're meaning Iceland, sir?'

'Yes, it seems likely,' replied the captain. 'I'm to command the *Pearl* as she returns from the Mediterranean and eventually head north. The girl's a fine-enough ship, but she's no lioness.'

Without another word we spent the next several minutes drinking deeply from our cups.

ॐ

Captain Williams went on to discuss the details of the

new commission, but I became lost in my own thoughts as I frantically scratched at the underside of the wooden table. It was clear the *Pearl* was a much smaller ship, lacking the recent outfitting and gunnery of the *Lion*, and that Captain Williams was dismayed about what seemed like a demotion.

However, all I could think about were my own selfish needs, and the conversation blurred into the background against my growing melancholy.

Serving under anyone else was something I had never really considered. What if the *Lion* was given over to one of those lordlings who felt nothing but contempt for her crew and was neglectful of our upkeep? The thought of serving aboard a poorly-run ship made my stomach turn over.

Again, as if reading my mind, the captain raised an eyebrow in my direction.

'Don't worry, Mister Frobisher,' he chuckled. 'This is far from my first change of station, and you've many years ahead of you, God willing.'

'Aye, sir,' I replied. 'But, the *Lion* won't be the same without you.'

I instantly felt my blunt remark might be taken as insincere. Thankfully, Patrick raised his mug and was followed by the rest of the table in a cheers. Even the Frenchmen joined in, and Etienne piped up that he knew a good captain when he saw one. Given their physical similarities this caused a round of laughter, and Captain Williams had a sheen to his eyes.

'It's good of you lads to say such,' he quietly stated through a pull of ale. 'Although if a Frenchman is saying I'm a good captain, it probably means I'm no better than at running a ship than old Guillaume over there, eh?'

Etienne feigned indifference with a flourish of his

hand, but the stocky sailor named Jean grinned and pointed over at the innkeeper.

'Je parie que Guillaume ferait un bon travail de gestion d'un navire, si sa nourriture et ses boissons sont un bon signe.'

At this the captain looked thoughtful for a moment, and nodded. 'Indeed, you have the right of it, monsieur. I've no doubt Guillaume would do a fine job in my shoes.'

The fact Jean had deliberately switched to French was not lost on us, but his wicked grin showed he knew men of such high station as the baron and captain would have no trouble understanding, and that it was all meant in jest.

'Well, the day of my departure is months away if not longer,' the captain went on. 'And, his lordship has just informed me of something this morning. Indeed, it was the main reason for our sojourn and will either seem like the best news or the very worst, that's all down to one's outlook on life.'

The baron leaned in closer to the rest of us, and, after indicating for Etienne and his companions to do likewise, he began to speak in a conspiratorial whisper.

'There is news out of Algiers,' he began. 'It has been quiet for years in these parts, but word of corsairs has been growing over the last few months. In particular, the name Ali Reis keeps coming up, but it has mostly been through tavern gossip and details are vague.'

The baron took a moment to drink and nibble some of the cheese on his trencher, then grinned and stroked his beard.

'That is, until we... *extracted* further information from a prisoner earlier this week.'

His look made it clear that questions about how the

gaolers of Saint Peter Port gained their information were not to be asked.

'We know the corsair goes by Ali Reis and claims to be a son of Ali Bitchin, that Venetian turncoat who ended up owning half of Algiers some thirty years past. It is difficult to tell whether or not this is true, even the prisoner is dubious of such claims, but this pirate does command a small fleet of between four and six ships out of Algiers.'

Without thinking I muttered, 'he reminds me of my father.'

The circumstances surrounding my lineage were well-known to the crew, but Etienne's company and the baron looked puzzled until Henry Every brought them up to speed. Baron Hatton smiled and returned our attention to the reports of growing corsair activity.

'Well, let us hope he lacks the prowess of your esteemed grandfather then.'

'What relation does the prisoner have to this heathen? All you told me was that he was found lurking around the docks.' Captain Williams poured the baron another mug of ale as he inquired after his source of information.

'Well, he's out of Algiers, for a start,' Baron Hatton replied. 'He was fishing for details about our munitions and supplies before he intended to stow away on a trade galleon for either Spain or the Sicilies. The man is adept at staying hidden and has no lack of confidence in his skills, given that he has been here for over a month. If it had not been for one of the fishmongers reporting him to the town guard the spy would very likely have made his escape undetected.'

'Any indication of a raid in the making?' Bill asked as he finished off the dregs in his mug.

'It seems likely, although when his man fails to return from Guernsey it may cause this Ali Reis to look for greener pastures, rather than try to attack forewarned defenders.'

The baron likewise finished off the last of his ale and started tidying up his trencher.

'Whatever the case, I'd like you to keep the *Lion* close by,' he said. 'At the very least near Jersey or off Sark. Monsieur Beaumont, if you could relay a similar message to your own captain it would be greatly appreciated by the people of Guernsey. When it comes to the Berber pirates we stand nothing to gain, and everything to lose.'

Etienne nodded in agreement and promised he would pass on the baron's words to his own superiors.

'I thought Sir John was supposed to have settled this mess, once and for all.'

Henry grumbled this more to himself than anyone else. Captain Williams nonetheless responded, 'Oh, there are always rogues and scoundrels luring men to their causes with promises of riches and slaves. We may have enforced treaties with Tunis and Algiers, but such men care little for such things and often act against the wishes of their own pashas.'

As we finished off the ale and rose to leave the Baron Hatton wished us well, and with a wave to Guillaume and Jacques the nobleman left to tend to his daily affairs. After Etienne told Patrick to give Jeanne his regards the Frenchmen followed suit and made to return to their own lodgings. Between our light brawl and subsequent drinking we had taken a liking to Etienne's men, and we told them the usual drunken offers to keep in touch and meet up for drinks in London, although it was unlikely to happen. They responded with similar notions of dining with them in grand chambers of Versailles and being introduced to the gentry of France.

Absolute nonsense, of course, but it made for a light-hearted end to the afternoon.

With the captain's business in Saint Peter Port concluded there was nothing left for us to do but muster the crew and return to the *Lion*. The five of us stood to leave, and, after graciously thanking Guillaume through slurred compliments, we eventually staggered our way down to the harbour. Once aboard the rowboat and watching the bustling town, Captain Williams spoke to us with a a grin that reached the corners of his eyes.

'Well then, maybe if God in all His wisdom sees fit to send us the heathens we will get to see our claws and fangs in action, eh?'

It then dawned on me that for all my nerves about meeting such pirates face-to-face in battle, the captain was relishing the thought of unleashing the full power of a ship of the line before his transfer to the *Pearl*.

After returning to the ship I was permitted an early night by the captain and all of the other Sailmakers were still on leave until the next morning. As I lay in my bunk with the room slightly spinning I ate a slice of salted beef I had taken from the mess earlier. My mind was tumbling over itself and I had trouble trying to keep calm.

One moment I was pondering what Tom and Michael would feel upon hearing I had been killed in service, while the next I was feeling pride and confidence, with images of the *Lion* firing a full broadside into the oncoming enemy and utterly destroying their decks and rigging. I thought of my father and his claims to be a son of Sir Martin Frobisher, and wondered how that man felt prior to going into battle against the Spaniards.

Surely all men felt their stomachs roll and had the shakes, or did this make me a coward? I would learn the harsh truth of such emotions in the years ahead, but at the time it was all I could do not to pull my coarse blanket over my head and hide from the world.

The next several weeks passed in the usual routine of daily tasks in patching sail or attending the various needs of the crew. With every passing day my apprehension about hordes of corsairs leaping on to our hull seemed to lessen. Also, being around the confidence of the captain and the rest of the crew greatly bolstered my own sense of security.

When I was alone with my thoughts it was a great comfort, and most of the time I was too busy with duties to contemplate future events. About midway through the third week after having left Guernsey we sighted French pennants in the vicinity, and despite the complicated relationship between England and France I felt glad of their presence.

For the time being England and France were maintaining a fragile peace, and one would hope they would likely come to our aid against any raiders intent on dragging slaves back to the Barbary Coast. I thought about Etienne and his sister Jeanne back in England, as well as Alice Dunholm and Alderman Samuel at Cripplegate. Pride in my quick promotions within the navy and the contrast between life at sea and my dour life back in London often helped to improve my mood.

Whenever I was working on a sail I would inevitably think about the Corams and Bollards, and I wondered if Tom had left the family home yet. I liked to think they were out fishing aboard *Bess* whenever they had some time away from work, and I often smiled to myself at the kindness the two ferryman had shown us that day on the river. Part of me felt guilty that I couldn't remember their names, but then so much had happened since then it felt like a lifetime ago. Robert and Stephen I wanted to say, something like that. I could picture their faces and one of them had been a giant of a man, so at least I could still picture them in my mind.

Sometimes I reflected on the slaves we often encountered in port and wondered what their lives must be like, but it was hard to fathom. Sure, we were worked to the bone aboard the *Lion*, but even those of us pressed into service were still our own men to some extent. Or, at least we liked to tell ourselves that. It certainly didn't feel that way as a cabin boy nor landsman. But whenever I saw one of the many dark slaves running about to attend their masters, my mind raced with questions:

Why did no one else, excepting perhaps the captain, seem to give a shit or even acknowledge them? Why were they rarely seen at sea on the decks of our fleets, yet so common in port? How was I the only one thinking about where they came from, or what their lives were like before such bondage? Or, were they born into that station? Why was there the occasional Irish or northerner fallen on such a life?

On the few occasions I had tried to bring up such ideas the rest of the crew had either laughed or lost interest within moments. Henry Every claimed it was 'just the way life is' and Bill Pritchard had told me 'because they're not sons of England like us.' At that moment I refrained from my usual comment about my mother being Welsh. No one seemed to really have many answers hough, and I was left to ponder such things alone during the time in my hammock.

Thoughts of corsairs dragging me off into such a life would sometimes keep me up at night, but I resolved never to let that happen at any cost. Then, one early morning in August, as the Sun was beginning to rise, there was a call from the crow's nest which brought every man above deck. My nerves quivered and I felt a stone settle in the pit of my stomach as I listened to the man's words. Several sleek ships bearing sails shaped like the fins of an enormous shark had been spotted off the Norman coast. It became clear very quickly that Ali Reis had decided to make his move.

Chapter 10

The Coast of Normandy, 1679 AD

Things proceeded much more slowly than I would have thought.

After hearing the call to stations my vision was filled with images of impending bloodshed. The memory of Will Baker's corpse crumpled in a heap on the wharf filled my mind for the first time in months. He was to that point the only man I'd killed with my own hands, so I suppose it was only natural that his sneering visage would appear alongside thoughts of battle.

Still, the corsairs' sails were little more than specks on the horizon visible through the spyglass. It would be hours before we could close the distance and engage them, and that was presuming we managed to head them off and gain the advantage over the smaller, more nimble vessels. I had been aboard long enough and witnessed enough test rounds to picture the scene in my head.

First, the *Lion* would fire off a few test rounds of solid shot with her large pounders to try and gauge the distances and hopefully cause their powder stores to explode with a bit of luck. A direct hit against the enemy's munitions was one way to bring a quick end to the exchange.

Second, we would likely close the distance and release a round or two of chain shot to rip apart the enemy's masts, sails and rigging. Despite their simple design, really just two half-cannonballs joined by an iron chain, they caused devastation to a ship's mobility when used effectively.

Third, as we sailed closer a few rounds of grapeshot to harry the men above decks would be unleashed. These canvas bags filled with small rounds would bring utter havoc to any poor soul caught in their wake, rendering them no more than scattered shards of bone amidst pools of blood and tissue.

Finally, the captain would have men on the pivot guns and sakers trying to keep up the pressure on the pirates, while our pilot and crew did their utmost to position us alongside the smaller craft.

That would be when the *Lion* would show her worth as a third-rate ship of the line, and why she was to be feared by any who would incur her wrath.

The outcome of our full broadside was indescribable.

Yes Baltasar, I mean that in the truest sense. It wasn't a matter of amazement or awe, I mean it took days for my mind to really come to terms with what transpired in front of my eyes. It was… pour me another drink. Good man.

To say we destroyed the first two corsair ships doesn't even begin to sum up what I witnessed.

They simply ceased to exist as coherent, man-made things, and instead became floating masses of timber, unbound rigging and fire. One moment they had been low-lying, swift arks upon the water. Then, well…

I remember hearing the call and every gonne from our port firing as one voice. As I watched from above deck at the stern, clasping the small dagger one of the marines had handed me in my shaking hand, our attack ripped the opposing rowing portholes wide open. Our marines stood positioned with their muskets readied, but there was no need.

Not only was the corsair ship torn to pieces at a distance of perhaps no more than twenty yards, but another in the process of manoeuvring close by was clipped along her bow on the starboard side. The resulting damage to both caused them to begin taking on water and sinking within what felt like seconds, but was more likely several minutes.

It is hard to get a sense of time passing, when men are swarming all around you and the din of a fight at sea bombards your ears. Everything seems to be happening at once, yet somehow slowed to a snail's pace. Through the smoke and utter chaos I heard men screaming in tongues I could not understand, but their meanings were all too clear.

I saw several men throw themselves into the sea whilst engulfed in flames, only for them to swiftly realise they were unable to swim. There were a few who tried to pull themselves up on to flotsam between the gap, but our marines started placing wagers and began their target practice with deadly effect.

The remaining Barbary flotilla consisted of two square-rigged ships more akin to our own, albeit on a smaller scale with a single gun deck, and three remaining smaller craft like the ones we had just annihilated. I still think to this day the corsairs thought to continue their attempt to claim the *Lion* as a prize, but our broadside had put such ideas to rest. Instead, the remaining marauders tried to use their lighter builds and advantages of speed to retreat down the coast of Normandy, likely with the intent of finding a secluded bay to regroup and plan their next course of action.

From what I gathered in conversations with the crew, such direct assaults against a man o' war were uncommon. Generally the Barbary pirates fled and to later resume their *razzia* on small and undefended towns. I had been unfamiliar with the word, but Captain Williams quickly explained it was more or less a raid with the focus of taking slaves for trade. Such victims were often sent over vast distances to Constantinople or other cities within the vast realm of the Turk.

Ali Reis must have been feeling especially bold that day, or perhaps some lust for power was driving his thoughts. Likely he felt confident in his own numbers, but after the total loss of two raiders became unwilling to risk further damages.

We made a half-hearted attempt at pursuit, but it was clear to every man aboard this had already been a good outcome for a day's work, and that our chances of gaining on them while a strong westerly blew against our sails was unlikely. However, fortunate was truly against the rogues on that warm summer afternoon.

Just as we were beginning to loosen the rigging and slow the chase, another shout rang out from above. This time there was a different cadence to our barrelman's call, a slight undertone of humour in his words. I had trouble hearing at first, but as our crew ceased their many tasks to listen the reason for the man's high spirits became clear: Three French warships equal to our own were advancing up the coast in the direction of the pirates.

I felt a sudden jolt to my shoulder and turned my head to find Henry Every giving me an ear-to-ear grin.

'Good thing we asked 'em to join us for a round, eh mate?'

I chuckled. 'Just be glad we're not currently at war with the Sun King, or right now we'd be well and thoroughly fucked.'

Ali Reis and his men were slaughtered outright.

For some reason I had expected the captains to enter talks and parley with the self-proclaimed heir to Ali Bitchin. I suppose in hindsight this was foolish of me, given our overwhelming strength upon the arrival of the French. Still, the number of clearly European sailors aboard the two larger ships was probably one reason I had entertained such naive notions. The backgrounds of the few hundred men were of no consequence, and their throats were cut over the course of about an hour. Both the courts of King Charles and King Louis were in agreement over the threat of piracy out of the Barbary States; no prisoners would be taken and the navies had full authority to execute such men without trial.

Ali Reis himself was somewhat underwhelming. I had been expecting something out of the tales of the Orient and a man clad in fine silks and all manner of jewelry. Instead, he was no different in his appearance from that of an olive-skinned merchant, and he would not have looked out of place currying favour with potential customers in the markets of London as a trader out of Spain, the Italian cities or any number of Mediterranean nations. Ali Bitchin himself had been born a Christian out of Venice, so perhaps the corsair's claims were not entirely false.

It is of no consequence either way. The man's head adorned the *Lion*'s yardarm as a warning for months afterwards, and any claims to wealth or fame died with him.

He had been frothing at the mouth and calling down what must have been curses, but Lieutenant Selby calmly walked over and sliced a neat gash across the man's neck without the slightest hesitation. It was a dirty business, but the four captains either nodded or looked away in silence. It was usually custom to hang such pirates from the yardarm, but everyone was in agreement to dispose of them quickly and throw the bodies overboard.

The reactions of both the onlooking crews and the prisoners awaiting their fates covered every possible emotion. Some, like our own lieutenant, wore cold expressions of detachment, while others visibly fought to fight back tears or sick. What I recall to be most disturbing were those few men who had the corners of their mouths turned up.

I've killed many men since the days of Will Baker giving me grief, but it's never been something to relish in or remember with fondness. I confess, there were a few individuals I felt strongly deserved their ends and I was content enough to send them to the Devil, but generally it was just something that needed to be done.

There are men though, who take great pleasure in watching others squirm and beg. I didn't know it at the time as I stood on the deck watching the executions aboard the defeated vessels, but in the years ahead I would become a close acquaintance of one such fellow. Edward Teach was one of my closest confidants in later years, but the man was an absolute bastard.

Here lies Blackbeard, *requiescat in pace*. A demon to his enemies, and an arsehole to his friends.

Well, at the time I was unaccustomed to such things and the spectacle made my stomach turn. Once the last of the cries faded away, I thanked God the captain had promoted me swiftly out of the station of cabin boy or deck swab. Blood doesn't wash itself out of wood grain.

Lion and the three French ships, which I learned were named *Arc en Ciel*, *Éclatant* and *L'Invincible*, had at first surrounded the two square-rigged vessels to press home our overwhelming strength. However, once they were subdued *Arc en Ciel* and *Éclatant* left to pursue the smaller corsairs ships which had managed to scurry away with their combination of sail and rows of oars.

It was unlikely the French would manage to overtake them by this point, but I think it was more a matter of principle and pride on the part of the captains. Also, it would be easier to agree terms of the spoils between the *Lion* and *L'Invincible*, as the latter was clearly in a position to negotiate for the two absent man o' wars.

Her *Capitaine de Vaisseau*, as the man insisted on being referred to upon introductions, was one Jacques-Auguste Maynard. He was a French knight who had commanded *L'Invincible* during battle near Ouessant against the Dutch the year before, and given the captain of *Arc en Ciel* was a marquis, it was fair to assume Captain Maynard a very capable leader for such a nobleman to defer to the man's authority.

Well, that's one explanation. Or, it perhaps had something to do with the fact that *L'Invincible* was a giant second rate with seventy-two cannons of various sizes. She didn't quite dwarf the *Lion* nor the others, including the prizes, which Captain Williams suspected to be of Spanish origin from the cut of their masts and decking, but *L'Invincible* was without question the most formidable warship present on that warm summer evening. It seemed only sensible for her captain to assert his claims regarding the substantial spoils of battle.

While the two captains retired to the main quarters at the stern of the taken corsair ship to commence negotiations I pottered about checking our own sail for tears or damage in order to look busy. There were a few small rips and holes from the paltry resistance the *Lion* had met prior to unleashing her broadside, but nothing we couldn't swiftly repair given a few days. I waved as I noticed Jérémie Orenbuc standing at the stern of *L'Invincible* but he was busy with a task and it took a moment for him to notice and return the gesture.

There was no sign of his companions, but I took a measure of comfort in knowing they were somewhere aboard. Then, I realised if hostility broke out concerning the division of spoils our recently-forged friendship would amount to nothing. Should things turn ugly it would not make any real difference, and I did not cherish the thought of having to fight them in earnest. With such dark thoughts on my mind I continued checking the sails and rigging, the familiarity of the task helping to assuage my mood.

※

After what felt like several hours the captains returned with the crews to their respective warships in order to relay the outcome of the negotiations. A small number of men were left aboard the two prizes, but they would be brought up to speed afterwards if they hadn't already been privy to the decisions.

Captain Williams came aboard with a broad grin on his face, and as one the crew visibly relaxed. Their fidgeting and anxious gazes mellowed as a sense of eager anticipation swept over us. I wasn't quite so sure, as such a smile could have resulted from thoughts of engaging the French to claim *L'Invincible* while the other two vessels were still on their patrols. I quickly shook off such an idea.

Our captain could be impulsive and coarse, but he was a navy man through-and-through. The courts of England and France were currently maintaining a fragile peace, and he would not be the type to bring about open warfare for his own gain. I gave one of the landsmen a pat on the back as I shuffled into a position to better hear the outcome of the day's work. Captain Maynard, a primly-dressed man with a bright periwig and a gaunt face, was already declaring the terms of the agreement to his own men. He bore a similar expression and his men seemed to be receiving the news well. Finally, after what felt like an age Captain Williams beckoned everyone closer within earshot and spent the next several minutes explaining how we were to proceed.

'Next time we're back home we should pay a visit to one of those fancy knocking shops,' Henry Every said jovially as we made our way to get a couple of mugs of rum in celebration.

'What, so you can spend all your coin and wake up a much poorer man than before?' He had obviously been expecting my answer, and was ready with one of his own.

'Well, a much poorer man, but a much happier one all the same.'

I chuckled at this as our chaplain James Whitworth rolled his eyes after overhearing the remark.

'I do recall a story about a certain someone waking up next to baskets of his own detritus and fleeing the establishment. Perhaps you are not in a position to judge your peers, Mister Frobisher. Better to leave such matters to God.'

With guffaws from Henry the dour-faced bastard made his way ahead of us towards the mess. Still, he had said it with a slight curl at the sides of his mouth, and even the colossal prick was in a good mood after hearing the earlier news.

'Well, he has a point I suppose,' I said.

'That he does,' replied Henry. 'We deserve a good bit of leave in any case. It's been weeks since Guernsey and if I have to spend another night with you lot I'll dash my head against the wall.'

'If you're going to do that, at least have the decency to use the main mast and leave all that nonsense for the cabin boys to clean up. I hate cleaning up shit.'

We both broke out in laughter and the sound of singing from across the water told us the Frenchmen were in similar high spirits. A night of drink and good tuck awaited. Daniel Everett was going to make his best stew, which was always popular with the men. Adding to the night's feast the captain had agreed to break out the best brandy of his own stores, along with several good chains of cured sausages from Saint Peter Port.

The rest of the evening was drowned in a heady mixture of strong spirits and full bellies, with outlandish tales from our best storytellers, farting contests and arm-wrestling. We ended the night near sunrise bellowing out several shanties before collapsing into our bunks. Praise God and all His angels both captains had agreed to a late start to the day. Both men were well-aware of the results from pressing men to work without rest and after a night of revelry.

The raucous behaviour was well-justified.

Our captain had been shrewd in his parlance with Captain Maynard. Likewise, the French leader had asserted his claims with every attempt at gaining the better spoils. Thankfully, both had proved reasonable and the resolution of terms were very agreeable to both sides.

The French would take both ships as prizes, given the skirmish had taken place within their own waters. Other men may have been insulted, given it was the Lion which had actually engaged the corsairs in battle. However, Captain Williams was no man's fool.

Rather than try to debate the waters, he agreed to the terms on one condition: Anything aboard not bolted down was to be taken as spoils by the Lion. Captain Maynard had been swift to make his own stipulation, and insisted any cannon or munitions were excluded. This was a bit of a sticking point for us, but Captain Williams was aware both ships held substantial cargoes from earlier raids after having left Algiers. The division of spoils was agreed upon, and both captains were satisfied with the outcome.

The French squadron would escort the two captured vessels to their nearest port with men from each of their crews keeping the prizes under sail. Such square-rigged ships would either be configured for further use in the French Navy, or would be put to other use. In either case, the French captains stood to make a tidy profit from the Sun King following such success, not to mention from the shipyards and potential buyers if the ships were deemed unfit for naval service.

The *Lion* would certainly not leave empty-handed either. Before the French departed we would scrape every single piece of furniture, foodstuffs, private belongings and all other items from the pirates' holds.

Or, at least those goods we could carry without our waterline riding dangerously low. There were a number of slaves in the lower holds to be sold as well, and the captain had decreed their profits would be distributed in equal shares between the men, excepting any English or French captives who would be handed over to the authorities at the next home port. Such men who could not provide any evidence of their status through family or employers would likely end up pressed into service, unless they demonstrated skills better used elsewhere.

A shipyard is always in need of a good smith or cooper.

The situation regarding women or children who couldn't prove themselves was worse. They would be turned out on the streets or end up in some manner of indentured servitude, under the guise of paying their upkeep and care during the return to England. A sad fate, but thankfully the holds of the corsair square-riggers were mostly a mixture of Spanish men along with a few younger lads out of Gascony and Brittany. There were around sixty such captives, after removing two English and French families from the group, both of which had confidence in their liberty due to having extensive relatives to vouch for them. I felt slightly torn between my growing thoughts about keeping people in bondage and the lure of receiving my first spoils of war.

Sadly, my desire for coin and reputation came out on top as it often would in the years to come.

I had grown up with ethereal visions of grandeur from my father's tales of Sir Martin, but with none of the more tangible, material wealth to back up such claims. A small wooden box left with Alice Dunholm contained my worldly possessions, and most of those were paltry things such as letters or poorly-drawn portraits. Thoughts of new clothing and hot sides of beef with good Portuguese wines filled my mind.

I did my part alongside the rest of the crew in shifts to transfer the many barrels and loose items across the boarding planks to the Lion. We had two heavy platforms designed for boarding actions, but the men had put together several makeshift ones to speed up the process as well. Mostly random bits of timber James Adams and his carpenters had provided for the job, they were sturdy enough under foot to support the weight. Or, at least we all prayed such was the case. I for one could not swim particularly well, and had no wish to end up crushed between the two massive hulls.

All told the looting took the better part of the day, as we had to bring ourselves alongside both corsair craft and make sure we were well-secured each time. After a few tentative trips to test the planks, the movement of goods was underway at a rapid pace. Barrels of various spices and dried rations were abundant, and various expensive textiles for making cloth stood in rows leaning against the sides of the hold. There were also three chests of Spanish *reales* in a mixture of silver and gold coin, and I had no doubt these were a large part of the earlier discussions surrounding the division of spoils.

In his usual all-knowing manner, Captain Williams gave me a wink while going in the other direction with one of the smaller chests clasped against his stomach. Despite its smaller size the weight was obvious as the man was puffing out breaths.

Indeed, I had to help one of our marines carry the second chest across to the Lion, and I can still recall the rough iron handle digging into my palms. Coin may be heavy, but a thick wooden chest with iron fittings is heavier for a good reason: It makes theft cumbersome and awkward. After making a few further trips back-and-forth I was invited by Mister Effingham to assist with combing through the corsair's correspondence as one of the literate members of the crew.

Ali Reis may have looked like a common merchant and struck an unimposing figure, but after ransacking his quarters it became clear he was no mere stall vendor. The man had been a masterful trader and deliberately masked his achievements.

The captain's quarters aboard the vessel he had personally commanded were modest in their decoration. However, one look at the detailed manner of his logs and personal records reflected his intricate knowledge of trade. Ali Reis had known many of the most up-to-date prices and demands for products in most of the major ports along the Barbary Coast. Also, his clarity of writing in Spanish looked clear to my eyes, and Captain Williams confirmed my hunch after reading through several letters.

'This was a man who knew his business, and did it well.'

'It's a shame I can't read Spanish nor this script,' I said and held up a letter written in the language of the Moors. 'I agree though, sir. There are almost no corrections I can see, and his figures are very neatly organised.'

Captain Williams nodded thoughtfully. 'Well, to be honest I can barely read Spanish myself. French and Latin sure enough, but even those poorly. Still, I can speak enough to get by when need be.'

He picked up one of the pages from the pile on the

desk I had been looking through.

'As for this, it's the language of the Mahometans known as Arabic, and you'll find its use everywhere from Baghdad to Toledo. Surely this isn't the first time you've seen it?'

I took a moment to compose my response, and the captain busied himself pouring over the various records.

'No sir, I have seen it in London on display at stalls several times, but this is the first I've ever really seen it written across an entire page in its entirety. Mostly I'd only seen one or two of the shapes displayed on pennants or fabric, I'm guessing the name of the stall or trader.'

'Likely Shabir ibn Musa if it was up your way,' he said. 'Lanky fellow with a wispy moustache selling pottery and cloth?'

I nodded. 'I used to see him for weeks at a time at market, he usually set up his stall in the summer months.'

'Aye, I've bought a few bolts of fine cotton from the man before. He's old blood from Granada, family been tradin' there since the Moors first came over. He has to pay a tax of some sort to maintain the business these days under their own King Charles, but he travels back and forth plying his wares throughout the year.'

At this Captain Williams handed me a bundle of various letters and pages wrapped together with a length of light cord.

'There will be plenty of time for us to contemplate the heathen tongue, Mister Frobisher, but if you would kindly take this to my own quarters without delay. Tell Lieutenant Selby I will be along shortly, and send for Mister Bridgeman to attend my quarters. The man spent a few years making sails in Portugal and I remember him saying something about being able to read a little Arabic.

It may have been false boasting over cups, but in any case he may be useful.'

'Yes sir,' I replied and took the stack of papers into my hands. I returned to the Lion and after informing Ben about the captain's orders I began work on one of the sails which had slight musket damage to its seams and needed patching. A pile of similar cloth sat in the corner of the sailmakers' shop which had been brought down in my absence, but it looked to be about two days' worth of work for myself, Ben and Henry.

I had taken a liking and sense of satisfaction to such work, as it kept my thoughts focused on the task at hand and prevented me from picking or scratching at whichever object was within reach. As I drew out the threads and lines to begin the repairs, I made a mental note to go above deck and wave farewell to Etienne and his men before the French ships were ready to depart. Then, my thoughts turned to how I might use my cut of the spoils to impress some of the girls back home, or how I might spend it to help out the Corams or Bollards.

Suddenly, I felt a strong sinking sensation in the pit of my stomach. For all the nerve-wracking experiences of the last year, from seeing so-called monsters of the deep to witnessing hundreds of men killed with no remorse, I felt an all-encompassing longing to see my friends and the people I cared for again.

I wanted to go home.

Chapter 11

London, 1682 AD

Home.

Ever since the encounter with the corsairs I had been receiving less time on leave with opportunities to visit London. Tensions were high between France and the Habsburg rulers across Europe. Louis XIV was seeking to expand his own borders whilst Spain was struggling with internal division under an inept ruler.

The continued advance of the Ottomans in the east was keeping the emperor preoccupied as well, giving the French another excuse to expand their borders. As a result of the rising sense of tension the Admiralty had kept the fleet deployed as best possible, with leave only given as an absolute necessity when the crews were pushed to their limits.

I was now a young man of eighteen years of age, and, apart from the desire to get away from the familiar sounds and smells of life at sea, my curiosity at how my friends were faring was overwhelming.

There had been growing tensions at home between the king and Parliament since his brother and heir had accepted the Roman creed. Ultimately Parliament had been called to a close and King Charles was ruling through his own court. For all of the rising concerns over the clear Papist beliefs of James, the Duke of York, I just wanted to visit the closest thing to a family I had known during my youth. I had received a letter from

John Coram in mid-October informing me his son would be home for Christmastide this year. Tom had been away from London aboard various merchant ships, and I was boiling over with excitement at the thought of hearing about his life at sea.

For my own part, apart from the experience with Ali Reis most of my time had consisted of mending sails while anchored in the Narrow Sea. My spoils had consisted of two months' pay, but had long been spent on the usual vices in port. God help me, but I'm a terrible one for putting coin aside. Still, I had saved enough from my wages over the last few months to buy a few modest gifts for Alice Dunholm, the Corams and the Bollards. I intended to get something for Alderman Samuel as well, as thanks for his many years of care despite the occasional lashings.

After an early morning farewell to Henry Every and a few other members of the crew who were already awake I had arranged for a coach to London at a fairly reasonable price. The trip had been uneventful and we made good time so that I arrived into the city with plenty of daylight remaining. My backside was grateful to be free of the road, and with a swift payment to the driver I made my way into the familiar sights and sounds of Southwark.

It had not taken more than perhaps two hours to find everything I needed to buy at the various markets and storefronts on the way to Cripplegate. Despite some Puritans and the more dour-faced members of society still arguing against the restoration of Christmas festivities, for the most part England had been glad for its return following the years under Cromwell. One had only to look at the number of merchants and stalls with their bustling trade to realise the popularity of the season to the everyday Londoner.

After various rounds of haggling and discussions over prices I had come away feeling quite content in my purchases: A bolt of fine woolen fabric for Bethany Coram alongside an ancient-looking map for her husband John, an amber pendant encased in pewter for Alice, three matching silver rings for myself, Tom and Michael and two legs of lamb with a few small pouches of herbs to help with the meals. Finding something for Alderman Samuel had been more difficult, as I was unsure how he would receive any sort of gift from someone who had for all intents and purposes ignored his counsel. After examining the wares of several shoppes I settled on a fine belt with intricate designs and patterns etched into the leather.

When I was about halfway to Cripplegate I also purchased a few pies and small items to give out to anyone who should randomly cross my path during leave, as I had no intention of being caught empty-handed upon receiving any small tokens myself. There was an air of good-natured frivolity to the city I had not felt in years, although this was likely enhanced by the fact it was my first time home for the season since joining the navy.

Well, that's not entirely true, I had been allowed a single day away from port the previous winter, but Tom had been away and the Thames had been bursting its banks with severe flooding. Upon arriving home this winter I had found London blanketed in layers of snow. People of all ages were frolicking and even the poor seemed to be in better spirits than usual. The bitter cold had likely stirred feelings of charity to a fever pitch alongside the spirit of the restored Christmas season, and

I recall seeing one beggar with a thick woolen cloak over his shoulders and a mug of mulled cider clasped in his hands.

No doubt the cloak and serving of hot drink had been gifted by one of the nearby merchants. Thoughts of the many less fortunate who would inevitably die from the cold and starvation this year tried to force their way into my mind, but with a pang of guilt I pushed such dark ruminations down. At least this man seemed content enough with his piping hot flagon.

As I turned on to one of the streets leading northbound for Cripplegate I felt inspired to my own act of selfless behaviour. Two children had been huddling together in one of the small alleyways under a paltry-looking sheet of old canvas, and I went over to kneel down by them. They recoiled in terror, and it made my heart sink in the knowledge that such urchins had likely experienced only fists and harsh words from their elders over the years. Still, I was no stranger to the life of an orphan myself.

'Easy lad, I know all too well how tough things can be.'

'We 'ave nothing, already told 'im we found this cloth back 'ere and Caroline said we could keep it.'

I raised my hands in supplication. 'I take it Caroline is a local worker or goodwife then?'

'She said it's ours if we be needin' it, honest you can ask her yerself,' the thin boy nearest me replied. I chuckled at the ridiculous thought of taking a shoddy bit of worn canvas from two snipes. Not exactly a high point in the life of a Sailmaker's Mate, eh?

'I've no quarrel with you nor your sister, I take it?'

The boy nodded cautiously and I decided to be blunt in my approach. It dawned on me that the new shirt I had purchased this morning as a bit of self-indulgence probably made me look fairly well-to-do in their eyes. So, I turned slightly to the side and lifted the hem up from my back.

'You think I gave myself these marks then?'

Their eyes went wide and it was clear they had sharp-enough minds to take my meaning.

'Was it your Da' too? Me and Millie ran away when he...'

The girl fidgeted and began scratching frantically with one finger against the canvas before speaking. 'We went back but he's dead from the red fever.'

Fuck me, but that small gesture of hers did more for their hardship in my eyes than anything they could have possibly said, including that their father had passed.

'I never knew my parents, but I wasn't always the best-behaved boy.' I winked and this brought a smile to his face. 'What's your name? Are the two of you planning to just sit here all winter and hope to avoid beatings?'

'I'm Daniel and this is Millie,' he replied.

'A pleasure to make your acquaintance, Master Daniel,' I said in the most grandiose manner I could with a slight bow of the head. This made them both openly laugh and I went on.

'I was in all honesty planning to give the two of you a few shillings or some food, but I think I can do you one better.'

At this they looked puzzled so I continued.

'I know a man not far from here who runs an almshouse and orphanage. The two of you are what, ten or eleven?'

'I think we're ten and nine but no records,' Daniel answered.

'Well, I can't make any promises he will take you in, but if you want to come along we can go see him. I was on my way to pay my respects anyway with a gift for the season,' I said and patted my satchel. 'At the very least it will get some warmth into you rather than sitting here in the cold.'

After a few moments passed, the looks on their faces quickly revealed the error of my approach. No doubt Daniel and Millie had been lured by people with false promises and trickery in the past. I did not even want to contemplate the horrors the two youths had been privy to as a result of such mistreatment. Again raising my hands in the air, I decided on being earnest as the best course of action.

'My name's Lewis Frobisher. I'm a sailmaker aboard the *Lion* in His Majesty's fleet. I won't lie to you, the man we're going to see has given me more beltings than I care to remember, and he is not exactly kind-hearted. That being said, he is fair and more often than not I brought them on myself by being an utter bastard.' I paused to let the words sink in.

'He keeps a clean and God-fearing home, and makes sure those under his care are provided with enough food and shelter. When you get older Alderman Samuel also does his utmost to try and find you employment of some kind. He can come across as fearsome, but I vouch for his character.'

Several long minutes passed as the two children absorbed my offer. To my surprise, it was Millie who answered rather than her brother.

'Is he… I mean… does he…'

The girl couldn't quite voice her question but one look instantly gave away her meaning.

'No, no Heaven forbid,' I quickly cut her off. 'There's no funny business like that under Samuel's watch. God preserve us, I don't even want to think what would happen to any man caught doing that at Cripplegate.'

Then, I winked at her and with a wide grin said, 'I think Samuel would put the cripple back in Cripplegate, if you take my meaning?'

This caused a round of open laughter and they both nodded their agreement.

I gave both of them a small mutton pie the three of us stood to make our way towards my old home about twenty minutes away on foot. They were both wiry but not at the point of severe hunger. Daniel was slightly taller, but both had crops of black hair and matching brown eyes. The boy had a swollen lip and bruise on his right cheek, but otherwise there were no clear signs of injury. At least, nothing readily visible to a quick glance, but I had no doubt there was a great deal of pain hidden underneath. As we made our way along the streets of London all I could hope for was that we found Alderman Samuel in a good mood.

※

Cripplegate was lively upon our arrival. It had become fashionable in recent years to adorn trees and windows with tinsel, a sort of weaving of metal threads which added a festive look to the typically dull structures. There was no sign of old Adrian Thorpe who had kept watch over the grounds since I could remember, but a new man who introduced himself as Charles Parsons greeted us.

He was, like Adrian himself, a former soldier and at first Millie was frightened by the long scar running from his ear down past his chin. However, the man clearly had a better way with young children than Adrian who was more at ease with the older residents of the almshouse.

Charles took one of the hanging pieces of tinsel and held it up against his face in the manner of a false beard. Then, he proceeded to pick up a handful of snow, rolled it into a tightly-packed ball and hurled it at Daniel. This brought shrieks of laughter from his sister who copied the man's assault with a small snowball of her own.

'Is Master Samuel in his offices, or is he away attending to his affairs?'

'He's over in the kitchens sorting out something to do with the provisions, last I saw,' replied Charles, as he swiftly ducked an incoming projectile from Daniel.

'I used to live here for years before joining the navy,' I said. 'Old Adrian will vouch for me, Lewis Frobisher is my name. I just stopped by to wish good Christmas tidings on the alderman and a few others who might still be around.'

'No need to fetch Adrian back from seeing his wife-to-be just to check such a thing. Anyone who spent any time here will know the alderman's favourite bit of scripture.'

'So whether you eat or drink or whatever you do, do it all for the glory of God, Corinthians,' I quickly fired back with a pursed smile. I must have heard that line a dozen times per day whenever Samuel was arranging my studies.

'Right you are,' Charles guffawed. 'He's told me that twice already this morning.'

'Only twice? I'd make a joke about you being a holy man, but… well, it's Christmas so perhaps not.'

'I take it you remember your way to the kitchen?'

'All too well,' I replied. 'How else can you get a decent meal in the middle of the night?'

We shared a few minutes in combat with Daniel and Millie, ultimately deciding it was in our best interest to concede defeat after Charles received two small handfuls of snow down the neck of his coat. He feigned rage but made it clear there was no harm done as he returned the gesture right down the back of Daniel's shirt when he wasn't looking. Two men threw scowls and hostile looks towards us as they were leaving for work, and Charles quickly returned to his station with an embarrassed look on his face.

I nodded an apology in his direction, but it didn't stop him from laughing when Millie stuck out her tongue and mocked the two men after they turned the corner. I nonetheless indicated for the two rogues to follow me to the kitchens by way of the wing reserved for the orphanage. After a minute of shaking themselves free of snow, the three of us entered the doorway and were instantly grateful for the shelter from the wind.

No one paid much attention as we made our way through the halls of Cripplegate in search of the alderman, as the remaining orphans and staff were quickly going about their own affairs. It was Christmas Eve and no doubt most would be hoping to gain a few pennies caroling, or preparing the Yule logs for the evening ahead. There were plenty of opportunities to make a bit of coin during the two weeks surrounding the Feast of the Nativity. Setting up the stalls for apple-catching, hanging the mistletoe or bay leaves, delivering the boars' heads and helping in the kitchens all required a steady supply of labour throughout London.

Even so, it was not enough work to ensure everyone

ended up with a full belly, and the more timid or disheartened such as Daniel or Millie were left watching with envy. At least the two siblings were in high spirits as we entered the kitchens, although we nearly knocked over a maid hurrying in the other direction which earned us a quick scowl. Thankfully, Alderman Samuel had not left and I raised my hand in greeting, whilst the children stared in barely-disguised hunger at the various dishes being prepared.

'What makes you think we have space for two more?'

I had been expecting the question, and I was ready with an answer I hoped would satisfy the stern-faced man without coming across as too desperate.

'Well, I noticed at least four empty cots on the way in. What's more, they seem bright enough to me, able-bodied and not shy of working. Daniel can read, or at least enough to point out a few signs on the way up from Walbrook.'

'They seem well-enough,' nodded Samuel. 'Still, it's another pair of mouths to feed and times have been hard with the weather the last few winters.'

I nodded in agreement, rather than disagree on a well-known fact. The last few years had brought an unusual amount of cold weather, with the Thames freezing over for months at a time. The crops and harvests had been poor as well, and despite the late-December revelry the signs of hardship were clear if one looked closely.

'True, and hopefully God in His wisdom will provide for them as for all good Christians.'

Samuel raised an eyebrow at this, knowing I had never been particularly devout. I was not generally blasphemous to the point of needing disciplined, but nor was I enthusiastic about services. The alderman was many things, but a fool was not one of them. I quickly realised he saw through my attempt to tug on his sense of piety. Nevertheless, fortune was with the two waifs that afternoon, as he decided to play along with my ruse.

'Indeed He will, Mister Frobisher,' he chuckled at addressing me as an adult. 'Yet, who's to say I'm to be the instrument of their salvation, hmm?'

I took a deep breath and decided to take the plunge.

'Well, Master Samuel, you and I have had our differences over the years, there's no denying that. But, even when my backside was throbbing I never questioned your genuine love for justice, charity and all good Christian virtues. It's largely thanks to your lessons I was able to strike out for myself, and I thank you for it, sir. So, I would ask you to take Daniel and his sister into your care, not as a request from Lewis the jumped-up stray, but from Mister Lewis Frobisher, Sailmaker's Mate of the Royal Navy.'

At this I received one of the rarest sights, one which I cherish to this day. The corners of the man's mouth perked up into a genuine smile, one I could tell he was using every power of self-control to mask.

'That's all very fine, and I am genuinely pleased to hear about your improved lot in life, Mister Frobisher,' he replied. 'It seems only fitting, given your family name and Sir Martin's legacy. Alas, there's one thing which gives me pause: Why do you care?'

My mouth opened and swiftly closed. Alderman Samuel knew I was not typically one for helping others without gain. Sure, I treated Tom and Michael well enough and tried my best to be a decent sort, well, most of the time, but dragging two foundlings halfway across London was something different altogether. I leaned closer across the small table to speak more quietly, as the two children were busying themselves helping the cook in exchange for small morsels.

'She scratches,' I said.

'What, you mean...'

I nodded and shrugged my shoulders. 'Just the same, I've seen her do it a few times when she looked worried.'

'That still doesn't answer my question though, it's just a nervous tick, what of it?'

Upon hearing this, I sighed in exasperation. The truth is, I really wasn't entirely sure what had possessed me to take on such a burden, particularly not on a day when I already had several plans of my own.

'Honestly, sir, I don't rightly know,' I said. 'When I saw her sitting there scratching away in a panic, the few shillings in my hand felt... wrong, somehow. It was as if I had to somehow do better for them than offer a few days' worth of life. What's the point of serving His Majesty only to come home and find this lot huddled in the shadows, their ribs poking through?'

I sat back and shrugged again, unsure what to add to the explanation.

'That...' Samuel paused for a moment, 'is precisely the type of answer I had hoped to hear. Genuine, heartfelt compassion through Christ, during this most-blessed of seasons. I truly believe you were offered an opportunity today, Lewis. What's more, you were open to receiving the message.'

The man placed his hand on top of mine and gave it a squeeze.

'I will gladly take them in, and see your act of kindness is not wasted.'

With tears in his eyes, the man stood from his small

wooden stool and beckoned for me to do likewise. Daniel and Millie looked up with their forearms covered in flour as they understood my discussion with the alderman had been concluded.

'The alderman has kindly agreed to let you both stay here under the care of both himself and his staff,' I told them. 'I can tell you from experience it won't always be easy, and you will have to follow his rules to the letter, but you won't lack for food nor company. What say you?'

'Will we ever get to see you?' Millie was on the verge of tears, but it was Daniel who asked the question. I could tell he was trying his utmost to seem brave, but fear of the unknown is arguably the most terrifying of all.

'Hah,' I barked and cracked my back. 'This place couldn't be rid of me if it tried.'

Without hesitation I swiftly plucked a chunk of white loaf from the counter and plopped it into my mouth, all while artfully avoiding the ladle aimed at my hand. The cook tutted but had clearly taken a liking to the young imps and muttered something along the lines of 'the scoundrel's always nicking our tuck.'

Once they realised I was not leaving them entirely the two youths warmed to the idea of staying at the almshouse. It wasn't quite an 'orphanage' like we see in London these days, largely thanks to the efforts of my good friend Thomas Coram, but, despite the alderman's bluster and severity, Samuel was never one to turn away starving children. Part of me felt a pang of guilt, since it had been over a year since I last visited Cripplegate, and I resolved to make more of an effort to return. Or, to at the very least try and write letters with tales from life at sea to entertain them. As the alderman showed the newly-acquired orphans a rare smile and welcoming manner, the thought occurred to me:

'I feel bad for only just noticing, but where's Miss Dunholm?'

After saying my farewells to the residents of Cripplegate, both new and old, I carried the letter as I began to make my way down to Southwark. It would be dusk by the time I arrived to visit Tom and Michael, but that had never stopped me before. It was bitterly cold outside and the wind was coming up from the Thames as a gale, but my mind was preoccupied with the letter Alice had left for me prior to her departure from Cripplegate the previous month. I could no longer contain my curiosity, and I decided to duck into a small nook off the main thoroughfare to read it. Once I had pulled open the small droplet of wax I began to read:

Dear Lewis,

I hope this letter finds you well. Alderman Samuel agreed to hold it in safekeeping until your next return from the Lion. It's not how I had hoped to exchange our farewells, but time is pressing and I cannot delay any further. You may think poorly of me, for all my talk of staying put and refusing to settle down. But, I've had an offer unlike any before. I'm to sail for Port Royal and the West Indies in the coming week. It's not that I was lying to you or anyone else about not wanting to change my life, but his tales of the blue waters and beautiful coasts won me over. I won't go into detail since I'm sure it's not what you want to hear, but his name's James and he's a prominent officer in the fleet. We're to be wed at some point once everything is in Port Royal is prepared. I do hope we can still communicate through the alderman, and that you won't be too displeased at my good fortune.

A voyage at sea and a life away from the filthy streets of London, I'm sure you can not hate me for wanting such things. You are probably wondering about your belongings. I kept the box with me, as something to always remind me of my young friend from the kitchens. I hope that doesn't cause you any grief. I left your family papers and any personal affects with Samuel, I just took a few of your own letters and the box for myself. Mary helped me put my thoughts into letters, in case you're wondering why it's not my usual chicken scratching from the kitchen lists. I will try to write you and let Samuel know how I may be reached once we have settled into our new lives. Perhaps someday you may be able to pay a visit through the fleet, although James told me the Lion is still on patrol duty and keeping an eye on the French. Take care of yourself Lewis, and may you find happiness,

Your friend,

Alice Dunholm
15 November

I finished reading the letter and lowered it to my side in one hand. Alice had finally shaken off her apathy and decided to leave the kitchens of the almshouse and orphanage. She sounded very pleased at the life which awaited her across the Great Western Ocean. Indeed, it sounded like a comfortable home, with a prosperous husband-to-be and all manner of exotic adventures. She had also had the foresight to leave my family belongings with Samuel, and Alice seemed like she genuinely valued our friendship with the offer of keeping in touch. I should have felt grateful for having been treated so well over the years.

I curled up the letter and threw it into a pile of frozen sewage, then stalked off back into the street.

Chapter 12

The Pool of London, 1682 AD

It was the first time I would manage to see Tom Coram in three years.

There was no sign of Charles Mason or his crew as I approached the recently completed restoration of London Bridge. I had not seen the man in years and was disappointed at not being able to wish him well. The storefronts once again lined both sides of the structure, and the quality of his craftsmanship was evident.

    I considered buying a few extra baubles and gifts as I walked past the facades, but I already had a fairly heavy satchel across my shoulder and my mood was still sour from Alice's message. Instead, I settled for a small bushel of tinsel for the Corams to hang from the thick wooden rafters which supporter their humble roof. I didn't even bother to haggle over the tuppence the woman was asking.

    When I returned to continue my walk along the bridge the wind grew into a blistering gale. As people hurried past with their faces buried into their cloaks I felt strangely out of place. I couldn't quite put my finger on it until reaching the south bank of the Thames, but as I watched a tall, lanky farrier rush along with a bundle of fabric held up in front of his face it clicked: I was a sailor after all. Englishmen were by no means strangers to the biting winds or cold, but during these years of severe winters my time at sea had inured me with a greater toleration for such things.

Actually, no… that's a load of bollocks, meu amigo. I remember being frozen to my core, the only difference was I had become too proud to show it. You wouldn't catch me scurrying along like some animal seeking shelter. I'll admit, my clothing was better suited to the weather though.

The instinct to wrap my cloak across my exposed nose finally overpowered my pride as I was within sight of the familiar series of jetties and larger docks. Our new captain, a man out of Cheshire by the name of James Melior, was a stern, old dullard with no sense of humour, but he never neglected our winter gear. Apart from my newly-purchased linen shirt, I was clad in a thick woolen cloak smeared with wax, a coarse leather full-sleeved coat and I wore two layers of linen hose under my dyed flaxen trousers.

Sure, I wouldn't be going to pay homage to the king anytime soon, but it kept the wind at bay and stopped the snow from melting through to my skin. I had spent slightly more than I would have liked on my wool-lined boots, but they were better than the standard issue and worth every penny that Christmas Eve.

As I carefully made my way down to the Pool of London, dodging snowbanks and patches of dark ice, I spotted two small specks moving about on the frozen Thames. A wide grin crossed my face as I was willing to bet good money on Tom and Michael refusing Bethany's summons to come in from the cold. Knowing those two idiots there was no way they would be able to resist causing all manner of mayhem in such conditions.

When I say the Thames was a frozen over, I don't just

mean it had bits of frost or sheets of ice here and there. The entire stretch in either direction was chalk-white. You would have about as much chance of drowning as stumbling upon a hoard of Spanish dollars with a note saying to line your pockets. That being said, I had no doubt Bethany would be on the verge of sending poor John to bring them back indoors. Big man that he was, there was never any question who ruled the roost.

To his credit, John Coram knew when to pick his battles and when it was a much better idea to roll with the punches. Well, not literally—Mum preferred to use a ladle—but I'd be lying if I said we hadn't laughed at Bethany lightly thumping the man on the top of his head on occasion. I laughed to myself in recollection of one such evening after supper with the Corams and gingerly walked down the ice-covered dock.

The very moment I came up to the entrance my earlier doldrums disappeared. With one look at the cracked timbers and feeling of warmth seeping out from within the small hovel I felt well and truly home. Our old punt *Bess* was hauled up from the water and lay swaddled in a few layers of rough linseed cloth. Suddenly, an arm taught with cords of muscle clenched itself around my neck and dragged me into the shack.

'Look what I found loiterin' about, tryin' to take our tree I wager.'

'Oh dear, what do you reckon? Shall I chop him up and put him in the mince then?'

There was a roar as John lifted me into a bear hug and his wife immediately rushed over to join in. I felt something collide into my back as a giggling eight year old Lucy threw her shoulder into me. Her sister Jane, who would soon be fifteen in January, was more aloof as usual, but she gave me a warm smile nonetheless and a quick hug once her parents finished fussing over me.

'Enough, enough,' I protested in jest. 'I'm a grown man now, what will the neighbours think of such affections?'

Goodwife Coram swiftly proceeded to pick up her wooden ladle and knock me on the top of my skull, to the peels of laughter from her family.

'I come bearing gifts of food, drink and my own company,' I said. 'That is, presuming there is space for one more at such a busy table this cold Eve of the Nativity?'

'Oh, we've still a good few hours until caroling and the Midnight Mass at Saint Olave's, and you look like a man who could do with a hot meal.'

Bethany looked me up and down after her comment before going on.

'You're not all skin and bones anymore though, Lewis.' She poked my ribs with a frown. 'I've tried for years to fatten you up and the navy does it for me.'

John rolled his eyes at this in mock annoyance.

'It'll be the work to thank for that,' he joined in with a look of satisfaction on his face. 'Life aboard ship does that to man.'

'Oh come on, I saw the both of you last year,' I said. 'I can't have put on that much weight in the meantime.'

'That's what you think, belly boy,' Lucy replied with a squeal as she thrust her arms around my midriff and squeezed. I turned with a growl of defiance and hoisted her over my shoulder with threats to throw her in the snow. Jane had vanished, and I figured she had likely gone out to fetch in the boys from the river. As I was horsing around with Lucy I overheard John speaking quietly to his wife:

'I said to call it the Midnight *communion* from now on, and sod what Canterbury says about it.'

'Yes, yes I know, it's just a habit and slipped out. I agree though, my sweeting. The deacon's just behind the times, you know how he is.' John nodded and gave his wife a squeeze around her shoulders with one arm.

Whatever issues the man had with Rome, tonight of all nights was not the time for such things. I've said before he was generally stern and not one for displays of affection, but there was never a man who got into the spirit of Advent or Christmastide like Johnathan Coram. He was always keen to get the fir wreaths up at the end of November and went out of his way to either craft gifts for his children or procure something special through his connections in the East India Company. No ritual nor tradition was too small to escape John's fervour, and the tree standing about two yards tall in the corner of the small home was the latest addition.

'Popular with our fellows in the Rhineland, but I hear they hang candles from them. They must live surrounded by stone.'

John gestured at the entirely wooden structure surrounding us.

'I remember reading about Luther's followers doing such things to celebrate the season,' I replied. 'But, this is the first I've seen the like outside of churches. Even Cripplegate never had one, but we did hang plenty of other decorations up.'

I set down my pack and dug out the parcel of tinsel. Lucy clasped her hands together and asked permission to string it over the tree. While I took a seat at the table with a mug of spiced wine thrust into my hands, the three of us sat in quiet comfort watching the youngest

Coram untangle the ball of metal threads. She was about halfway through spiraling the strings around the tree when the peace and quiet was utterly shattered.

'Where the He… erm, where by God have you been?'

Having skillfully avoided blaspheming Tom pulled me into a hug and gave me a few thumps on the back, much in the same way his father had done upon my arrival.

'Same as you, from what I hear, I said. 'Although I've never been anymore more exciting than Cornwall so far.'

Tom bit his tongue, and I could tell he was resisting the urge to tell me about some far-flung trip to the Caymans or the like. His skin was much darker than I had ever seen it, and his forearms had taken on the texture of rough leather. To be honest, our skin was cracked and split from the constant salt coming off the waters, and if we had stood side-by-side in our work clothes the only real difference would have been the tone of the man's skin. He had always been a portly child, and now at the age of fourteen the three years of service in the merchant fleets had added a hard edge to his usual girth. Thomas Coram, despite our difference in age, was not a young man to be trifled with.

'I brought you something from the Floridas,' my friend replied, unable to suppress his desire to boast any further. 'Michael as well, but you lot will have to wait until after we eat.'

'I won't say no to that,' I said. 'I picked up a few trinkets and things of my own. After we leave for Saint Olave's I was going to stop by your's Michael. I've a leg of la—'

The temperature of the room seemed to plummet, and the look on Tom's face made my voice catch. One glance at the Corams, along with Michael's own clenched expression, told me everything I needed to know.

'When?' I managed to ask through a choked throat.

'Two months past,' Michael replied. 'I didn't want to put it in a letter, not when you would be home so soon. They would have wanted me to tell you in person.'

I nodded. Stephen and Agnes had always been good to me. I had never become quite as close to the Bollards as the Coram family, but that was due to the fact I tended to help out John with his work more than anything else. Still, Michael's adoptive parents had always given me a friendly wave or a kind word as I went about my tasks. My spirits sank and threatened to cast a shadow over the evening, until I felt a hand squeeze my shoulder.

'Don't let it get you down, Lewis,' Michael said. 'I was there at the end and we said our farewells. Nothin' to be done, we even had a chirugeon visit from Vintry who said the same.'

I could tell Michael was trying his best to keep an even expression on his face, but the corners of his eyes betrayed his emotions.

'They were good folk, taking you in for those years,' I replied while giving his own shoulder a firm grip.

'What will you do now?'

'They left me their affairs and the home is rightly mine, but I've no desire to live alone with their shades, friendly as they may be.'

As I began handing out the various gifts in my satchel to rounds of hugs from the Corams a thought occurred to me. I decided to broach the subject once everyone was content with a belly full of mulled cider following supper. With any luck, I might solve Michael's problems and my own in one fell swoop.

'Do you think he would take me on?'

As the rest of our Christmas party strolled along the south bank of the Thames, mingling with other families making the trip to Saint Olave's along the way, I hung back in discussion with my two closest friends.

'You've years of experience mending bits of sail and rigging,' I replied. 'We're short two Sailmaker's Mates and have been for ages. It's just a shame Captain Williams had to shift over to the *Pearl*, with him I'd have no doubt. Still, the new captain may be a dullard and a bore, but he runs a tight ship and knows his business.'

'I heard Henry Williams is over commanding the *Constant Warwick* since the summer,' Tom piped up alongside us. 'She's a fine ship, escorted me and a few cargoes to the Barbadoes a couple of years ago for Sir Richard Dutton.'

This was the first I'd heard of the transfer and chuckled.

'He'll be glad for the extra cannon then,' I said. 'I had drinks with some of her crew last they were in Portsmouth and they seemed proud of their recent outfitting.'

'Listen to him' Michael cut in. 'Barbadoes as if it weren't nothing.'

Tom grinned. 'Listen, just because the pair of you choose to laze about back here with frozen plums between your legs doesn't mean we all do. Some of us are just built for greatness.'

He said the last with a haughty flourish in his false accent, one usually reserved for mocking my own occasional sense of self-importance.

'Apologies, your highness,' I drawled. 'Perhaps once

our conversation is finished you will let us bask in your glory all the way to Church.'

Tom slapped our backs and quipped something about it costing us a few pounds, then went ahead to check on the rest of his family. The wind had let up since the afternoon, but it was still a cold evening. If it hadn't been time for the midnight services the streets would have been deserted.

'Anyway, I will put in a good word for your skills. At the very least, we can always do with another cabin boy or deckhand.'

'Ugh,' my friend coughed out. 'I'm getting too old for emptying piss pots.'

'Hmm, I don't know about that,' I said. 'I was about fourteen when I started out, and it's not uncommon.'

'Still, if you could get me aboard working with the sails…' Michael trailed off. 'That would be a Godsend, Lewis. I would leave my boat and tools for John to expand his trade, that goes without saying.'

'I'm more worried about how you'll fare if things go to shit with the French again.'

Michael sighed and rolled his eyes.

'Do you think it's likely?'

I paused for a moment to consider my response.

'Louis has been causing trouble,' I said. 'He's already taken Strasbourg and Orange for himself over the last year. I wager it's not long before someone decides to punch back and we get dragged into the mess. To be fair, Charles has never pressed his personal claims on France, but I'm sure Louis would relish the chance to put a end to such ideas, once and for all.'

Michael argued the depth of his love for England as we walked along the street leading to Saint Olave's amidst throngs of other locals who had made the trip along the river. It wasn't the nearest church to the Coram home but they had been married there years ago by the deacon. Over the years it had become something of a family tradition to make the short pilgrimage for the Christmas and Easter services.

'It's not your loyalty that concerns me, more the bit of French in your accent.'

'Fuck's sake,' he said. 'You can't be serious.'

I raised my hands in a conciliatory gesture, not wanting to provoke a genuine argument minutes before entering the church.

'It's barely noticeable anymore, I'll give you that. But, some of the crew might catch the rare drawl or bit of speech and become suspicious.'

Michael raised an eyebrow. 'Surely it's not unknown for sailors out of Calais to enlist under King Charles, given he's half-French himself.'

'True,' I replied. 'We have three aboard the *Lion*, but they all have thick French accents and are plain about having joined up. So long as they perform their duties and get stuck in when there's a fight after the pub no one really cares. There's some banter and the like, sure, but nothing more than calling them yaldsons to which they usually say we eat dogshit for food.'

'Well then what's the problem?'

'The difference is because they're openly French it's not really all that suspicious,' I went on. 'It's easy to just crack jokes back and forth, so long as there's no funny business and they go about their work. An Englishman with a slight hint of a French accent though…'

Michael understood and a frown creased his brow.

'I see what you mean,' he said. 'Well, what do you suggest?'

'Be honest and open right from the start,' I responded as we approached the stone entrance to Saint Olave's which had miraculously survived the Great Fire. 'Tell everyone you were born French but grew up in London, obviously I'll vouch for you as well.'

I reassured my friend about having my full support as we made our way into the ancient stone building. It was named after one of the Christian kings of Norway who had helped our own Saxon rulers many centuries past, but the interior was simple in its design. Douglas Fergusson had once told me a little bit of its history over a few mugs of ale when we were discussing our plans for Christmas. We had been on leave during a refit in Deptford and the Scotsman always seemed to know a good deal about London's past. In fact, his knowledge of such matters was well-known. Douglas was often our go-to man for directions or when we wanted some obscure point clarified, usually the result of a wager.

Saint Olave's of Southwark had for the most part been plundered following the reign of Good Queen Bess, and there were signs of water damage to its foundations as well. Grim masonry and signs of its neglect or decay were everywhere, but the priory and attendants had done their best to offset the depressing scenery with all manner of festive decoration.

I've no doubt attending regular prayers would have put me to sleep in such a place, blasphemer that I am, but the deacon had arranged wreaths, trees and candles in various colours of wax throughout. Small reconstructions of the Nativity made from straw and pieces of vegetables lined one wall, and I smiled when a small placard represented the one created by the orphans at Cripplegate.

I remembered making a dozen such small Bethlehems as a child. It was one of the few times when we forgot our lots in life and came together. Well, the promise of treats and a few extra shilling to the 'best' manger scenes didn't hurt either. We had never really been told where our displays ended up once they were collected. This was the first I could recall seeing one at Saint Olave's in any case.

My back stiffened as I briefly recalled Will Baker stomping on our turnip-headed Saviour one morning. I'd be lying if I said it was from pangs of remorse or a desire to repent. If anything, I was glad the fucker was dead. I've cut down men in their prime since that day, but thoughts of Will always haunted me. It was likely a combination of his youth and our personal history growing up together at Cripplegate, for better or worse.

Actually Baltasar, forget that. There was no 'better' with Will. He was a monumental arsehole every step of the way. I didn't mean to kill him, that much is true, but the prick got what was eventually coming to him, one way or another. He pissed off too many people every time he opened his mouth. Oh don't look at me like that. I told you I'd cut out the tall tales, but I never said I grew up to be a saint. Damn it, I've forgotten what I was saying. What? Ah yes, Christmastide. No, I think I'd better wait until talking to these men of yours until having another cup.

In any case, I didn't want dark thoughts to take hold of my mind on such an occasion with the few people in my life who I truly loved. I can't recall the vicar's name from that year, but he did a competent-enough job of leading the midnight communion. To be honest, I spent most of the time looking for attractive girls along the pews or elbowing Tom in an effort to make him cause a scene.

Once the full liturgy was finished we slowly made our ways back out into the cold, ambling pleasantly and wishing the other parishioners well. It was perhaps an hour into Christmas Day and the wind had renewed its fierce attack upon any exposed skin, so we hurried back to the Coram household at a brisk pace.

Once the hearth was glowing I stayed up for about an hour talking quietly with John, Bethany and Tom. The girls had quickly collapsed into their bedding along the wall and Michael had gone home to his own bed after saying goodnight.

'How about you Tom, will you go back to the merchants or is that you home for good?'

'Nah, I haven't even told you the half of my stories from the Indies,' my friend yawned. 'I'll go back out with the Spring trade, more likely than not. When is your leave up?'

'I'm expected back the second day after Twelfth Night,' I said. 'Captain Melior was pretty generous with the shifts, but I will likely pop back to the *Lion* before then to see how the men are getting on. My friend Henry wanted to show me a few of the new pubs in town and…'

Bethany gave me a wry expression, but one I understood immediately.

'And… some of the erm, clothing shoppes in Fenchurch maybe.'

Tom guffawed openly while his father showed a barely-visible smile.

'Mate, I've spent time in Nassau and Port Royal, if you take my meaning?'

'Well, I won't get into detail about such things on Christmas, at any rate,' I said in a solemn tone, hoping to avoid awkward moment in front of Tom's parents or subsequent ladle to the head.

'Besides, it's not like I have to take over from Da' anymore, with another Coram lad on the way.'

It took a moment for Tom's words to register. He tilted his head towards his mother and my jaw nearly fell off. In all the commotion of getting ready for supper and the night's events, I had never noticed the small bump on Bethany's stomach. In my defence, she had been covered in thick layers of fabric to avoid the winter evening.

'He feels the same as Tom,' she said. 'Another boy, I'm sure of it.'

'Tom gives us a portion of his wages, and along with my fishing we're hoping to spruce up the house with some new walls,' his father added. 'Besides, he's away more often than not these days, so we could probably do with three rooms. There's a carpenter nearby who might give me a good deal, done him a favour before. It would mean a walk away from the docks in the morning, but that's no trouble.'

After a few minutes sitting together and watching the flames dance in the hearth, John rose to put his hands on Bethany's shoulders.

'I'm more worried about these winters the last few years,' he continued. 'Good, stout walls and a roaring hearth are what we need to think about.'

Stunned, I found my voice after a moment.

'Have you given any thought to the baby's name?'

'We were thinking possibly Stephen after Michael's father,' Bethany said. 'But, there are already too many by that name around the Pool, so we thought about Richard or Johnathan.'

'I'll not have the boy stuck with my name,' John grinned. 'So, we decided to go with something different. I think your own Mum would have approved.'

I wasn't sure what he meant and the look on my face must have said as much.

'No one can question me as a true Englishman, with a Thomas, Jane and Lucy to…'

'And Sarah,' interrupted Bethany.

'Aye, and a Sarah to my name,' he went on. 'So, we're going with something a bit different this time. It only seems fair his Uncle Lewis has something in common with the tyke.'

'Please tell me you're not naming him Lewis, or Heaven forbid, Llewellyn. Besides, I've never had Tom call me uncle before.'

This brought a round of laughter from the Corams who were still awake.

'True, but you both grew up together. Now you're an adult and practically family, especially once we marry you off to Jane some day eh?'

'My money's on Lucy,' chortled Bethany. 'The way she fawns after Lewis, she will be a terror when she's of an age to court. I worry about that girl, but you didn't hear that from me.'

We all nodded in unison. There was nothing really wrong with Jane at all. She was comely enough and polite, but there was no sign of any connection between the two of us whatsoever. I don't think the shade of her late sister tormented her thoughts anymore, but Jane had become so accustomed to such manners they had stuck with her after childhood. Lucy, despite her youth, shrieked with delight whenever I came back from time at sea. Even so, childish impulses often end up as nothing more than that. I pushed thoughts of Alice Dunholm to the back of my mind and avoided scratching at the underside of the small table.

John eventually broke the minute of quiet.

'Anyway, it's only right Baby Owen should call you uncle. You've been as a brother to Tom for years.'

'Of course,' I replied, my voice catching. 'I would welcome such a thing, gladly. We've an Owain on the *Lion*. He's a big brute of a man from a town in *Gwynedd* I won't even try to pronounce. Good landsman though and someone you want on your side.'

'We can tell him Lewis is his distant relative from the heathen Welsh marches,' Tom spoke for the first time in a while. 'Mum's expecting him sometime in the summer.'

We spoke quietly for a little while longer before turning in for the night. As I huddled into the makeshift bedding in one corner of the room, something I had done countless times before, I drifted off to sleep with a stomach full of roasted fowl, pies, spiced drinks and thoughts of what the latest addition to the Coram family would be like.

My last thoughts before falling into slumber were that I had to find a way to come home and see young Owen in the years ahead. The years ahead would be full of strife for both myself and England as a whole, but I swore to do my utmost to visit more often.

Chapter 13

His Majesty's Ship Lion, 1685 AD

The king was dead.

Captain Melior had addressed the crew in the early hours of a wet February morning with a rare display of heartfelt emotion. You could say what you wanted about the man, he was uninspiring at the best of times, clad in old-fashioned attire complete with ruffs and speaking in flat tones, but his sense of loyalty to the crown was apparent. It was with a grim sense of determination that the man brought the rest of us up to speed concerning the dispatch he had received in the middle of the night.

King Charles, the second of his name, had suffered some form of 'episode' a week prior and had only just recently passed away. There was all manner of muted discussion surrounding potential poisoning by the Catholic members of the court, or even by agents of his own younger brother James, Duke of York. The man was next in line to the throne, a point which only served to fuel such rumours. Charles had been known for his many mistresses and as an enthusiastic, vigorous lover, but his untimely death left him with a bunch of bastards and no acceptable heir to carry on his legacy. Instead, the crowns of England, Scotland, Ireland, along with any claims to lordship over France for that matter, passed to James. The man was a known Papist, but at the time the Parliaments seemed willing enough to accept his inheritance. The attempts to assassinate both Charles and James two years earlier had caused a wave of sympathy for the man as well. In the first year of his reign people largely overlooked the king's religious tendencies.

However, it soon became very clear the eldest bastard of the late King Charles had no intention of fading quietly into obscurity. Within a few months we were informed of plots to overthrow James II by the eldest of Charles' bastards, James Scott, the Duke of Monmouth. The crew of *His Majesty's Ship Lion*, as we'd finally taken to calling her in keeping with the orders from the Admiralty, was directly involved in opposing the rebellion. Before I bluster on about our role in resisting the usurper it's worth mentioning a few developments aboard ship and at home which transpired before that small invasion in late May.

It had been just over two years since I had brought Michael along to enlist and the young man had acquitted himself admirably as a Sailmaker's Mate. My concerns over the subtle French lilt of his accent had been unfounded; not only was he an excellent mender of canvas, Michael also took it upon himself to sew and repair the men's kit or personal effects for a very reasonable price.

He quickly became known as the Jack of all trades where anything involving a needle and thread were involved. We worked closely together and in January of the year 1685 I had been promoted to Sailmaker following the transfer of Benjamin Bridgeman to a second rate bound for the Plymouth and Massachusetts colonies. I had many new responsibilities, such as arranging the new sails from their lofts in port, or liaising with Mister Effingham about needed materials and requisitions.

Thankfully, our quartermaster had become one of my good friends in our years at sea together, and as a result there was rarely any major disagreement or conflict between us. Along with Michael there were two other mates working directly under me. Henry Every had thankfully been elevated to one of the *Lion's* midshipmen and we managed to avoid the awkwardness of rank. I was glad for my friend's new position. He had been a member of the crew for several years longer than myself, and I felt more comfortable with such an arrangement.

Furthermore, I had been true to my innermost thoughts from that frigid Christmastide two years earlier. Four times I had been back to see the Corams with Michael in tow. Tom had been on leave twice and the three of us had gone fishing several times with varying levels of success. The last time had been in October of the previous year, and, amidst squalls and heavy rain lashing across the Thames, we had brought back a substantial haul to the delight of his family.

I had settled into the role of 'uncle' with greater ease than I had expected. Owen Coram, with his mother's shock of blonde hair and bright blue eyes, was a complete menace. At first I had been unsure how to handle such a youngling, since most of the children I had grown up with at Cripplegate were past the toddling age. I had quickly become comfortable holding the wriggling form during my first visit, and as he continued to grow I couldn't help but wonder in awe at just how quickly the boy changed. During my last visit he had been able to walk in short bursts while babbling to himself. With his increased mobility our opportunity for causing havoc increased significantly.

One evening the new Coram home, a sturdy wooden affair about two miles up from John's workshop on the wharves, was alight to the sound of Bethany merrily chattering with her daughters as they went about fixing supper or spinning the loom. I recall the sound of their voices that night and even Jane's soft laughter could be heard, along with Katheryn Wooler's who was becoming increasingly fond of Tom.

The feeling was definitely mutual, and the two were by this point expected to wed. My friend's increased status as a man of the companies and associate of the guilds had greatly smoothed over the situation with her father. The man had taken a liking to Tom's eagerness to learn everything about trading. Gone were the days of his incompetence with letters and stubborness; Tom Coram by age seventeen had matured into a reasonable fellow with a keen eye for turning a profit.

Unfortunately for Kat and her companions, we were not entirely without a sense of mischief. After a few minutes, the feminine tranquility and decorum was utterly shattered, as a naked boy of two years came bounding into the house, while swinging a soaking wet eel in each of his tiny hands. Shrieks of complete terror broke out as pandemonium descended and various pots were knocked from tables. For my part, I was bent double outside with John, Tom and Michael in stitches. We were barely hidden behind the two round oak posts supporting the entrance, but our loud snorts and choking breaths gave us away.

It had been worth the ensuing barrage of ladles and wheels of cheese aimed at our heads. The women of the household were not averse to playing pranks with the newest addition to the family either. I distinctly remember John waking with fury one morning to a pair of chubby buttocks thumping against his head, as Lucy howled with laughter and continued to bounce the gurgling cherub up and down.

Spending time at home was vital in helping me to cope with life at sea. I know for a fact Michael felt the same way, because he told me as much over a drink one evening aboard the *Lion*. Things had been increasingly tough over the last two years as concerns over French expansion continued to grow. The Sun King had successfully defeated the Habsburgs and Genoese with bloody reprisals last Autumn, and the Admiralty was keeping us ready for engagements at all times.

The Duke of York and heir to the throne was on cordial terms with Louis XIV for the most part, but the situation at home was fraught with tension between followers of the Protestant and Catholic persuasions. Even so, James had received the crown at Westminster Abbey in April with throngs of well-wishers lining the streets. Parliament had come close to excluding him from the throne of England due to his Catholic faith in the years preceding the death of his elder brother, but the late king Charles II had dissolved Parliament on each occasion.

Despite the early support for the new sovereign of England, Scotland and Ireland, it became clear his reign would be a tumultuous one. Both of his daughters, the princesses Mary and Anne, had been raised in the Protestant fold under the wishes of their late uncle. The former had been married to Prince William of Orange, who had been fighting against the French for years. Not only was the man seen as a strong defender of the Protestant faith due to his direct involvement in the conflicts between the Dutch Republic and France, he was also the nephew of our own James II of England through his mother's side.

I remember at the time of Monmouth and Argyll's rebellions in the spring of 1685 the entire situation made my head spin. The Catholic James II had been able to claim the throne due to his elder Protestant brother dying without an heir. However, the late king's eldest bastard was about to launch an invasion of the country alongside an invasion of Scotland by Archibald Campbell, the Earl of Argyll. The years ahead would see James' nephew and daughter launch a far more successful invasion, once again sailing from Holland. To put it bluntly, England had become a nest of adders wearing different stripes.

Oh, they are arriving now? Excellent. Baltasar, if you could have them assemble by the firepit behind the kitchens I will be down after I relieve myself. I'll continue my story once you return. Fetch them a few flagons and something hot to eat. That should give us some time to wrap it up, I've never known a sailor to turn away a free meal. Remind me to tell you about Monmouth when you get back, oh and I could do with some water.

The Duke of Monmouth, eldest illegitimate son of Charles II, had wasted no time in preparing to seize the crown. Barely a month after the coronation we received word of an impending plot from the Admiralty. *His Majesty's Ship Lion* was to patrol the southwest coast of England between Dorset and Cornwall. The orders were unclear as to what we were to expect. Anything from several warships to a squadron of small fishing boats was to be intercepted where possible.

There was one small caveat: Captain James Melior despised the new king.

Where our former captain Henry Williams had never shown any great concern for matters of religion so long as the men did their duty, Captain Melior was about as fervent a Calvinist as I have ever met. Normally a morose and emotionless man, without any of the spark nor ease of conversation we all enjoyed under Captain Williams, the one topic sure to bring his piss to a boil was the Church.

'Aye sir,' Michael said. 'Saint Olave's, no less.'

'Well, you've given me no reason for doubt in your years of service,' replied our grim-faced captain. 'Still, how do I know you're not some conniving French dog playing the long game, eh?'

My back was aching from a long shift of mending the winter wear-and-tear of our sails, and as my friend stood under the man's suspicious onslaught I scratched a finger violently against the underside of my sailmaker's bench.

'Well, it was good English folk who took me in, and I grew up surrounded by the like. Anglicans, I mean. I've been to midnight communion at Saint Olave's since I was a young lad. Way I see it, I owe fuck all to France or the Vatican, sir. Not like they ever done anythin' for me.'

This last remark caused the captain to nod approvingly. Not quite convinced, but at least his unease was appeased for the time being.

'I'll back him, captain,' I said. 'Michael's about as much of a Papist as I'm one of those savages from the land of Carolina.'

'We shall see,' he replied drily. 'Very well, be about

your work then.'

As he stomped off with his old-fashioned ruff swaying around his neck I turned to Michael.

'Well done, mate. I doubt it could have gone much better.'

Michael sat back upon his own small bench and viciously plunged his needle and thread into the thick sprawl of canvas.

'I suppose I should just be thankful I still have a job,' he muttered. 'The last of the "Frenchmen" aboard.'

For a few minutes we both sat in silence and focused on our repairs. As my other two subordinates returned, a slightly obese young man by the name of David and another whose name I have entirely forgotten, my thoughts turned to old Ben Bridgeman. I felt a pang of loss at having lost both my former captain and Ben to other ships in the fleet. I wondered how they would have dealt with the rising mistrust for French members of the crew after the death of our Merry Monarch.

It was true, our holier-than-thou captain had dismissed the few French members of the crew from service in March. It was unjust, as the men had done nothing to earn such poor treatment, but the death of King Charles had revealed a side to James Melior we had never seen. Sure, the man had always been clear about his views and the crew knew him to be a strong church-goer, but with the return of a Catholic ruler the captain saw conspiracies at every turn.

The fact he shared his own name with the man did not help matters.

I sighed and quietly spoke in hushed tones to my mates.

'Just keep your heads down and get on with what I tell you,' I said. 'Do what the captain tells you and don't go looking for any trouble. Unless, of course, you'd rather get a good view over London from atop a spike?'

'I think I'll stick to fixing this sail, if it's all the same to you, sir,' quipped David.

'It would have to be a bleedin' great trunk to keep your noggin propped up,' added the younger man. I want to say 'Oliver' but his name escapes me. He was one of those people who could enter a room and no one would even notice. At any rate, I remember him being a decent enough sort. David just raised a fist towards him in mock anger.

'What the fuck are these orders, though?'

I turned back to Michael who put down his needle for a moment.

'I know,' I replied while doing likewise. 'Our chances of finding James Scott and his men are pretty slim. If he were coming in force with anything worth the *Lion's* bite we would have heard by now. More likely he's trying to sneak ashore, and the men are fed up with quick manoeuvres just to interrogate cod fishermen or free merchants.'

'I suppose that's something,' my friend said. 'Could you imagine if we had to board every company ship as well?'

David grimaced at the comment and a shudder ran through the four of us.

'Anyway,' I went on. 'Just be about your work and leave plots of kingship to our betters. I'd wager this whole thing blows over while we're at anchor or on routine patrols. If anything, the Duke of Monmouth has already landed and we're keeping busy to stop the men from talking.'

The last thing King James needed was for rifts in the Royal Navy to appear in the first year of his reign. My loyalties had been tightly-bound to his elder brother since enlisting, but I was not overly religious and didn't care much for such debates. My oath and sense of pride had been tied to the person of Charles II as the man behind my new life in the fleet, rather than any of his views or particular decisions as king. So long as the Admiralty paid my monthly wages and allowed me to sail the seas aboard the *Lion*, our ruler could believe in the ways of Mohamet for all I cared.

༄

'But it's fucking treason…' Henry Every whispered.

'Don't even voice such thoughts,' I interrupted.

'Lewis, this isn't some drunk baker calling the king a prick after a few too many cups.'

I was becoming genuinely angry and struggled to keep my composure. My friend was right, but the whole crew was torn between ripping the captain's throat out or defending him at sword-point.

'Well what in God's name do you expect us to do?'

'We tie the bastard to the main and send word to Plymouth,' he growled through clenched teeth.

'Do you have any idea of the risk?' I was ready to throttle one of my closest friends since coming aboard the *Lion* for the first time. 'Most of the men are with Melior.'

Henry gave me an even stare and crossed his arms.

'Look,' I started. 'I'm no coward, and you know that. But, there are better ways to bring the arsehole down than by cutting men we've known for years into red ribbons.'

My words apparently hit home, as the thought of fighting his way through the crew broke through his rage. We had endured the hardship of a life at sea together and drank with them on countless occasions. Henry could be a firebrand, but he was not foolish nor keen on causing pointless destruction.

'What then?'

'When we're next refitting or in port, we spread some rumours amongst the public houses. Stories of how Captain Melior let the Duke of Monmouth slip through under his watch. About how he told the crew of the *Lion* the man was a prosperous merchant.'

Henry looked at me in confusion.

'It's important we keep the crew free from blame,' I explained. 'I for one don't want our girl's reputation dragged through the mud.'

At once I could tell my friend was beginning to see the subtlety of my plan. His face quirked into a grin and he relaxed his hands into his pockets, all signs of tension and threat of violence fading.

'Agreed,' he said. 'Better by far to just see Melior shoulder the charges of treason. I've no love for the Pope either,' he conceded. 'But, I'm a king's man to the bone. The duke may have a fair cause, but it makes him no less a usurping bastard.'

'Right, so we wait until port then spread the story. Be sure to mention the field guns and muskets hidden on that second ship. The man even looked like Charles, right down to his chin.'

To be fair, I'd only ever seen portraits of the late king, but I kept my mouth shut.

'I'll have a quiet word with those of us who want to watch Melior hang,' Henry said as he pursed his fingers against his lips. 'Tell 'em to spread the word when we're next ashore, especially to the barkeeps and usual gossipers. "Captain Melior deceived his own crew and allowed James Scott to land in Dorset" or something like that.'

The two of us sat for a long moment huddled behind a large store of barrels in the cargo. If anyone came looking it would just seem like I was sorting out the large assortment of sail and tack laying in a pile nearby. One of the oars for the boats was resting against the cloth, and I smiled at the thought of our punt *Bess* back home. I wondered if any of the Coram girls were allowed to take her out, or if Tom still went fishing with Kat.

Then, an idea struck me and I grabbed Henry's shoulders.

'It's perfect,' my friend said after I explained the stroke of genius the oar had stirred in me.

'They ferry the nobles across the banks constantly,' I said with barely-concealed excitement at the idea of letting the story slip to Robert Smythe and Simon Beecham, the two ferrymen who had saved my life years ago.

'I still see them now and again,' I continued. 'We go for the odd mug of ale at the Swan together sometimes. They're probably sympathetic with the duke, to be honest, but above anything else they're insatiable when it comes to exchanging any morsels of news with passengers.'

'They'll have half of Middlesex spreading the tale before the call to evening prayers,' Henry snorted.

'Half of England more likely. There's nothing we can do about him letting the usurper pass unhindered this morning, but we bide our time and work from the shadows. This isn't Will Baker with a head full of iron. String up a captain of the fleet to the main mast, good reason or no, and how do you see that ending for you?'

'Alright, alright Lewis, you've made your damned point,' Henry threw up his hands in defeat.

'There's something you haven't considered either,' I said. 'A point which gives us even more reason for caution.'

The man was always quick to catch on. Say what you want about his later years and great acts of piracy against the Mughals, but Henry Every was someone who could always be relied upon to think on his feet and react.

'What if the Duke of Monmouth is successful?' he mused.

'Well the southwest is full of supporters for any number of Protestant beliefs, not just our own Church of England. There are Lutherans, Calvinists and Presbyterians throughout the nation as well. I confess, his chances are probably slim given King James received word of the plot and has issued commands for its suppression. You never know, though. God knows there are plenty of folk who would rather see a different Stuart on the throne. One with less... *difficult* personal beliefs.'

Our small conspiracy was interrupted as Daniel Evatt came down into the hold in search of foodstuffs and various items for the evening meal. As the Ship's Cook he was accustomed to bumping into me in the lower sections of the ship since I had become the Sailmaker, and I raised my hand in greeting. Henry departed to go about calming those members of the crew who were considering mutiny, although thankfully no obvious signs of hostility had been shown to the captain. Insofar as he was aware, no one had noticed the 'merchant' closely resembling the departed Charles II nor his stores of weaponry and cannon on the small sloops. In reality, myself and several others had put the pieces together and reached a similar conclusion. Lieutenant Selby was one such man, and we exchanged a glance but said nothing.

The rest of the afternoon was spent attending to the sails and instructing David on some of the more challenging repairs while Michael did the same for the other mate. Captain Melior remained in his quarters apart from one brief tour of the decks, and he seemed blissfully unaware of how close he had come to a very dangerous situation. By nightfall as we doled out portions of Jamaican rum it became clear Henry's words had their intended effect. Men exchanged knowing nods or quick gestures, but none made outright attacks or tried to stir up trouble. There was no question they would be telling every whore and acquaintance back in England that Captain James Melior was a treacherous dog.

Whether or not many of them despised King James was of no real import, or at least it seemed that way to me at the time. What mattered was that word spread and he would be called to account by the Admiralty directly. I would learn over the next few years that religious opposition to the king greatly exceeded my own estimations. This became particularly clear following the birth of his son and heir, James Francis Edward Stuart, who we now often refer to as the 'Old Pretender'. However, in that spring of 1685 it seemed Parliament and people on the whole were still willing to support the younger brother of the departed Charles II as their newly-appointed sovereign.

Unfortunately, looks can be deceiving.

Chapter 14

Putney, Hundred of Brixton, 1685 AD

'There was no mistakin' the man's colours neither.'

Sweat beaded on the foreheads of both ferrymen as I told them of Captain Melior's complicity in the recent attempts to overthrow the king. It was a stifling evening in mid-July on the Thames and the clouds of pests were infuriating, even with the small fire Simon had lit near their ferry station. Between the humid weather and the heat coming from the flames the three of us were sweltering uncomfortably.

'I sometimes forget you're good with that sort of thing, letters and what not.'

I bit back a retort about the matter being one of heraldry rather than literature and continued.

'A star between two crescents on a yellow shield, I noticed the design on a few of the men when their cloaks were blowing in the wind.'

'Well, it's no matter anyway,' Robert Smythe spoke as he swatted at some terror hovering just out of range. 'The king mopped up Monmouth and Argyll easily enough.'

My friend was right enough. The two rebellions had been put to a swift and merciless end by the king's officers. The Duke of Monmouth had been executed at the Tower of London about a week earlier, and the Earl of Argyll met the same grisly end about a month prior. It was still a bit unclear what had happened at the time, with reports and gossip still coming in through the various taverns and town criers, but what eventually became clear was how poorly organised both attempts had been. The king's men had utterly routed Monmouth at the Battle of Sedgemoor in the first week of July, and a series of skirmishes in Scotland had put an end to Archibald Campbell's ambitions.

Apparently the duke had proclaimed himself king upon landing at Lyme Regis, but no one really seemed to give a shit. The Earl of Feversham had outflanked the man and swiftly rolled over his half-trained followers. So much for the eldest of Charles' bastards.

'I heard they had to give 'im the chop eight times,' murmured Simon, the big man padding a hand gently at his own neck as he spoke.

'Five it was,' Robert disagreed. 'Heard it from Samuel, and you know what he's like.'

Samuel was the Swan's innkeeper and well-known for being a good source for the latest sordid bits of information.

'In any case, it doesn't change what I said.'

The two ferrymen looked at me with serious expressions on their faces. I'd long since paid them back for their help years ago with rounds of food and drink, but talk of treason was not something to be taken lightly.

'Well, it's only treason so long as James is the one leading the parade.'

'You do realise even saying such a thing could be seen as—'

I knew what they were getting at. As the two older men bickered I mulled over the latest news. There were rumours the king was planning to prorogue Parliament as it argued his appointment of Catholics into positions of high rank commanding the royal armies. Charles II had often clashed with Westminster over the question of succession, but James lacked the personal charisma and popularity of his elder brother. He was becoming increasingly heavy-handed in his treatment of his ministers and anyone with a mind for such things could tell the winds were shifting. The last Oak Apple Day had supposedly caused him great annoyance, with most Londoners shouting their love for the departed Charles rather than the current monarch.

We didn't know his kingship was quite so precarious at the time, given the fate of the recent rebellions, but the man was hanging on to his extravagant ermine coats by a thread.

'So what's the plan?'

I mulled over Simon's question for a moment and finished chewing on a piece of gristle from the platter of meats at our table.

'I'd rather not end up hanging from the gallows, so I figure it needs to be a careful bit of work. The man's a traitor to the crown, but I don't really care enough to risk my head over the matter. Melior's just a bastard who deserves flogged or at the very least to lose his captaincy.'

'Fair enough,' Simon said. 'Take it he's an arsehole?'

'He runs a tight-enough crew,' I replied through a mouthful of beef. 'But, the man's as cold as they come, barely gets to know the men and treats a few of my mates like shit.'

Robert grinned. 'Sounds to me like you miss old Henry Williams running the show.'

I felt my spirits sink at my friend's words. 'Now there

was a captain who knew how to get things done. Too right I miss that leather-faced bastard. I think he's still over on the Pearl, last I heard.'

'Well, I doubt we can offer you much, Lewis,' Robert continued. 'But, I wager we can strike up casual conversations about a certain James Melior when the right passengers are within earshot, what say you Beecham?'

'Works for me,' the big man answered. 'Lewis 'ere has always done right by us, figure we can manage that at least.'

'Thank you both,' I said in hushed, conspiratorial tones. 'Just don't go sticking your necks out, if anyone asks just say you overheard the tale at the coaching house or in town.'

At this the two men gave me an appraising eyebrow before raising their tankards with a laugh. After a quick cheers followed by a long pull of the ale Robert noticed my confusion.

'Lewis, the two of us are likely the worst gossips in the south of England. We know tales about the bishop to make milkmaids blush. But there's a responsibility to being in-the-know, you see—'

'A good twattle-basket never reveals their sources,' I finished for him with a grin of my own. Simon's eyes lit up and he tapped a finger to the side of his nostril. The ease with which my friends took up my cause raised my mood, and we spent the next hour stuffing ourselves at our usual corner table of the familiar coaching inn.

For all of my mastery of letters, sometimes I can be an absolute lackwit.

In my half-drunken state I had turned down my friends' offers of a berth for the night to sleep it off in favour of making my way back into town. I wasn't sure whether I would call upon the Corams for a place to sleep or make my way back to the inn where I had paid for a room whilst on leave. In any case, I was adamant about taking in the cooler night air after having suffered under the blazing midsummer Sun throughout day. Despite their concerns and shouts of me being a 'fucking idiot' I set out from the Swan in Putney in high spirits.

The problem with going for nighttime strolls on the outskirts of London is that it's a very easy way to get a knife lodged in your back. It didn't help that the stretch of woodland and unlit paths stretching from the ferry crossing along the south bank of the Thames was notorious for highwaymen and darker deeds. I suppose as a man in my prime at twenty-one years of age I cut a hard-enough figure to discourage most typical robberies, with my broad shoulders and corded arms gained from years at sea. Still, if anyone was serious about having a go at my coin purse or fine boots the drink fueling my steps would become a serious disadvantage.

About an hour into the drunken shambling I was beginning to wish I had stayed with the ferrymen for the evening. It was not quite pitch black, as the moon reflecting from the banks of the Thames provided enough light to make my way. However, it was hard-going and I nearly tripped up on tree roots or uneven footing several times. My back was aching as the drink gradually started to loosen its grip, and the familiar drumming at my temples began its incessant rhythm.

At least I had the good sense to fill my skin with water prior to leaving the inn, and I sat upon a flat outcrop of stone to rest for a moment. The night was eerily quiet compared with the usual noises aboard the

Lion or at Cripplegate. No water fowl made any sound and only the water of the river gently lapping against its banks broke the silence. It must have been late into the night by this point, given it was almost August and the Sun did not fully set until well after Vespers or Compline.

As I rested my legs and drank the still-cool water from my skin my mind turned over the prick Melior. I didn't have any particular reason to hate the man personally, but his treatment of Michael alongside his treason against the king had gotten under my skin. If he had been less stone-faced and zealous in his views I might have even let it alone, but there was something about the way he treated the crew of the *Lion* that infuriated me. My mind poured over such thoughts until I noticed a formless shadow out of the corner of my eye, and a feeling of utter dread clawed upward from the pit of my stomach.

The man stood with hands upon his hips in the middle of the narrow path. He was positioned between two large oaks on either side and had clearly chosen this particular spot for the ambush. A Spaniard-style tricorne hat was lowered across his brow, and a dyed length of fabric hid the brigand's features below his eyes. I couldn't make out the exact colour of his attire beneath the moonlight, but posture alone made his intentions clear. Without a word he raised one arm in my direction, clasping an old flintlock pistol and gesturing to the side of the path. I cursed myself for having left my knife with my kit at the inn and rose to my feet. It would have been better than nothing, but I'd spent enough time alongside Lieutenant Selby and his lads to know better than to try and fight someone wielding a loaded barrel from close range.

'You'd do better up at the heath,' I tried to sound calm. 'Rich lordlings and the like, all you'll find on me is a shit coat and a few pennies.'

'Turn around,' the man said in a gruff, no-nonsense voice. 'Keep your hands behind your back while you do.'

'There's really no ne—'

The sound of the flintlock being drawn back put an end to my meagre attempts at delay. With rising terror I did as commanded and felt thick rope being wrapped across my wrists and tied off. With a shove between my shoulder blades the man indicated to keep walking along the path. At first I thought whoever we were going to meet must be somewhere nearby, for the thug to be so brazen about taking me hostage. Then I swiftly remembered that very few people would risk this stretch of water in the middle of the night, and there was a good chance we could walk all the way to Southwark without seeing another soul.

My mind raced as I tried to think of an escape, but the man's sour breath at my neck constantly reminded me such ideas were mere folly. Any attempt at conversation was met with a rough jab of the pistol into my lower back, and I abandoned such notions after about twenty minutes. Why had he not just taken my belongings and either left me standing at the side of the river or floating face-down in it? It didn't take long for me to realise the prick was more interested in my person than my coin.

This brought a fresh wave of fear as thoughts of buggery or worse raced through my head. I quickly dismissed such dark thoughts after a moment; the man had not leered in any way and something about his composure didn't fit with such notions. At the time I couldn't quite put my finger on it, but it was as though he was experienced at taking hostages and seemed emotionally detached from the process. It reminded me of a member of the crew following out orders, just without the usual grumbles or half-hearted complaints.

Suddenly, I was jolted from my thoughts as the man slightly stumbled behind me on a large patch of roots. As I tried to adjust my arms to take some of the weight off my chafed wrists the demon at my back gave me yet another rough prod as he regained his stride. However, I was walking in front and as I felt around with my fingers a small flicker of a plan began to take hold. By the time we were about an hour into the swift march my plan had developed into a raging inferno, and I had to be careful to keep my captor in the dark.

෴

The thing about being a Sailmaker, with years spent years sorting out rigging, is you know a half-arsed knot when you see one. *No, Baltasar, forget that.*
You know a half-arsed knot when you *feel* one.

A gap about the width of my little finger was all I needed. In his haste my tormentor had tied a shoddy and half-arsed overhand hitch, but he had forgotten to check it was fully-tightened. At a cursory glance it seemed solid enough, but if you leave even the slightest bit of slack that's enough for it to come undone. For about fifty strides after loosening my bonds I continued to adjust my shoulders as if in agony.
'I'm not goin' to tell you again,' the fucker said.
'Well, it would help if I had any feeling in my hands.'
'You don't need them hands to keep a move on,' he

growled.

That's when I saw it.

A large, coarse stump with roots spreading out like a spider's web was coming up in the middle of the small pathway. I just prayed to whoever was listening that he would stumble rather than accidentally fire off a round through my spine.

I've never been especially devout, but I still pour the occasional drop in remembrance of that dark evening. Events could easily have ended in my demise, with my fine calfskin-lined boots ending up in the belly of some enormous beast lurking in the depths of the Thames. Instead, I let my rage take the tiller.

As I lurched out-of-step past the large trunk the highwayman tripped himself up as expected. Thankfully, rather than pulling the flintlock's trigger he focused on regaining his balance. That was all the time I needed. Time felt like it slowed to a crawl, but within seconds I had dropped the rope from around my wrists and was atop the bastard.

It wasn't a fight. There was no sense of contest or trying to test our brawling experiences against one another. I simply choked the life out of him.

I poured everything I had into my grip around the man's throat. An all-consuming anger coursed out through my arms as thoughts of Cripplegate, Alice Dunholm, Captain Melior and years stuck at anchor in the Narrow Sea fueled my desire for vengeance. Poor Will Baker with his head caved in even crossed my mind for a brief moment.

At first my former master tried to free his arms to punch at my ribs, but his limbs were pinned to the rough ground in a good hold I'd learned from the Scot Douglas

Fergusson. We'd been deep into cups and fancied a spar, but I ended up in much the same position on my back. I barely understood Douglas at the best of times, let alone when the man was drunk, but I understood the lesson well-enough: Don't let your opponent move.

I can be stubborn and pig-headed, but one thing you can never accuse me of is being forgetful.

The man's breath reeked of pickled onion and some unknown variety of cheese. I could taste the sweat coming from his forehead as I closed my fingers even tighter. Gradually his resistance wavered and only served to make me press harder. After what felt like an age of the world, his eyes bulging from their sockets, his body went limp. I continued to squeeze for another minute or two just to be sure the deed was done.

After sitting back from the corpse I took a long moment to regain my breath. Then, I began to rummage through the man's long-coat and pockets. A bit of coin or anything valuable would be a good find, let alone anything explaining the reason behind my attempted abduction. Sadly, apart from the old flintlock there was nothing of any real value. I decided to leave the decent-looking coat after consideration; better to not have any visible links with the man on returning to London.

As I dragged the still-warm figure over to the river the makeshift veil fell from his jaw. A cold sensation went down the length of my back. I was profoundly grateful he wasn't a crewmate or anyone I knew from the *Lion*, but something about his face did look familiar. Alas, despite my best efforts I couldn't place him and instead proceeded to dump the body into the softly-flowing river. While using a thick branch to help submerge the shapeless lump I pondered just how many men had met their ends in this very manner, being disposed of as little more than a rubbish tip into the great waterway.

Once I was sure things had been taken care of properly I pulled my way back up to the path from the riverbank using the branches of the surrounding oaks and alders for leverage. For the next couple of hours I walked in a daze in the direction of Southwark, having decided to try and call on the Corams for a night's rest. John and Bethany would no doubt be cross at a half-drunken lout hammering at their door in the hours when no decent folk were out of bed, but I reasoned one look at my face would put an end to such complaints.

I vaguely recall passing one other man when I was cutting through Lambeth and Saint George's Fields on a familiar shortcut, but he paid me no mind. Even if he'd been planning some thievery I wager the look of murder painted across my face would have given him pause. Not long after I collapsed out of exhaustion for several minutes in the middle of a field before continuing on my way to the Pool of London. The Sun was still nowhere to be seen by the time my aching and battered form staggered along the wharves. I took a long breath to gather myself as best possible, and rapped quietly at the door.

After a minute two shining eyes glared at me from the opening crack of warm light. Then, I heard soft cursing and a hand reach out to pull my arm inside.

'Lewis, what the f—'

'Good evening Jane, but now's not the time. I can barely stand, let alone listen to your spinster's prattle.'

'Evening, is it? You could have fooled me, and if you call me that again I'll show you *exactly* why I'm still not Lady so-and-so. Come on then.'

With a squeeze of her hand and a quick hug I made

my way into the familiar fisherman's hovel.

'What will you do?'

I had shore leave until tomorrow evening and John had insisted on walking me back to my room at The George over in Southwark. Jane and Lucy had given my clothing a quick wash while I was asleep, but I now owed them both a favour apiece. The youngest Coram daughter spent most of her time doting on little Owen these days, but she had an evil sense of humour and I dreaded the day she would call in my obligation.

'I have no idea,' I sighed. 'Far as I can tell he was acting alone, but then why not just rob me and be done with it?'

We pursed our lips and walked side-by-side along the streets of Southwark. Noises of all kinds poured out from storefronts and passersby so there was no real need to keep our voices down.

'Well, my advice is to watch your back and keep your head down. The entire thing stinks worse than the Pool these days.'

The attempt at a jest fell flat. The stench of rotting fish and salt on a hot midsummer afternoon was nothing to laugh about. Even so, John's words made sense.

'If I could just remember where I'd seen him before,' I said. 'Eyes too close together, a squat face and thin, cracked lips. Hmmm…'

We arrived without any incident at The George not long after midday. Locals often referred to the inn by different names such as the 'Saint George' or the 'George and Dragon' from years past, but its new sign displayed a theatre troupe underneath the current one in bold white letters. The inn was well-known for putting on shows with patrons watching from the galleries, and innkeepers from the days of Good Queen Bess had turned a pretty penny as a result. My room set me back more than most, but that summer had been my first leave in ages and I felt like indulging. The food and drink were fit for nobles' tables and bedding consisted of fine linens with down pillows. There were cheaper options on offer as well, but I had paid four nights' expenses upon arrival for one of the better rooms on the uppermost floor.

As I closed the latch to my door and sat upon the bed I tried to recall where I had seen the highwayman's face before. With a belly full of good tuck and a night's rest I was feeling much sharper than the night before, and the answer came to me while I was in the middle of untying my boots. I paused, with one boot held in my hands, and knew exactly where I'd seen that ugly mug before: The docks at Portsmouth.

I was sure of it. The man's narrow eyes and squashed face were often seen above broad arms carrying wares aboard the *Lion*, along with any other ships of the fleet undergoing resupply.

My teeth ground together as realisation dawned.

The only reason I recalled his otherwise dull expression was because I occasionally saw him talking with James Melior and one of his acquaintances. So there was a connection of some kind, but I'd done nothing to show any outward hostility in front of the crew. In fact, I'd been a model sailor and gone about my orders with aplomb. Why then, would Captain Melior have any reason to send the rogue after me? It wasn't as if he knew about…

Daniel Evatt. The Ship's Cook.

The toad must have overheard my conversation with Michael in the cargo hold and carried wind of it to the captain. I'd counted Dan as one of the crew I got along with since first embarking on a life in the navy, but when I got back aboard there was going to be a reckoning.

    I picked up my dagger and turned it over in my hands, admiring the polished finish on the hilt and the elegant curve of the iron blade. Then, I continued to undress and lay back for a few hours' rest before going down for supper.

    My dreams were filled with visions from the night before, my hands circled tightly around my assailant's neck. However, it wasn't the highwayman's face staring back at me but the bloated, rosy-nosed image of Daniel Evatt. There was going to be a reckoning indeed.

Chapter 15

Portsmouth, 1685 AD

I found him sitting at a table with a landsman from the *Pearl*.

After having made the short trip from my coach into the docks of Portsmouth I saw Daniel Evatt and the stranger laughing outside one of the warehouses responsible for ships' victuals. The other man had the familiar grease and stains of a cook about him as well, so I figured the two had just placed their requests for provisioning and were killing time. Typically that sort of thing would have fallen to our quartermaster, Stuart Effingham, but it wasn't particularly uncommon for cooks to end up ashore with orders to sort things out for themselves.

Nor was it uncommon for a certain sailmaker to be told 'take the ledger along and get what you need.'

Dan didn't show any sign of surprise at seeing me return from leave, but he would have had plenty of time to see me coming down the main thoroughfare from the coaching station before I laid eyes on the two of them. I made my best effort not to seem suspicious and offered them both a casual wave of greeting.

'How's things, Dan?'

'Just finished a civil discussion about a few barrels of salted fish and pease,' Dan nodded at his companion. 'Arthur here was hoping to starve the good men of the

Lion, but I saw to that.'

The man-pig turned his gaze in my direction with a chuckle and nodded. While the docks were not known for graceful physiques nor beautiful faces, Arthur was something to behold. He made Dan look like a God-born Adonis, even with his pox-scarred jowels and signs of heavy drink. With tiny ears, a flat face and turned-up little nose, Arthur bore the unfortunate and uncanny semblance to a large hog.

Now, I've never cared much about such things, certainly not where my crewmates were concerned, but I'd be lying if I said the man's features didn't fill me with an odd sense of marvel. All the same, I tried to ignore my impulses and returned the nod.

'Lewis is what my friends call me,' I said jovially. 'The rest don't.'

This brought an approving guffaw from Arthur, yet no look of discomfort from Mister Evatt whatsoever.

Disconcerting.

'How were the lovely, one-toothed *belles* of Cripplegate anyway? I hear all three of them are in heat this time of year.'

Dan's awful attempt at wordplay made both Arthur and myself groan.

'Never made it up to the old stomping grounds,' I replied with a false yawn. 'Mostly spent time out in the countryside or living the rich man's life at *The George*.'

This brought a whistle from Arthur, who spoke for the first time.

'Good place that,' he said. 'Best cider and greens anywhere in London, or so I'm told.'

'The cider lives up to the reputation, as does the fare. It's not often I treat myself, so I figured God would forgive me a few days' sloth and gluttony. He knows I'll be making up for it over the next month or two, having to survive on this knave's cooking.'

While my erstwhile friend Dan, a crewmate with whom I had experienced many nights of drinking and carousing by this point, bellowed a laugh and rolled his eyes across the small table at Arthur, I felt a sudden desire to be bold and take a risk.

'In any rate, shore leave was just what I needed. Good tuck and a soft bed, the fresh air of the countryside. It was to die for.'

Still, nothing.

Daniel Evatt didn't even so much as pause in his laughter.

I decided not to push my luck, and after wishing them both well I continued on my way towards the piers. The last thing I needed was the man running off to Melior or putting a knife in my back while I slept. For the life of me, I couldn't think of any alternative to Dan having informed on myself and Michael to the captain. I was either missing something entirely, or my friend Mister Evatt was a thespian worthy of Shakespeare himself.

I was deep in thought when a familiar, rough voice called out my name.

'Mister Frobisher, it's been far too long! Come, join me for a quick one, won't you?'

The dark cloud hovering over my head lifted as I looked over to see Henry Williams, Captain of *His Majesty's Ship Pearl*, raising a clay mug in my direction.

'Of course, sir,' I answered. 'I'm in no immediate hurry and not due at my station until this evening.'

I sat down across a small wooden table from my former captain, almost identical to the one at which Dan and Arthur had been sitting. The only real difference was the better location near the tavern away from the worse smells of the port. Being an officer had its perks, a point which became a major source of contention in the years to come.

'How's life aboard the *Pearl*, sir?' I asked. 'God, it must have been three years since we've last had a proper chat. I saw you now and again between leave, but you always looked to be in a hurry.'

Captain Williams gave me a wry expression.

'Well, if you want to know about the *Pearl*, you'll have to ask her captain, William Botham,' he said. 'I spent a couple of years running the *Constant Warwick*, a solid forty-two gonner, but these days I'm in charge of the *Cleveland*.'

My puzzled look caused a short bark of contempt.

'Thirty men, and eight cannon. Barely more than a fishing trawler or cog. But, she's fast and then some. The Admiralty wanted someone with experience at the helm since we do plenty of quick transports for lords and their families. They even let me hand-pick my crew, so all things considered I have no reason to complain. Pay's excellent as well.'

I must have looked downcast, because as I opened my mouth to speak he interrupted me with his familiar power to somehow read minds. Of course he was just good with people, but at times it could be downright unsettling.

'You're wondering why I didn't ask you to serve aboard the *Cleveland*.'

It was a statement rather than a question.

'I still think fondly of our lioness, Mister Frobisher,' he went on. 'It gladdens me to think some of my lads are still taking care of her. Perhaps one day we shall have the opportunity to sail together once more though, I'd like that.'

I smiled. The man always seemed to know the right thing to say, for all his gruff manner and impish sense of humour.

'I'd like that as well, sir,' I said. 'We miss your leadership and good nature. The crew still speaks fondly of you, those of use who were around at the time. God, sometimes it feels like a lifetime ago.'

'Aye, the sea will do that to man,' he agreed. 'How are things aboard the old girl anyway?'

Captain Williams listened to my tale with his hands tucked into the pockets of his dark blue overcoat. We had moved away from the tavern to an empty passageway behind one of the shipyards, as if on a casual stroll together. In port the walls tend to have ears.

'That's… a bad business, Lewis.'

'Yeah, it's one thing to have enemies coming at you within view, another entirely when they scuttle about in the shadows.'

'And you're sure it was Mister Evatt?' Henry Williams frowned. 'He never struck me as the type to fuck over his own. But, you never truly know,' he paused. 'Well, with a few exceptions, I can't imagine you going behind Mister Every's back or that Frenchy's I hear you brought into service.'

'Well-informed as ever, sir,' I chuckled. 'Too right, I grew up with Michael and our friend Tom in the Pool. I'd sooner cut off my own leg than put them in danger.'

'We're being followed. No, don't look just listen.'

I avoided the instinct to check behind us and followed the captain's lead. He gestured with a thumb at a large cluster of wooden kegs resting next to the shipyard. I copied his movement of resting my back against one of the barrels, and the two of us acted as though we were taking a short rest.

'It's Joseph, one of the slaves we brought back from the Barbados before your time. I think he's still owned by the Company of Shipwrights, works about the docks most days. I've never had any problems with the boy, or man these days I reckon, we should see what this is about.'

The slave noticed our attention and came running up, bowing his head. Clad in rough-spun flaxen trousers and a matching shirt, I'd never really considered just how itchy and uncomfortable it must be to wear such attire while performing heavy lifting throughout a midsummer's day. Even the lowest pauper at Cripplegate would have been hesitant to wear such rags. Joseph didn't seem to have any visible signs of punishment though, and looked solid enough; I would see wretches barely clinging to life while crammed into ships' holds in the years ahead, but upon meeting this dockyard slave I was still largely ignorant of just how cruel man can be.

Will Baker was a living saint by comparison.

'Afternoon, sirs,' Joseph began. 'I weren't sure if it was my place to say anythin', and I didn't mean to pry or listen in while cleanin' the st—'

'Relax man, you're making my heart race,' Captain Williams interjected. 'Take a moment and start from the beginning.'

Joseph collected his thoughts and I remember being impressed with the man's ability to calm his nerves. It was clear he was reluctant to tell us what he knew about my encounter on the banks of the Thames. Once his breath became more stable he began to speak, his eyes always searching for something to focus on other than

Captain Williams or myself.

Well, I was frantically picking at the back of a wooden barrel, so who am I to fault others for their twitching?

'I was washing down the walls of the company offices,' Joseph began, 'and I heard one of the masters offering fifty guineas for any proof of Papal plots.'

Captain Williams whistled. 'That's no small sum of coin, enough to keep a man for a few years in reasonable comfort.'

I had been expecting it to be difficult to understand Joseph, never having had much direct experience with slaves, but despite the unfamiliar accent he spoke clearly. As he continued it became obvious the man possessed a keen intellect and the common sense to avoid being caught eavesdropping.

'Twas one of your men off the *Lion* who I saw nodding, he was sayin' for that amount he heard a thing or two. This was a few days back, but I just heard them again a few minutes ago and the two of 'em were watching your backs with murder in their eyes.'

Joseph paused and looked directly at Captain Williams.

'The first bit was free, as a gift for your kindness over the years, sir,' the slave went on. 'Surely it's worth a few shillings to hear the rest?'

'Or I could just drag you down to the guild-master and have him beat it out of you,' the captain said with a glower. 'Out with it.'

Joseph's reaction made it clear he had no desire to incur the anger of his masters, and as he gently reached up to his shoulder I suspected signs of the whip had left their brutal mark upon his back. I was no stranger to lashings myself, but not in the way I'd heard it described from Henry Every. My friend had once said he witnessed a man in Jamaica whipped to the point his bones were showing through.

I grimaced at the thought as Joseph quickly told us the rest of his tale.

After Captain Williams confirmed it was indeed James Melior offering the coin, my stomach turned queasy upon hearing the rest. I was to have been taken to a small outcrop branching off from the path in Putney and 'questioned' by Melior and two of his men. The thought of being tortured and then disposed of into the Thames made me shudder. When we asked how Joseph knew such a thing, my worry quickly turned to rage.

'The cook was saying it wasn't his fault you escaped, and that he had lived up to his side of the agreement by telling about your chat with the Frenchman. Your captain disagreed and said the deal was off.'

Dan Evatt, you fucking bastard.

৪•

We spent the next few minutes trying to pry any other valuable information from Joseph to no avail. Even so, it was clear Captain Melior had it in for myself and Michael. I was starting to panic about my friend back on the *Lion*, hoping he was still in the sailmakers' workshop and free from immediate danger. As we turned to leave, Henry Williams dug out a solid gold guinea and placed it in Joseph's hand. The man's eyes went wide with delight, and despite my worries I couldn't help but chuckle at my first captain's favourite type of jest: Make a man shit himself and then shower him with good fortune.

'I'm going to shove Selby's rifle right up the fat fuck's arse, I swear to…'

I trailed off mid-sentence as Joseph gave me a curious

look.

'Sirs, I think there's a misunderstanding, and I don't want no innocent man to pay the price. The cook was thin as a rake, shock of red hair and skin to make the worst whores in Paris turn away.'

Captain Williams gave me a puzzled expression.

After a second of confusion on my part I shook my head in a mixture of relief and anger.

'Christopher Wheyton,' I said. 'He's after your time, Cook's Mate. The little rat-faced fuck must have been out of sight in the hold but helping Dan with something. No, wait…'

I tried to recall the cargo hold as best I could from the night we had laid our plans to ruin Melior's reputation.

'He was there, I just never paid him any mind,' I continued. 'But, I do remember him looking over at us briefly while hoisting a sack of grain atop his shoulder.'

'What do you want to do, Lewis?'

'I want to open the fucker's throat,' I growled, ' see how he talks then.'

Captain Williams simply raised an eyebrow, and twitched his head towards the warehouse. Joseph took the hint and with a curt nod and thanks he returned to his daily chores.

I sighed and knew my act wasn't fooling anyone. Sure, I'd killed a couple of men by now, but never in cold sport.

'First, I want to make sure Michael is alright, I replied. 'Then, I might stop by the kitchens to see if Chris is around, or ask about if he's not.'

We began to make our way slowly up the rest of the backstreet, ceasing our conversation briefly as two coopers passed us in the other direction.

'I'd suggest going directly to Dan,' he added. 'I've

known Daniel Evatt for years, and he'd sooner serve up his own leg for supper than turn someone over to the likes of James Melior.'

I nodded in agreement. 'We've been mates for years as well and always gotten along, so far as I could tell anyway. Still, I'm not sure what good dragging him into this mess will do.'

'Well, for a start he will definitely know where Christopher is. On top of that, you will need to muster as many supporters as possible if you want to find evidence of Melior's schemes against both yourself and the crown.'

'That's true enough, I suppose,' I replied as we came to the main concourse of Portsmouth's dockyards. Captain Williams leaned in close and quietly said, 'I'll dig around a bit as well with the Admiralty and see what I can turn up, but for now I'd suggest keeping your head down and a pair of eyes on your back at all times. The same goes for your mate Michael and anyone else who might have a grudge against the puritan prick.'

Unsure how I was ever going to get a decent night's rest again, we parted ways and I hurried back to the ship. As I walked along the wharves, weaving between fellow crewmen and slaves, my fear over lying awake at night was quickly discarded.

The Royal Navy has changed in many ways since my time aboard *His Majesty's Ship Lion*, but there is always one constant: At the end of every day, you're either exhausted, drunk or both.

Sleep is never an issue.

I felt a weight fall from my shoulders as Michael came bounding up, gesturing we should head back in the direction I had come.

'Melior's in a right mood,' he said. 'Even by his usual standards the man's being a monumental arsehole to the landsmen right now.'

'There's good reason for that,' I muttered.

I brought Michael up to speed as we walked in the direction of the stores. He had been going out to try and find me anyway, so we decided upon a mug or two of ale at the same tavern I'd met Dan and his crony earlier on.

'Jesus Christ, Lewis, we're in over our heads here. I knew he wasn't right in the head, but trying to have you questioned and…'

'And killed,' I finished for my friend. 'Aye, chances are I wouldn't have walked away from the meeting.'

'What should we do?'

'For now Captain Williams has the right of it, I think. Stay focused on our work and try to blend into the background, hopefully Melior's wrath will turn elsewhere. We need to be sure of our friends and keep an eye out for any members of the crew who pay us unwarranted attention. On top of all that, we should watch for anyone who has reason to hold a grudge against our 'captain', and try to recruit them to our cause.'

'That's all well and good, but so long as he's in command we're pretty much fucked in the long run.'

'True enough,' I sighed. 'At least there we know where he is though, do you really want to leave service once your terms are up, only to worry about knives in the dark wherever you go?'

'It's no worse than worrying about knives in the bunks,' Michael replied with a hint of venom.

'Nah, I wager Melior's more the crafty type, if his attempt to take me is anything to go by. I think we'll be safe enough aboard ship, and he knows we are well-liked by most of the crew. If anything we have more to worry about on leave. He's a giant prick and has it out for us, but he's not completely useless at running the ship, you know that.'

I waved to Dan who was now sitting by himself, and he gestured us over to join his table.

'He's going to make our days a living nightmare though.'

With a bemused smile at Michael I slapped his arm and shook it.

'Yes. Yes, he is.'

Dan was fairly deep into his cups when we sat down, but not to the point he was incoherent or struggling to sit upright. One of the younger lads brought a fresh round of drinks and a few morsels of cheese with pickled onions. I handed him a few pennies and we raised our tankards to clank them together.

'Thick as thieves, the two of you,' Dan quipped.

'Like brothers, we are,' I said. 'May as well be, you know we grew up together around the Pool.'

'Thought you were up north in London?' Daniel Evatt asked with a slight slur. 'Aldersgate or thereabouts.'

'Cripplegate is where my poorhouse was, close enough,' I answered. 'But, I spent any free hours I could down at the Pool with Michael and a few other friends.'

'Sounds like it beats growing up in…'

Dan trailed off and a serious look came over his face.

'I couldn't say much earlier with Ugly Arthur around, but the two of you are in serious shit.'

'Tell us something we don't know,' I yawned.

'This is no joke, Lewis. You—'

'We're being watched by Melior who intends to have

our necks strung up from the gallows?'

I had decided to take a chance on Dan's friendship. There was no way to be sure he wasn't in league with Christopher Wheyton or the captain, but if you can't trust someone you've been to brothels with and helped peel carrots, then who can you trust?

Dan's eyes widened. 'How could you possibly know that? I only just heard about it a few hours ago.'

'Because our esteemed captain has already made one attempt.'

We were trying to speak softly and there were no other patrons outside, but the three of us quickly finished our flagons of ale and retired to my workshop to continue the discussion away from prying eyes or ears. It wasn't unusual for Dan to pay us a visit when he wasn't busy preparing meals, and it would seem much less conspicuous than the three of us wandering off. Thankfully my sailmaker's mates were still ashore so we had a measure of privacy.

'I remember seeing the two of you in the hold, but to be honest I didn't pay it any mind. I just figured you were getting canvas or whatever else you layabouts need for the sail.'

'I'd make a joke about your food, but I know better than to bite the hand that feeds.'

Dan grinned. 'A wise decision. So you thought I went and told Melior for his bag of guineas?'

'I didn't want to think that, but until someone mentioned Christopher I had completely forgotten he was with you.'

'Well, who's to say the only reason I didn't take the coin was because I never got the offer, eh?'

My heart felt like it stopped in my chest at hearing

those words, but one look at Dan's ear-to-ear grin put me at ease.

'Bastard,' I muttered. 'So what, Chris just up and told you?'

Michael sat in silence and appeared deep in thought as Dan played with a bolt of canvas between his fingers before continuing.

'He was worried, said he made a big mistake and didn't know who else to talk with about it.'

I opened my mouth to say something, but decided to not interrupt.

'Anyway, eventually he told me that Melior offered up a big purse of guineas and Chris had told him about your plans to smear his reputation as a traitor. The lad is a fucking moron, you know that. He always jumps before he walks, but he's always been likeable enough on leave.'

That much was true, I thought to myself. I didn't know Christopher Wheyton nearly so well as Daniel Evatt, Henry Every or Bill Pritchard, but the boy had a quick laugh and good nature about him.

'His greed got the better of him, that's my guess. We'd best have words with him, I imagine you have a few questions of your own, Lewis.'

'I do indeed, and as much as I want to ring his scrawny neck, it was fifty guineas at stake. When I was at Cripplegate I would have done pretty much anything under the Sun for such a fortune.'

Michael spoke up for the first time since we arrived back aboard the *Lion*.

'Do you think Melior was really going to hand over the purse?'

'Probably not,' I admitted. 'But, Chris had no way of knowing that and took him at his word.'

The three of us sat for about a minute in

contemplation. I broke the silence by asking when and where Dan had last seen his Cook's Mate.

'I sent him off for some salted beef and rum not long after,' the Ship's Cook replied.

'Right,' I said as I got to my feet. 'I guess we'd better start with the kitchens then victual stores in port.'

'Let's stick together,' Michael proposed. 'It will take a bit longer, but right now I'm not in the mood to split up and get a dagger in my spine.'

Dan and I both nodded and we went above deck to spend our few remaining hours of leave searching for the informer who had told Captain Melior of our plot.

To this day, Christopher Wheyton was never found.

Chapter 16

Amsterdam, Republic of the Seven United Netherlands, 1688 AD

I was now twenty-four years old, and James Melior was no longer a traitor.

In the years since the attempt on my life things had rapidly deteriorated at home.

James II had maintained a precarious hold over his throne following the first year of his reign, but his support had dwindled over the course of three years. He had tried to promote tolerance for other faiths, and the English were having none of it. Most folk saw it as an attempt to reinforce the Roman creed at the expense of the Church of England, and his imprisonment of seven bishops last summer for refusing to read his terms only bolstered such views.

The people along with Parliament had been turning against the king for years. He lacked the charisma and easy manner of his elder brother Charles. While he may have possessed some personal tendencies towards the Catholic Church, Charles II was savvy enough to at least hide it from the public and his ministers.

Personally I just don't think the Merry Monarch gave a shit about such things, so long as they didn't impact his spending. From what I'd always heard about the man, I feel like he'd rather be feasting and admiring art or the female form. Never too old for a romp, eh Baltasar? Well, it could be worse. At least your eyes still work.

Are the men gathered in the yard, then? Good, we can let them finish eating and head down after I finish my story.

In any case, we had a Protestant Dutchman set for coronation in the months ahead, and a certain puritanical captain couldn't have been more elated. After James and his Modenese queen had produced an heir to the throne, Parliament had practically begged William of Orange to take the crown.

James at least had the good sense to realise his cause was utterly lost. He fled to the courts of France with his family, including his newborn son, James Francis Edward Stuart.

Aye, that's the one. Got his arse kicked up in the Scottish Highlands last summer by General Wightman. I suppose I should feel sorry for the man, given I earned my first wages in the navy from his uncle, but I stopped caring for lords and ladies years ago.

William and his wife Mary had entered England with overwhelming support from its people. The latter was a niece of Charles II and first in the line of succession following James' flight to the continent, but William could hardly be expected to defer in matters to his queen nor act as a mere consort. Such a style of rule was unthinkable.

Instead, it was expected they would rule together as equal regents, in a similar manner to how Philip of Spain and Mary Tudor had briefly governed more than a century ago. I remember thinking this sounded like a recipe for disaster, but it turned out to work rather well. This was doubly true when William was away at war and Mary was left to her own devices in London.

It turns out having a functional relationship does have

its advantages.

Unfortunately for myself and my crewmates, it severely hampered our ability to expose Melior for his earlier treason, and we still had no proof of his involvement in my own brush with death other than the testimony of a slave. We could hardly expect the crown or Admiralty to string the man up for having allowed the Protestant James Scott to slip through and stir up rebellion against a Papist.

My own desire for vengeance had become more personal as well. I was never a religious man in my younger days, and my abduction was a much greater source of fury than any grand scheme of politics. What really got under my skin was how little James Melior seemed to even acknowledge what had happened; he would sneer and treat us like the drippings of a cesspit, but not much worse off than most of the crew.

The fact he couldn't care less about having tried to kill me set my blood ablaze.

Every time I saw his ruffed collars and pudgy, leather-worn face I wanted to gouge his eyes out, or open his stomach on to the main deck for all to see.

Such thoughts were the reason myself and several other crew were huddled within a small room at the cheapest brothel in Amsterdam on a cold December evening.

We were going to kill the whoreson, consequences be damned. What better place to layout such plans?

The small conspiracy consisted of myself, Michael Bollard, Henry Every, Bill Pritchard, Stuart Effingham, Daniel Evatt and two new seamen by the names of Jack Fuller and Henry Morgan. The latter deserved to be part of the plot by virtue of his name alone, sharing it with the late rogue-turned-governor of Jamaica, and the two men could barely contain their utter loathing for Captain Melior.

We had decided upon meeting in secret at a place highly recommended in the *Het Amsterdamsch Hoerdom*, and even Bill's eyes nearly bulged out of his head as we made our way along the street by one of Amsterdam's many canals. All manner of debauchery, from topless barmaids to drinking competitions, was in full form alongside the many vendors trying to ply their questionable wares.

Eight drunken sailors fit in perfectly.

Despite our sinister intentions, I recall being surprised by the sheer opulence of the city. *Lion* had taken on provisions in the Netherlands before, but this was our first proper shore leave as relations with the locals had greatly warmed since our recent wars. William of Orange was soon to be crowned King of England, Scotland and Ireland, and arguably the *de jure* King of France, but he was also the Prince of Orange and *stadtholder* of the Dutch Republic.

The English and Dutch had never really held any particular hatred for one another, at least not compared with how we viewed the French. Most of our wars had been over trade and control over the maritime routes leading into Europe. Now though, we began to feel like cousins of a sort.

Alright, perhaps I exaggerate. They were still happy to fleece us at ridiculous prices at the shops, but at least they did so with a smile. In any case, Amsterdam was clearly prospering and made most of London look like utter squalor; only the few streets around the Tower which had escaped the Great Fire could begin to compare.

Canals weaved their way alongside well-paved streets, and many buildings were built from superb masonry and covered with a wide range of paints. Vines and branches were found everywhere, and I tried to imagine how the spring must have looked, with flowers bursting from every crevice.

To be fair, London was not entirely without its charms despite having been engulfed by flames twenty years earlier. Charles Mason's newly-repaired London Bridge was a point of pride in those days, but for the most part we were in awe of the fine clothing, cleanliness and overall sense of affluence which seemed the norm in Holland.

The two beggars we did encounter on the way up from the wharves both had steaming bowls of some unknown stew in front of them and blankets, the latter coarse and undecorated but of good, thick wool. I'd grown up on the streets for long enough to know how the darker aspects of city life are often hidden from view, and that Amsterdam like London had its sad, hungry secrets, but for eight men on shore leave the place felt like a dream.

The only downside was that no one in my company was in any mood for a night of frivolity, or so I thought upon our arrival at the whorehouse.

'So, that's it then?'

We sat with our hands clasped around mugs of mulled wine, a small light flickering from the fireplace behind Henry's chair.

'I suppose so,' I answered Bill. 'It's crucial no one learns of our involvement, I figure poison's the safest option, what say you?'

'Makes sense to me,' Dan grumbled. 'No blood, and hard to trace back to any of the crew.'

'We still don't know that fight at the King's Arms was his doing,' Stuart interjected. 'That big bastard with the knife was after your head, sure, but he looked the type to kill his own mother for a tuppence to begin with.'

'I'm sure our ruffled up cock Melior was behind that one as well,' I said through clenched teeth. 'First leave in ages, and someone comes at me with a blade for no reason?'

'Poison seems like a bleedin' waste,' Jack said in hushed tones while playing with his own small, easily-concealed dagger. 'Would rather stick 'im with Jane here.'

'I'd rather not see you swing,' I said in response to his blunt comment. 'But, believe me when I say the feeling is shared.'

For a few minutes we sat quietly as noises of doors being unlatched came from the hallway. We pretended to discuss the various tits and arses on display at the establishment, lifting our voices in forced-but-raucous laughter. I reckoned the master of the house would be by again shortly to inquire about our 'tastes' for the evening, but he had been happy enough to offer up a room for good English silver. Our ruse of heavy drinking before choosing our companions for the evening would only hold for so long though. We needed to wrap things up quickly.

'I figure next time we're back home in the new year,' Henry Morgan added to the discussion. 'Stu was telling me the "captain" usually enjoys a meal with one of his friends the first night back. Hire a professional to slip in, lace his grub or ale, then slip out unseen. We just have to make sure the man's well-paid.'

Henry Every began to laugh and clutched his hands together. Naturally we all turned and waited for him to enlighten us.

'I think I can do us one better,' he said. 'I know a crook from Bishopsgate who runs a good trick. He goes collecting alms from homes, claiming it goes to the nearby churches. Looks the part as well, has the holier-than-thou act down to a fine art. More often than not he gets invited in for a meal. Willard's a famous glutton and can't abide church folk either, which helps us. I would have to talk to him, but I can more or less promise he will be our man for the right amount.'

'Good, it's settled then,' I concluded, and the men's nods confirmed it. 'Next we're in London, we introduce Melior to our mutual friend, Willard.'

'Good riddance,' piped up Michael. 'May the fucker choke on his own bacon.'

As we raised or flagons in agreement, I felt a brief moment of guilt. Not at what needed to be done, but while looking at Michael thoughts of Tom Coram and his family crossed my mind. Part of me hoped John and his family would understand, but I knew they would feel deeply ashamed. It's one thing to kill a man when under attack, another matter entirely to have someone else do your dirty work from the shadows. Sadly, my desire for revenge and to stop Melior from abusing the rest of the crew or my friends won out.

'What now then?' Bill said after we downed the rest of our warm drink.

Jack grinned.

'Well, we're already here, aren't we?'

ઠ♦

The decision to spend the night at *de zoete boterbloem* was actually a pretty clever one.

A group of English sailors staggering back from a night of debauchery was far less conspicuous than if we had avoided the many vices and returned early.

At least Stuart had been clear-headed enough in the morning to suggest leaving in smaller groups at intervals. I was the last to leave with Michael and Henry Every. The three of us were close friends and it was unlikely to raise any eyebrows. A few lewd gestures from the crew at the state of us, no doubt, but that sort of thing was no trouble.

Most of them were probably up to the same mischief the night before anyway, they'd just had a chance to splash some water on their faces.

Chaplain Whitworth was another matter, as were the Ship's Surgeon Walter Crouch and our old friend Patrick Byrne. The former two had always been stiff, joyless types when it came to sin, but Pat was a shame. He used to love a good drink and night out, always getting us into any number of problems like the brawl in Guernsey with his French brother-in-law, but the man had adopted sobriety and a passion for the Bible in the years since. Captain Melior was of course perfectly content with the development.

God, had that really been ten years ago? I'd only been fifteen years old at the time, and getting into fights with Frenchmen.

I had seen Etienne Beaumont and his companions a few times in the years since, mostly through Pat and his wife Jeanne when they had us all over for a meal, but it had been a while. Between Pat's new-found morality and our deteriorating relations with King Louis, I had fewer opportunities to see any of them. Things would get worse in the years ahead as open warfare erupted across Europe, but that morning we focused on avoiding the less-jovial members of our crew on the return to our stations. As we dragged our aching figures down to Amsterdam's eastern harbour we were forced to stand aside several times, as carts with the familiar 'VOC' branding of the *Vereenigde Oost Indische Compagnie* rattled past on their way up from the numerous quays.

Signs of our own East India Company were everywhere as well, now that trade disputes between the English and Dutch were beginning to thaw. The companies operated free from crown or republic control, at least on paper, but any trader worth his salt knew better than to jeopardise the immense profits to be gained due to the recent turn of events. I had no doubt the holds of every ship at anchor would be laden with prized cargo, ready to be lapped up by well-to-do residents of Amsterdam and the rest of the Netherlands.

The eastern quays and harbour were truly something to behold. Trade cogs and vessels of all sizes crowded the wharves, and their crews moved to and fro like a colony of ants at work. Spices I still don't even know the names for filled my nostrils, while bolts of cloth so delicate as to be barely visible stood in neatly organised rows. Michael whistled as an expensive-looking vase with unfamiliar designs was carried between two Moselman slaves in the opposite direction towards the markets. I wondered if either of them had been members of Ali Reis' squadron those many years ago, but then I figured it was unlikely. From what I gathered through Captain Williams the smaller craft had evaded French capture, and we all but massacred the Barbary pirates on their man o' war.

I was regaling Michael with stories about the corsairs

while we grabbed a drink of water and a quick meal from one of the many stores lining the waterfront. Once satiated, we gave our faces a quick wash and steadied ourselves for a return to work. With any luck Bill and the others would have cleared the way ahead of us, with Melior distracted or on someone else's case.

I couldn't wait for Willard to pay him a visit, but for now we just had to survive until our next trip to Deptford or the Tower stores, assuming we didn't call in at Portsmouth instead.

As we turned the corner of the wharf and the familiar hull and markings of the *Lion* came into view, I cursed myself for not having known better.

If you ever want to make God laugh, just tell Him you have a plan.

'You reek of sin, both of the liquor and strumpet variety.'

I bit my tongue and was relieved Michael had the composure to do the same. We both stood at attention and prepared for the complete bollocking we were about to receive from the very man we were planning to murder within the coming months.

'Well?' James Melior inquired. 'Have you nothing to say?'

'Apologies, sir,' I gave my best attempt at sounding obsequious. 'We got a bit carried away with our wages and woke with a pounding in our heads, God's punishment right enough.'

'Atonement and prayer is in order,' Michael quickly added. 'Perhaps Chaplain Whitworth would be willing to read some passages for us while we begin mending the jib sheet?'

Clever. Appealing to Melior's religious fervor and inviting the chaplain to guide us in prayer was a good way to hide our true thoughts.

'Mayhaps I should just switch you both bloody,' the captain pondered aloud.

I knew he was full of shit. His prior attacks had been subtle and carefully orchestrated, either through sending highwaymen or hired thugs after me. There was no way he could expect the rest of the crew to put up with us being whipped raw for having been out whoring.

The captain gave us a long, appraising look.

'You're both on swab duties for the month, just be glad you keep your backs. Now, off with you.'

Without a second glance the sanctimonious prick turned and wandered off to berate some other unfortunate soul.

'What a tosspot,' growled Michael under his breath, once we were safely at work in the sailmaker's workshop. 'Lewis, what the Hell are we going to do? A month of swabbing the decks will drive me beyond reason, no?'

'I sometimes forget you more or less skipped life as a cabin boy,' I grinned. 'You could do with some toughening up, Frenchy.'

My friend punched my arm and muttered something incoherent about roast beef.

'I spent maybe a week on deck duties when I first joined,' he continued. 'My back still aches. Patching up these sails is something I have grown quite comfortable with, much more my style.'

'It will be a damned misery, but at least it keeps us near the rest of the men. Try to stay away from the galleries or gunholes wherever possible. I wouldn't put it past Melior to cause one of us to have an "accident" when no one is looking.'

'Do you really think he'd try to pull that?'

'Not really,' I replied. 'But, I try to prepare for the worst, that way you rarely end up being caught off guard.'

'What about Putney?'

'Oh come on," I protested. 'Me and the ferry lads had been drinking for hours, you can blame that cock up on the ale and cider.'

Michael paused for a minute, unsure of what to say.

'Was it… bad?'

I didn't need to ask what he meant.

'Worse than Will Baker,' I stared at the sailcloth in my hands. 'That was quick and a bit of a mistake, but the footpad, well… I saw the life leave his eyes and couldn't get his rank odour from my nose for days.'

'Are you going to tell Tom? When we get back home, I mean.'

Michael had yet to kill anyone, but as a good friend he never seemed to judge my actions nor hold my stained hands against me. I'd told him about Will and the more recent assailant, naturally, but I was unsure how to broach the subject with Tom Coram, let alone the rest of his family.

I had a feeling John might understand, but Bethany and Jane would never be able to look at me the same way again. The thought of losing their kindness and love was unfathomable.

Oh God, not to mention Lucy or Owen finding out.

The last time we'd been back home the little sprat had just turned six years old and I thought of him as a baby brother, as did Michael for that matter.

'Maybe…' I shook my head. 'I don't know. John knows I got roughed up, but I just told him the arsehole ran off. He doesn't know I—'

'Shh,' cautioned Michael. 'Things are best left unsaid sometimes. We'll cross that bridge when we come to it.'

The next several weeks consisted of wiping blood and sweat from the *Lion's* beams and planks, while also struggling to keep on top of our repairs. The winter had been particularly cold at sea, and we spent most of our nights dreaming of warm hearths, cotton bedding and down pillows.

At least we wouldn't freeze to death in our hammocks. One of the few advantages to being surrounded by snoring crewmates.

I was allowed to hang my bed away from the main crew in the sailmaker's workshop, as a perk for being one of the ship's officers, but in midwinter I generally hung it between Michael and Henry. Furthermore, given our ongoing plot against the captain I was wary about sleeping alone.

Finally, after a meagre celebration of New Year aboard ship we received orders to make sail for Deptford Dockyards for a minor refit, given the main mast had been having a few issues following the December squalls.

Perfect.

I met with my seven fellow conspirators at a rundown fisherman's shack just up from the Royal Dock at Deptford. We waited for about an hour before being joined by Willard, who had come with such high recommendations from Henry Every.

The look on his face made my heart skip a beat.

'Wasn't there,' the priestly-looking Willard stated bluntly. 'Still get my coin though, as agreed.'

'What do you mean he wasn't there?'

Willard turned at Jack Fuller's indignant roar.

'Just as I says, he weren't at the deacon's place.'

'But he's been there for supper every time we've been back through Deptford or the Tower Shipyards,' Bill looked puzzled. 'Are you sure you went to the right house?'

Willard didn't even justify the question with an answer.

'Fuck,' I said. 'I guess that idea's out, then.'

'Deacon Paul was generous enough, I tend to try it on with priests and the like. Will have to remember to try a bishop next,' Willard smiled through jagged, green teeth. 'Still expectin' my pay though.'

We thought better than making an enemy of a clearly dangerous man, despite Melior having given us the slip. Bill and Dan offered up a few extra pounds along with the original price.

Willard scooped up the dull coins, nodded his approval, and left without another word.

We ran into Patrick Byrne on the way back to the *Lion* and he waved us over. I was going to visit the Corams with Michael and intended to see the rest of the men back to our ship beforehand, but Pat asked if we wanted to share a coach into London. It was too good a deal to pass up, so Michael and I bade farewell to our six other companions and hopped into the small but comfortable carriage. Only an utter fool would look for trouble with Henry or Bill together, so I was pretty comfortable they would be fine.

Pat passed me a wedge of good, crumbly Cheshire and I relished the taste. For all of his changed ways since our nights of heavy drinking and carousing, he was still a good friend. That is, if you managed to look past his incessant references to scripture. Ten years ago he probably would have wanted to gut James Melior himself, but now…

Well, it was likely in Pat's own best interests that we kept him in the dark.

It was during the coach ride into London that we realised why Melior had been absent from his usual evening with the deacon; Pat informed us about a change to the captaincy of the *Lion* following this shore leave. Apparently he had heard the news directly from the bastard's own lips while discussing one of the Psalms in the ship's small chapel.

James Melior was headed for the Orient, to serve with the Venetians and their allies in holding back the Turk. The Admiralty had agreed to send him with a handful of other officers to assist with recruitment drives and training. *La Serenissima* was a shadow of its former self, but Venice was still a major threat to the Ottoman advances. I supposed they must be in dire straits if they needed the like of James Melior to help out.

We passed the rest of the short journey in amicable silence, or talking about trivial affairs. It was only when I arrived at the Corams' home with Michael that we heard the more significant news. John had caught wind of it through his peers on the fishing trawlers earlier in the day, and was filled with concern when we came knocking at their door.

England was going to war.

Chapter 17

Deptford Dockyard, River Thames, 1689 AD

His Majesty's Ship Lion was looking her very best.

From gunhole to crow's nest every visible piece of iron or woodwork was polished to perfection. Broad bands of thick paint in a rich, dark hue of yellow against black spread the length of her hull. I took particular pride in her rigging and sail, knowing from my own weeks of work that every sheet of canvas was either in pristine condition or mended to the best of my ability.

Well, mine and the rest of my sailmakers. Pride is a sin, after all.

The crew, officers and marines matched the *Lion's* display of power as a third-rate ship of the line. Lieutenant Selby was still with us after these many years, and, along with his men, he cut a dashing figure in his new uniform. The cut of cloth and large buttons were both finely-crafted by some of England's most skilled tailors; there were significant profits in producing officers' uniforms. His blood-red overcoat was trimmed at the cuffs and collar with the same shade of gold found on the sides of the *Lion*, and his matching officer's cap was emblazoned with the letter 'W' in white stitching. He could have been promoted up the ranks years ago, but the lieutenant made it perfectly clear he intended to stay with his men.

Indeed, this representation of the recently-coronated

William III was visible throughout the dockyard, from barrels of rum to kegs of powder. It was made abundantly clear who was now paying our wages.

The new kit wasn't just for decoration. Our marines were issued new muskets and sidearms fresh from the depots of London. As I stood admiring our beautiful lioness from the wharf I noticed George was busy showing one of the younger marines how to properly grease the barrel and flintlock. I knew from my years of service this was to reduce the lethal risk of the gun jamming up, but my own experience of muskets or other longarms was extremely limited. Pistols, cutlasses and knives were more my style of weapon, as I would discover in the years to come. I hadn't forgotten my desire to avenge myself upon James Melior, but with the fleet readying for war and his transfer it would have to wait. Instead, I busied myself with the endless work of a Sailmaker and waited.

We spent a fair amount of time learning how to fight as well. Each man o' war came with a compliment of marines, but going into action we figured it would be a worthwhile use of our time. Most of the crew were fairly competent brawlers to begin with, but there's a big difference between a drunken round of fisticuffs and a fight to the death.

Several of us would unfortunately learn that lesson the hard way, on the receiving end of a blade.

George and his soldiers were in favour of the training for the most part; he reasoned any extra support in battle if things got really ugly could only be a good thing. It rankled their pride as soldiers somewhat, but it was always very clear who the professionals were, and George dropped me on my backside on more than one occasion without even breaking a sweat.

I was stretching out the knots in my back when the new captain of the *Lion* came up beside me.

'Life of hunching over sail,' he smiled. 'I know that all too well, it's how I started out.'

I nodded my agreement.

Captain John Torpley had been transferred from his previous post aboard a fifth rate named the 'Success' and by all accounts was a decent-enough sort. He didn't speak much and there were rumours amongst the crew as to his… preferences, but I had no reason to dislike the man. So long as he didn't give me any reason for concern, he could bugger the Sultan's court in Constantinople for all I cared.

It was a common-enough thing anyway, but most knew better than to air such things in the open. That is, unless you felt an impulse to be strung up to the mizzen mast and left to die from thirst. Chaplain Whitworth and most of the crew wouldn't even hesitate.

No matter the circumstances, Torpley was a much better captain than a certain rat-faced, frill-covered goat's pizzle, I can say that much for certain.

'She's no three-decker like *Royal Sovereign* over there,' he went on, 'but, she's a real beauty.'

At first I felt a hot flush of anger at our new captain belittling the ship I had served on for over a decade. However, after turning my head farther down the wharves I had to admit he was right.

The old girl was an absolute monster.

While she was getting a little bit long in the tooth, the first rate had undergone a major refit over in Chatham about four years earlier. With three decks of one hundred cannon and full-rigging she was a match for any other vessel to be found on the seas. While not as agile nor swift as smaller ships, the hulking ship was still perfectly capable of fairly complex manoeuvres with a skilled crew.

The problem was if she managed to close range and unleash a broadside.

I'd witnessed our own such assault against the corsairs, and I shuddered at the thought of what utter devastation the *Royal Sovereign* would rain down upon her victim.

'That she is,' I replied. 'Louis will be swimming back to Versailles with his fine, silk britches around his ankles.'

That brought an open laugh from my new captain.

'That's what I like to hear. God knows their fleet can hold its own though… we're in for a tough one, what, with all the trouble in the Rhineland on top of everything else.'

Captain Torpley was right. Louis XIV, the Sun King and most powerful ruler in all Christendom, had far too much to lose in the coming war to back down without a serious contest.

'Ah well,' I affected a yawn. 'Won't be the first time we showed them a thing or two.'

'It doesn't take very much for we English to fight the French. King Billy must be cunning as a fox. By taking the throne he's more or less dragged us into a war to protect his own interests in Europe.'

Catain Torpley paused as if in deep thought.

'You know… we've fought one Louis after another for so long that I don't even know who's on top anymore. For every Azincourt there seems to be a Formigny to match.'

For some reason I felt a dire need to prove my own learning on such topics. Alderman Samuel would be proud, I think.

'True, but Louis himself has already managed to gain the upper hand against us ten years' past, and the last major battles between us were definitely to France's favour, granted they took place on land.'

The captain raised an eyebrow and I said something about not always having been a sailor.

'Well, then I suppose we're long overdue for a change of fortune.'

Standing there, watching the vast array of warships being armed for battle, it was easy to feel the resolve behind the man's words.

It had taken a while for John's rumours to prove true.

By the middle of the year of our Lord 1689, about six months after having first heard the murmurs of a coming fight with France, the king and queen openly declared war.

Once their coronation was out of the way in February, William and Mary had managed to bring Parliament over to their cause. They managed this feat by emphasising concerns over trade disruption and the attempts of James Stuart, our former king-in-exile, to scheme against us from across the Narrow Sea. With the English and Dutch firmly aligned through the person of William III and all signs pointing towards an alliance with the emperor in Vienna out of common interests, it seemed we could finally contain the French expansion.

Since as far back as I could remember, stories of the Sun King's military accomplishments and the might of the Kingdom of France had been told throughout England. No other realm could match its wealth nor power single-handedly. His borders had expanded significantly at the expense of Spain in the first two decades of his reign, and now Louis looked to continue expansion through the Netherlands and German electorates.

I had no desire to face Etienne and his company in battle, but I reconciled my sense of foreboding with the knowledge they very likely felt the same way. We'd shared too many meals and hearths for it to be otherwise. I just prayed it wouldn't come to that. Chaplain Whitworth even agreed to offer his services, which surprisingly I accepted.

It was one of the few times I visited the chapel of my own volition and I think he was eager to support my unusual piety, even if it did involve sparing the king's enemies. We were never friends nor close, given he'd caned me for blasphemy several times, but when it came to matters of the soul the man was blunt, honest and not one to mince words. He was like a rock in a stream, and, when you wanted your courage or backbone stiffened, James Whitworth was the man to ask. He didn't attempt any nonsense about them being French, he simply stated it was never wrong to care about our loved ones or to desire peace.

I'd never let the bastard hear it from my own mouth, but the hour or so spent in his company did relieve some of the darkness from my mind.

Michael, much to his credit, stood firm in the face of growing concerns from some of the crew.

Now that our friend Henry Every had transferred over the *Rupert* for a midshipman's position one of our most vocal supporters was unable to help our reputation with the crew. While the men didn't confront Michael openly about his background, we knew of murmurs when out of earshot.

The matter of his loyalties were laid to rest one afternoon while we were making our usual patrol in the English Channel, as some of us had taken to calling the Narrow Sea. Captain Torpley had casually asked how Michael felt about killing his own, to which he replied: 'Why would I have any desire to kill Englishmen, other than Dan for his filthy cooking, oui?'

This brought a chorus of cheers and hurrahs.

His mocking use of French at the end was an especially nice touch.

I knew my friend though, and over a bite of salted beef washed down with rum we returned to the question in private. Bill Pritchard had wanted to join us for the meal, but he must have realised three was a crowd upon seeing our faces. I told him to set a couple of mugs aside for us and that we'd join him in a few minutes.

'I know you never really get into it, never have,' I started. 'You're really fine with what's likely to happen?'

'Lewis, I can't even picture my parents' faces anymore, my real ones, I mean.'

'Stephen and Agnes were as re—'

'Oh, shut the fuck up, you know what I meant.'

I decided to do just that.

'Sorry,' Michael mumbled. 'I know they were, and I still pray for them at night. But, when it comes to France the name *Gauthier* doesn't even mean anything to me anymore.'

'Do you remember much from before the Pool?'

'Not really,' he went on. 'Bits and pieces, but I was pretty young when we left for England. It's sort of like trying to remember a dream. I can picture the colours in my head, and some of the smells have stuck with me, but not much other than that. I mean, Jesus Christ, Lewis, I've never even been to Paris.'

'Me neither,' I chortled. 'None of this matters anyway, you eat more *rosbif* than anyone I know apart from Tom.'

'The one great contribution of the English,' he laughed. 'I figure we get paid to patch up sails and fight if it comes to it. The king lines our pockets with coin, so it's only fair he gets to decide who we get stuck into.'

It was as if he had read my thoughts.

'My sentiments exactly, *mon ami*.'

'Ugh.'

&♥

We spent the first few months of the war as little more than glorified ferrymen.

James Stuart, with the full support of his French allies, had been stirring up trouble in Ireland ever since the spring. Its Parliament had welcomed him with open arms and passed a series of laws to his benefit. Tolerance for both Protestant *and* Catholic faiths had been decreed, along with all those involved in his fall from power being branded as traitors to the crown.

Suffice it to say, William and Mary were none too pleased.

Through the summer months into August we spent most of our time away from the main fleet. Admiral Herbert, Earl of Torrington, was in command of several dozen ships of the line in the English Channel, with more reinforcements en route from the Mediterranean and West Indies.

While nominally part of the main fleet, the *Lion* spent most of the summer and early autumn helping transport soldiers across to Ulster with the aim of stomping out James' growing strength. By the end of August, 1689, not only had Londonderry withstood a six month siege from the *Jacobites*, as we had taken to calling the followers of the deposed king, but Carrickfergus Castle had just surrendered to one of our generals after a brief week-long siege.

Marshal Scomberg, a *Huguenot* who was one of King William's staunchest supporters, planned to quickly move on Dublin and put an end to the insurrection. Unfortunately, a series of events hindered our hopes of a swift victory. Most of the crew, myself included, wanted this nonsense with Ireland to be over so we could rejoin the fleet under the Earl of Torrington.

Safety in numbers is as valid at sea as on land, after all.

The first major setback occurred within two weeks of our armies leaving Carrickfergus to march south towards Dublin. Marshal Schomberg had seriously underestimated the time required for the journey and ended up being forced to pitch camp just outside the town of Dundalk. Despite our constant efforts in shipping provisions and gear for the increasingly cold weather it never seemed to be enough.

I remember one of our new recruits, an Able Seaman by the name of William Carter, telling us the army lost close to six thousand men to sickness from September through November. At the time I fancied he was exaggerating the numbers as sailors typically do, but sadly I was mistaken. It became abundantly clear by the New Year that William III was livid with Schomberg for the setback, and the king was making plans to take direct control over the campaign.

Thankfully the French were preoccupied with enhancing their own fleet and showed no sign of coming to James' aid. Things were rapidly deteriorating, but that was at least one stroke of good fortune. Well, it seemed that way at the beginning of the year. However, by the summer the increased number of French warships would have dire repercussions for the Royal Navy.

To give James his due, the man had not remained inactive nor incompetent whilst Marshal Schomberg marched from Carrickfergus. Still styled by the Irish as James VII and II, he mustered a large field army and managed to deter our general from advancing on Dublin through a show of numbers. The Duke of Schomberg was forced to disperse his already-ravaged forces across Ulster into winter quarters. The first half of 1690 saw a temporary lull in the conflict, as James tried to maintain his control over most of Ireland. The French busied themselves with ship-building and offensives in Spain and Savoy while the League of Augsburg, of which we were members, continued to gain further allies across the continent.

Swedish Pomerania and Lower Saxony were two such additions, and with Spain officially joining our *Grand Alliance* my crewmates started to display a growing sense of confidence in our eventual victory.

We may have been a hodge-podge mix of English, Dutch and Habsburgs but we were united under a common cause:

To rain grapeshot and musket-fire down upon the French.

It was during this cessation of warfare in the waters surrounding England that I decided to write several letters. I'd been terrified in my first experience of ship-to-ship fighting with the corsairs a decade prior, but that had largely arrived without warning. Sure, we'd heard mention of Ali Reis and his squadron from Etienne Beaumont on Guernsey, but our encounter had been unexpected.

This felt different.

I suppose it was the result of our time spent in the Irish Sea and the tension from knowing a major battle was inevitable. The best I can describe the feeling is when you're about to dive into the sea from a cliffside, with your lover or friends goading you on.

You know there's no getting out of it, but you've yet to take the plunge.

This sense of impending dread wouldn't leave me alone until I finally decided to put my affairs in order should anything happen to me in the coming months.

Towards the end of March I had one of the many naval messengers to be found traveling in-and-out of Portsmouth deliver a bundle of letters on my behalf. I recall throwing him a few silver half crowns to ensure they were delivered promptly and into the right hands.

I had considered writing Alice Dunholm, who was by now surely living a life of comfort in Port Royal, but I had never kept in touch. There had never been anything romantic nor serious between the two of us, but her decision had continued to sting in the years since her sudden flight to Jamaica. She had been one of the few truly kind people from my childhood, and I couldn't help but feel a sense of loss and resentment at her betrayal. Instead, I silently swore to myself that if I ever made it to the New World there would be a reckoning. Exactly what form it would take I had no idea, but it would happen.

Nevertheless, I did write several letters to the few people I cared about. Michael gave me some fine paper and an inkpot of fine black liquid from his own stores in exchange for a few days' worth of my rum ration.

The joke was on him, the chancer, I had my own private stash of good brandy in the workshop.

I wrote to the Corams with general tales of my life at sea alongside my best wishes, but I withheld any information concerning the killings or our conspiracy against James Melior. If I were to ever discuss the subject with them, it would be something to do in person.

I sent several shorter messages to the likes of John Mason, Douglas Fergusson, Robert and Simon down in Putney and a handful of other acquaintances. To Alderman Samuel I penned a longer letter, one which took me several attempts to feel satisfied with. I'd never really thanked the man for his care and instruction during my years at the poorhouse in Cripplegate, and as a man in his mid-twenties I was able to muster the courage to do so. Once the missives were out of my hands I felt a weight lift from my shoulders.

Whatever should befall me in the coming months, at least the handful of people I cared about would know I gave a damn.

Things began to escalate rather quickly with the end of spring.

While the *Lion* sat at anchor on a warm evening in late June alongside nearly sixty other ships of the line, our sovereign had successfully made his landing in Carrickfergus. After mustering nearly sixteen thousand men, King William had moved from Chester over to Ireland without opposition. That was all well-and-good, but we soon learned from the Admiralty that our own circumstances were much less encouraging.

The French fleet had been spotted off the coast of

Cornwall near the end of the month. Reports reached us of between sixty and ninety ships of the line, with Captain Torpley guessing eighty to be a reasonable estimate. Dozens of fireships were also attending the larger vessels.

'We're fucked.'

I sat with about twenty of the crew at supper, the usual faces looking grim and forlorn.

'Those rose-smelling blockheads can't build ships for shit,' quipped one of the men I've long since forgotten in response to our surgeon's blunt remark.

Memories of our fight with the corsairs filled my mind.

'You've clearly never seen *L'Invincible*,' I muttered.

'Lewis has the right of it,' spoke a voice from the narrow stairway.

Captain John Torpley waved off any attempts at formality. He was a good captain and a few years older than most, which gave him an air of wisdom and confidence with the men. No frills nor ruffs for Torpley, just a no-nonsense, immaculately-maintained officer's uniform for him. He was the very image of the respectable, elderly commander.

Most of the rumour-mongering had died down by the summer of 1690. The men's thoughts on the matter hadn't really changed, if anything there had been further signs of his attraction to some of the more handsome members of the crew. A passing odd remark here and there, or a gaze lingering slightly too long upon one of them. It was more a matter of the crew deciding not to give a shit.

He treated us well-enough, paid our wages on time and didn't try to cut corners with the rations. Good, drink and clean food, none of the watered-down *grog* which was becoming more common across the fleet. If he'd tried anything on with one of us things may have been different, but the captain, if he did indeed favour such desires, had the good sense to keep it private. Even Chaplain Whitworth was content with the man's leadership in the absence of any real proof.

Personally, I couldn't have been happier to no longer have Melior lording it over us, and that must have influenced my perceptions of Captain Torpley. That's not to say I was going to let the giant knob off the hook for trying to kill me, but nor did I miss his constant cruel treatment.

'King Louis can put together man o' wars and crews to match any of our own, that's just a simple fact of life.'

'Like I said, we're fucked.'

'Not necessarily,' the captain continued. 'I could stand here and lecture you all about past battles where men were outnumbered and nevertheless won, but I won't.'

I knew where his line of reasoning was going, and didn't feel out of place finishing the thought aloud.

'Because for every one such battle, there are a dozen where numbers resulted in victory.'

He grinned.

'And here I was thinking you were all a bunch of wastrels, too drunk on King Billy's rum to use your heads.'

The captain picked up a mug from out of Dan Evatt's hands and downed it in one.

Henry Williams would have approved.

'Aye, chances are we're in some real trouble, lads.'

We sat in silence for a long moment, our heads bowed in varying degrees of despair.

'Why the long faces? Did you join up to spend your days scrubbing decks or picking weevils out of the stores?'

'I got press—'

The voice was silenced before the man could finish his sentence.

'I don't know about you lot,' Torpley went on, 'but I for one am sick to death of running back and forth to Ireland, just so those army layabouts can have their way.'

'If I have to scrub the fore yard one more time, I'll bloody end myself.'

'Well then, Mister Camborne, if your life is already forfeit, why not take a few bastards along with you first, eh?'

This caused a low rumble of agreement from the crew.

'Too right,' Dan said. 'We're outnumbered, but when has there even been fun in an even fight? Bill, remember them Flemish arselickers at the White Hart?'

The story was notorious.

Dan and Bill had soundly beaten the four drunk traders after one of them lost a hand of cards. They were both barred from going back to the inn, and I'd heard a fair amount of money had changed hands to cover the damages.

'The lily-livered Pierres won't know what hit them.'

Chapter 18

The Battle of Beachy Head, 30th of June, 1690 AD

It turns out there's a big difference between a few drunks out of Flanders and a French fleet.

Admiral Arthur Herbert, First Earl of Torrington, had taken one look at the enemy forces and known we were badly outnumbered. But, there's a thin line between glory and cowardice.

Queen Mary was having none of his complaints back in London. Her council of war included several high-ranking officers from the Admiralty, and the Treasurer of the Navy, Admiral Edward Russell, was one of the most vocal advocates for a swift engagement.

Torrington had been responsible for allowing the French to land supplies in Ireland following a smaller battle near Bantry Bay a year earlier. There were concerns regarding his previous defeat amongst the various crews of the allied fleet, but we knew better than to voice such matters aloud. Several ships of the line had been badly damaged though and required refitting in the year since, that was something no one could deny.

Whether or not the Earl of Torrington could lead with competence was irrelevant; he received his orders from the crown, and we got to work.

Battle is unimaginably brutal for the likes of myself and any common sailor. However, amidst the blood-soaked decks, with the smoke burning your eyes and the smell of shit and piss filling your nostrils, there's one perk to being a low-ranking officer: You don't shoulder the blame when everything goes to Hell.

Thank God for small blessings, I suppose.

As we set out under the growing sunlight on the morning of battle I was not yet accustomed to such horrors. In my years of service the only real fight worth mentioning had been against Ali Reis and his squadron of corsairs off the Norman coast, and that had been a decidedly one-sided affair. Approaching in line abreast to exchange cannon with a superior French force was another matter entirely.

I like to think I put on a brave face, and I managed to keep my bowels in check, but the fact of the matter is I can still remember the abject terror coursing throughout my entire body. Our head carpenter, Mister James Adams, pissed his britches. No one made any comment, and I wager more than half the crew were in similar discomfort once the French came into view.

It was Michael who broke some of the tension and tried to raise our spirits. We were one of the last ships to spot the enemy, given our position in the blue squadron under Vice-Admiral Ralph Delaval, as we were in charge of bringing up the rear of the English and Dutch fleet.

'Fucking French,' he bellowed. 'Surprised their ships aren't covered in lace and powder.'

I really know how to choose them.

His shout had the desired effect: Men returned the call with jibes and insults of their own, while the gunnery crews slapped the broad beams and double-checked their barrels. I was just about to head above deck to ready myself for the fight. Lieutenant Selby and his men wanted myself and a handful of others to assist in raking the enemy decks with musket-fire, and hand-to-hand combat should the need arise.

'You're a good hand with the rifle,' George Selby said upon my arrival. 'Trust in your lessons and just hold firm, God knows that's all a man can do.'

The lieutenant handed me a new flintlock rifle with a nod of approval. I had been expecting one of the older muskets and a spare smallsword or boarding cutlass, but this gun was superb and displayed no signs of wear. As I turned the weapon over in my hands, examining its fine combination of polished woodwork and sturdy iron, the marines presented me with a second piece of equipment.

My eyes must have gone wide judging from their grins. One of the marines, a Sergeant Dalton if I remember correctly, handed me a Walloon-style sword to hoop through my belt. With its thick hand-guard and narrow, slightly-curved blade, it was designed for stabbing into a foe, but there was enough edge to slash an opponent as a last resort. There was nothing fancy about it, but I could tell it had been looked after by its previous owner.

'Sorry we can't fit you out with any proper gear, but this will have to do.'

I thanked George and the men as they hung a few bags of powder and shot from my belt.

'This will do just fine, lieutenant,' I replied. 'We can't all go around with our noses up, strutting like peafowl, eh lads?'

A comment like that would have brought trouble from most, but the marines knew me well and I'd trained under them for years. I'd even helped one of them get ointments for his itch when we were in port, because the bastard was too ashamed to visit the apothecary.

We spent the next few hours under sail behind *His*

Majesty's Ship Anne, and the echoing booms of cannon could be heard through the thick fog of smoke covering the line of battle, where our vanguard and centre had already entered the fray. We were meant to be part of the red squadron under Torrington, but an issue with signaling had caused us to fall behind into the rearguard. As the screams and blasts grew louder, there was a growing sense of dismay above deck.

Despite the chaos, it was clear the French were gaining the advantage.

The enemy commander, Anne-Hilarion de Costentin, Comte de Tourville, had been no fool in making his preparations. His decisions after the battle... well, I'll come to that later.

To put it bluntly, we were getting pummeled.

It was unclear who was to blame for the situation. Some of us felt the Dutch white squadron under Admiral Eversten had gone ahead too quickly without the rest of the fleet, which allowed Tourville to strengthen his own van. Others blamed the Earl of Torrington and Vice-Admiral John Ashby for hanging back from the French centre and leaving the Dutch to their fate.

Whatever the truth may have been, by the time the *Lion* engaged in the rear action it had become clear we were in mortal peril. The Dutch were withdrawing from the line of battle, and our red squadron in the centre showed no sign of closing the distance to open fire upon their French counterparts.

I admit, much of this I learned after-the-fact as the news spread, but on the day I could still make out the Dutch sails fleeing and the lack of action from Torrington's line.

Then, my world exploded into madness.

The first shot missed the mark by about a yard, as the man had been suddenly jolted to one side as *Le Grande* rolled over a wave from her port. I couldn't make out which ship *Anne* was fighting with ahead of us, but the *Lion* was side-by-side the flagship of the French rearguard. Somewhere on her decks the Duke of Estrées was calling out orders to his own crew.

I cursed and ducked below the railing to reload my rifle. My hands shook out of feelings of overwhelming fear, as wood splintered and men died around me, but after what felt like an age I had readied another shot.

After a count to three I raised myself above the deck and tried to remember the rounds of training under the lieutenant. *Don't rush it... mark your man, gauge the distance... lead the shot, and fire.*

My second attempt struck the man in the side of his temple. Once the smoke from my muzzle had settled, I saw him laying face-down upon the deck, the entire right side of his skull missing in a pool of blood, brain and bone. Just then, a man to my right was flung backward as one of the loose halyards and its shackles came crashing into his chest. Rigging and line whipped around the decks after the enemy broadside had torn apart many of our fastenings. I could see a similar scene unfolding on the decks of *Le Grande* from our own volley.

'The fuck are you doing, Frobisher?'

I shook my head and coughed violently through the stink of saltpeter.

'Keep firing, you stupid cu—'

Just like that, Richard Dalton ceased to exist.

The sergeant slumped forward on himself and collapsed to the deck.

I reloaded as quickly as I could manage, but it was wasted as I missed my mark. This was my life for what felt like hours:

Fire, reload and repeat.

I later found out the action had taken all of twenty minutes.

It was during the battle, my first *real* contest, that I realised why our marines got to puff themselves up in fancy uniform, often with the better rations and drink.

Selby and his men were *counting* their kills, and they clearly had wagers placed ahead of time. The lieutenant's own tally by the end was fourteen men, with one of his subordinates coming in a close-second with eleven.

As a sailmaker with the most rudimentary of training I was obviously not included in the bet. But, I did manage one other successful mark to the approval of the men. My second kill took the man through his stomach, and I admit I felt a moment's sense of regret for the poor bugger.

Gut wounds linger for hours, if not days, and are amongst the most painful imaginable. On top of that, they are almost always a definite death sentence.

Finally, there was a lull in the cannon from below decks as the *Lion* and *Le Grande* both seemed to catch their breaths to assess the situation. We were outmatched by the eighty-gun second rate, but our crew had held firm and we now scrambled to repair what we could under the circumstances.

I was working on securing the lower jib sail to the bowsprit when I noticed the *Anne* was on the point of sinking about a hundred yards away. Thankfully for her crew the order to disengage and drop anchor came through a few minutes later. We were to rendezvous with the centre and make ready to sail back towards the

Thames estuary.

The French were gradually carried out of range by the tidal currents which overwhelmed the strength of their sails, and the battered allied fleet was able to breathe a collective sigh of relief. Unfortunately for the crew of the *Lion* we had one major barrier preventing us from retreating:

The Duke of Estrées decided to try a boarding action.

'Plug bayonets if you have 'em,' roared Captain Torpley. 'Swords and side pistols at the ready.'

'Goodall, get that hook sorted or I'll shove it up your arse.'

Men scrambled along the port-side of the main deck ready to fend off the French assault. Similar sounds of activity could be heard from the gunholes on the lower levels, as the men hoisted boarding pikes to thrust at oncoming victims.

I took up my position near the spar deck and clasped the Walloon sword in my right hand. A crewmate out of Belfast stood to my right, a long boarding pole in his hands. He batted away a grappling hook to the water below, but another found its mark and dug into the hull. I recognised a few choice phrases from the enemy jeers across their gunwale, *chiens anglais* and *putes de rosbif* being especially common.

Etienne's attempts at teaching me French hadn't been entirely without success.

Suddenly, my thoughts turned to Will Baker and my unknown assailant in Putney. While a cloud of guilt and remorse still hung over me with their deaths, moreso in Will's case than the footpad's at least, I felt no such conflict of emotion that afternoon. I'd just seen several of my crew killed as the result of the earlier French bombardment, and I would be damned if I wasn't going to pay them back tenfold.

For several minutes we managed to keep the enemy sailors at bay, but their superior numbers and own ferocity began to show. The first wave of the duke's sailors came aboard the *Lion*, and, with a grunt of dismay and anger, I was pushed back on the defensive alongside my fellow crew.

At least Etienne Beaumont and his men were not serving on *Le Grande* so I was saved from having to fight my friends.

Again, small blessings.

※

There is no sense of order when being boarded.

I've seen it happen over a dozen times in the years since Beachy Head, and in every case the attempt to control both sides quick becomes abandoned. Instead, men are left to pick out the enemy based on their clothing or voices, often unable to see one hand in front of their faces due to the smoke.

The same was true during my first experience with a boarding action. A swarthy French sailor, dressed in a loose-fitting white shirt with dark blue britches and brown woolen cap, came storming towards me. For some reason Daniel and Millie, the young tykes I had left in Alderman Samuel's care, entered my thoughts as the man approached. I pictured them shivering and clutching one another in the cold, dank side streets of London.

I suppose at the end of the day, fear is the same, no matter what form it takes.

Out of the corner of my eye I saw Ship's Master

Martin Campbell, the jovial half-Scot known for his expertise in all things relating to navigation, fall to his death up on the quarterdeck. I didn't have time to see what had brought the man down, as my own immediate threat was closing the distance.

The Walloon blade was gripped in my right hand. My lessons under Selby had been sporadic and by no means extensive. Nevertheless, I tried to keep my breathing steady. Then, I shifted my weight on to a balanced position between both of my legs.

None of it mattered.

Another of the lieutenant's instructions proved true: You can prepare until you're blue in the face, but at the end of the day anything can happen in a fight.

The sailor in the sweat-stained linen shirt hefted a large axe with fury in his eyes. I was planning to try and avoid the swing then run him through with my shortsword, but I never got the chance. Before either of us could make the first attack, our feet lost their grip and we both fell to the deck.

There was the pungent aroma of rum in the air. I saw the sweet liquor pouring out of nearby barrels which had been at the receiving end of the French swivel guns. As I clambered to stand upright my opponent was killed by a pistol shot to the head while he was floundering on his back.

'Fucker,' spat Michael.

'Thank God,' I breathed.

'Get up to the quarterdeck with the captain and take th—'

I didn't hear the rest of my friend's words.

A lance of searing pain split up my thigh. When I looked down in surprise and confusion, a slick, wet object was protruding from the front of my britches.

Before I even had time to absorb what was happening, an explosion in my shoulder threw me back several yards. My backside crashed violently into the starboard gunwale and I collapsed on to my side.

Pain. Never-ending, all-encompassing pain.

The blood-spattered deck and wails of dying men faded into the background, almost as if I was observing them from a distance rather than being an active participant in the slaughter.

Someone was kneeling in front of me, trying to say something. I didn't pay them any mind as my leg and shoulder coursed waves of red-hot agony throughout my entire body. After what felt like an age of the world the hurt gradually began to fade. It was still there, coming and going in pulses, but I stopped caring and let it carry me.

Then, someone punched me in the side of the head.

Anger erupted from every fibre of my being.

'What the fuck was... that for?'

'Good, you're not gone yet,' a familiar voice spoke hurriedly.

'Anthony, get him below decks and try not to disturb the wounds.'

I opened my mouth to protest, but everything faded to black.

I had never been so thirsty. Not even the worst nights out on leave began to compare with such a need for water. An angel answered my prayers, with a cup of the tepid but life-saving liquid raised to my lips. I drank greedily for a long moment, then lay my head back against the makeshift pillow. Once again, my vision failed and my surroundings disappeared.

This was my new life. Awake, drink and sleep.

Occasionally a memory of the taste of beef broth filled my mouth.

When I emerged from the endless *nothing* it was to dream the most disturbing and vivid scenes. I saw the Corams laying in death shrouds placed outside their small home. Alice being buggered by scores of corsair or French sailors. Charles Mason on a hangman's noose swinging from London Bridge.

The worst nightmare was one of Alderman Samuel sitting in his study, quietly reading through some tome in front of his fireplace.

Unfortunately, the heads of Daniel and his sister were resting on silver platters upon his table.

I was in no state to reflect upon any of the scenes. That would come later.

There was something else which interrupted my darkness on occasion.

A distant echo of sound, as though someone was trying to speak to me from underwater.

I wished they would just leave me alone. The effort to open my eyes just wasn't worth it.

'There he is, see? The twitching's a good sign, means he can still feel things.'

I was thirsty.

Colour and light burst into view, my eyes recoiling in pain.

'Easy, lad,' a low, husky voice said. 'Take it slow, you're alright.'

'The Fre—'

'Gone,' the reply came, as if anticipating my question. 'Gave us a hiding then got swept back out to sea. We're still accounting for the losses.'

I knew this man. Realisation dawned as my senses began to emerge. They felt dulled from a lack of use, but present all the same.

'Walter?'

The surgeon smiled down at me.

'You've my assistant Anthony to thank,' he said. 'The boy got you down to my station without too much loss of blood. He's the makings of a fine *chirugeon* when he's focused.'

I slowly turned my head to see a young man of perhaps fourteen sitting exhausted with his back against the workshop.

'It was you,' I said for no particular reason.

He knew what I meant.

'It was indeed,' Anthony yawned. 'You're surprisingly heavy for your frame.'

'Walter, my dreams…'

The surgeon nodded. 'Sydenham's *laudanum* sometimes has that effect, and we gave you several generous doses.'

'Fuck,' I said. 'I've seen it used before, when I was being pushed towards the life of an apothecary's apprentice as a boy. Always wondered what it was like.'

'Just don't try to move,' Mister Crouch continued. 'You're past the worst of it, nothing so bad once the bleeding was patched up and your pain taken care of. Still, those wounds will hurt like a bastard for a month or two.'

After one attempt to sit upright, I did not need to be told again.

It was another week or so before I was able to sit up and feed myself. Another yet until I was ready to walk gingerly across the surgeon's bay. A wooden shard about two hands in length had pierced my thigh from behind, likely from one of our masts being torn to pieces under enemy fire. The injury to my shoulder had come from an old wheel-lock pistol fired at close range according to Lieutenant Selby.

I was glad the man had survived, but was not surprised when he visited me. It would take the archangels and their entire host to bring George Selby down.

Others were not so fortunate. We lost close to sixty of the crew during the battle, including Master Martin Campbell, Quartermaster Stuart Effingham, Sergeant Richard Dalton, Jack Fuller and our Ship's Cook Daniel Evatt. Their bodies had been given burials at sea with word passed on to any family or loved ones through the command. While I would genuinely miss their company, I felt an overwhelming sense of guilt at not being able to properly mourn them. My sense of loss was entirely taken up by one casualty in particular:

Michael Bollard.

In our years together since he joined me aboard the *Lion* the man had become my closest friend. We had always been like brothers along with Tom, but in recent years we had drifted somewhat apart from our quick-witted friend. There was no real reason for this, and the three of us had always maintained our friendship. However, time apart from Thomas Coram, who now insisted on his full name due to rising prominence within the companies of London, had meant I relied even more heavily on Michael.

My friend had been the recipient of countless drunken tales of nonsense, and was my anchor when times at sea became especially difficult. We'd been on leave and fought together, often following some episode at a knocking shop or greedy tailor trying to fleece us. Michael was as close to a brother as I'd ever known, and, in the privacy of the sailmaker's workshop, I broke down and wept until my cheeks burned from the salt of my tears. I felt no regret, and the remaining crew were going through similar scenes, wrapped up in their own personal Hells. Sadly, their compassion didn't change anything.

He was gone. Somehow I would have to live with that.

Captain Torpley had approved my pension from the ship's scheme through the Chatham Chest, on the grounds I had received two substantial injuries preventing my continued employ. He made it clear I was welcome to return to service should I feel the need, and it was no exaggeration to say my ability to mend canvas was impaired.

My shoulder wound had done something to my left hand, and even with the utmost concentration it would randomly shake or tighten.

The captain in his good sense had waited until I recovered to bring up the matter of Michael's death and who to inform. I was grateful there were no letters sent ahead of my return to London. It felt right I should be the one to inform the Corams and their neighbours who also knew him well from Michael's years of work along the wharves.

On the return from Portsmouth I tried to find enough resolve to face the coming difficulties.

The Corams would naturally be utterly devastated by the news. John and Bethany in particular would be inconsolable, and I didn't even want to think about how Jane or her siblings would handle it. Robert and Simon down at the ferry deserved to be told as well. Then there was Katheryn Wooler, Thomas' former lover who had always enjoyed our mischief as an escape from her life as a rich merchant's daughter. She had been a good friend to Michael for years. Old Charles down at the fish market...

It was going to be horrible, but better they hear it from me than in some cold letter.

Given I hadn't been present at my friend's final moments due to my own injuries, I asked around the crew for any pieces of information to pass on. He had taken a gunshot to the chest and fallen on his back, but other than that no one had much to offer. I supposed honesty would be the best course of action; just tell everyone of his death in plain terms, but focus on what a formidable seafarer Michael had become.

During my recovery and later preparation to leave for London the full story of the 'Battle of Beachy Head' reached my ears.

His Majesty's Ship Anne had been scuttled, damaged beyond repair. Several other ships of the line were severely damaged, but it was the Dutch squadron in the van under Admiral Eversten which had borne the brunt of the losses. Seven man o' wars and several fireships were destroyed, while in the English fleet only *Anne* was sunk.

The French didn't lose a single ship.

It was a disaster for public opinion back home, with enemy control over the Channel and memories of the Spanish Armada a century earlier causing outright panic in the Protestant population.

Ah, Baltasar, you're back. They're still eating? Good, that gives us some extra time. Remember when I told you we'd return to the matter of the French commander? Well...

I remembered one particular lesson from Alderman Samuel.

He had been telling me of some old foe of the Romans named *Pyrrhus* from one of his dusty volumes. I don't remember much of the details nor where they fought, somewhere around the north of the Greek mainland I think, but I do recall the main point: The king won the battle, but lost the war.

Much the same could be said for Admiral Tourville.

He had soundly defeated our fleets at Beachy Head, to the point we were fleeing back to the Thames in disarray, but the man never pressed his advantage. In not pursuing Torrington, the French commander gave us time to regroup.

Our spirits were lifted by the news out of Ireland: King William had achieved a great victory against James Stuart at the beginning of July, one day after our own naval engagement. William's well-trained forces had defeated the Jacobite army near the River Boyne with minimal resistance, and he was pressing on towards Dublin and Limerick.

James himself had fled back to France, much to the delight of the Protestant communities in William's realms. At the time we were more concerned over the situation at sea. However, over the next two months our numbers grew to over ninety ships of the line at anchor in the once again, *English* Channel.

Despite our own good fortune and success, the French were nevertheless gaining the upper hand on the continent. The Ottoman advances in the east along the Danube, largely funded by French coin and weaponry, had provided an opportunity for King Louis to expand his own borders while the Grand Alliance was preoccupied elsewhere.

Last I heard during the coach trip to Southwark, as the bumps in the roads sent bursts of pain through my leg and shoulder, the Sun King was on the offensive in Piedmont and against the Savoyards.

I only listened half-heartedly to most of the gossip about the wars. While the stories did provide some comfort that our efforts had not been entirely pointless, I was no longer a part of that world having left service. The pension would at least keep me fed and I could figure out some form of accommodation easily enough. I certainly wouldn't be dining upon river sturgeon roasted with saffron anytime soon, but a mug of ale and beef stew were good enough for me.

My own task was daunting enough to occupy my mind for most of the trip, and thoughts of war faded into the background against the more pressing problem.

With every mile we came closer to London the sinking feeling in the pit of my stomach grew.

Chapter 19

London, 1691 AD

Things went about as badly as expected.

The Coram family wept openly, both at the sorry state of my own injuries and the news concerning Michael's death. Owen was by that time nine years of age, the spitting image of his stalwart older brother, and fully capable of grasping the fact his 'uncle' with the silly hair was not coming back.

It was even harder for the likes of John and Bethany, who had fed Michael countless times from their own larder and catch of the day. While it was perhaps a small mercy his adoptive parents, Stephen Bollard and his wife Agnes, had passed away ahead years earlier, I still said a prayer to the two of them on my first night home.

In a strange and unanticipated turn of events Jane, the eldest Coram daughter who was now verging on becoming a spinster at the age of twenty-four, came out of her typical aloof shell and broke down entirely upon hearing the sad news. Her sister Lucy, who had at first beamed at me with the usual twinkle in her eye until taking in my limp and thin frame, completely cut herself off from the world.

It was disconcerting and heartbreaking to see the two young women experience such a reversal of personality. We all try to cope with loss in different ways, I suppose.

Bethany did her utmost to be the pillar of strength for the family, as she always did. I knew Mum well enough to tell most of it was an act requiring every thread of commitment she could muster. John silently consoled his wife and daughters, allowing them to grieve and mourn at their own pace.

He was a good man, John Coram.

Say what you want about his gruff nature, but he was always there when it mattered.

Thomas took the news terribly when he returned to London two months later. I had considered writing to him instead of waiting for so long a delay. However, in the end I decided it was important to let him know in person.

We went to Saint Olave's to pray for all the Bollards' souls. When the girls, or rather, the *ladies* who I still thought of as the imps from my youth, were abed I discussed the circumstances of Michael's death in more detail with Thomas and his parents.

Lucy, Jane and Owen were battling their own demons and certainly didn't need to hear about such things.

'Sounds like a right ugly mess.'

I nodded as blurred memories of the battle filled my vision.

'Worst I've seen.'

'Nothin' you could have done, Lewis. I mean, fuck… look at the state of you. Thank God you didn't go over the gunwale as some stringy meal for the sharks.'

I smiled. The fact Thomas in no way held me responsible for Michael's death was an enormous relief. I felt as though shackles fell from around my shoulders. I had worried over the issue for months, unsure whether or not the Corams, Thomas in particular, would blame me for not having *done* something. Instead, they had taken one quick look at my battered, malnourished figure and known I needed help.

Walter Crouch had done his best to feed me during my recuperation, but when I left service my skin felt like it was hanging from my bones.

It stands to reason that my first port of call was Bethany's cast-iron pot.

'I'm just glad you're still with us,' Thomas continued. 'That bastard Michael would say the same. The arse still owes me five shillings from that hand of All Fours. I hope he at least took a few of the fu—erm, *froggies*, with him first.'

The false nonchalance was obvious, but then it was never intended to fool anyone.

'I'm no stranger to a fight at sea either. I've been thinkin' of buying some land in the colonies, maybe Massachusetts Bay or thereabouts, and we get trouble from corsairs now and then.'

I whistled.

'And to think you used to call me "Your Lordship" when we were younger. Listen to you… going off and buying up property. A proper member of the court.'

Thomas waved away my mockery but grinned.

'To be honest, it's not all that difficult now I'm well-known with the companies. Since the king sorted the colonies into a province there is more than enough land to go around, at least for anyone with the backbone to work it.'

My friend went into further detail about his plans, but my attention shifted towards his father. John sat with an odd expression on his face. It wasn't one of anger, he just seemed… *conflicted* somehow. I figured he was probably sad at the thought his son wouldn't carry on the family trade, yet fiercely proud of the man's rising success.

Suddenly, John's eyes lit up in response to a boy's yelp from the next room, after he was pinched and told to stop snoring. I'd bet my last penny Lucy had been the culprit.

The change in the sturdy patriarch's demeanour was as easy to read as any list from the quartermaster:

John Coram had a second son.

Thomas agreed to accompany me on my rounds to inform other acquaintances of the grim tidings. It was the first time we had spent in one another's company for what felt like years. There had been Christmastide and a few other instances, but our shore leaves tended to either overlap or conflict. Now that I was pensioned off, and Thomas had a substantial leave of his own following a lengthy voyage from New England, we were able to catch up properly.

We talked about the ongoing war with the French, but my heart wasn't really in it. King William had mopped up the Irish campaign and was continuing his efforts to support his allies on the continent. Admiral Torrington had been imprisoned in the Tower of London for his failure at Beachy Head. After being court-martialed the man was acquitted but stripped of his rank and position.

Thomas told me of the French advances in the Spanish Netherlands and a number of skirmishes, but as we walked in the direction of Putney my thoughts were elsewhere.

At first I couldn't help but think back to the brigand responsible for my attempted kidnapping years ago under orders from James Melior. The boot-licker had disappeared following his transfer of command, and my status as an invalid, incapable of exacting the desired vengeance on the man, only served to increase my anger.

Then there was the fact he was unlikely to ever be held to account for his treacherous acts against our former sovereign.

I had no problem with King William, from what I heard he was a fine leader of men and possessed a sharp mind, but Melior's deception had been underhanded and contemptible. My vow to make him pay for his crimes felt empty that day as I walked the banks of the Thames.

My second main concern was how the crew of the *Lion* were faring without me. Last I heard John Torpley was still in the captain's chair when they returned to Deptford for repairs. Henry Every had promised to come find me for a night out with the lads when next on leave from the slaver ship he now worked aboard, having left the navy not long after Beachy Head, but so far there had been no sign of them. There had been no word about Captain Williams either, and I hoped the rogue was alive and well.

One small glimmer of comfort was knowing Etienne Beaumont and most of his company had emerged relatively unscathed from the battle, although Jean de Chartres had been carried of by some form of pestilence in the years since our meeting on Guernsey. I remembered his ability to throw back rounds of ale. To this day I have never met anyone with such a bottomless stomach.

His friend Jérémie was a match when it came to food, and I chuckled aloud on remembrance of the large cut of beef the man had demolished within minutes at *La Belle Fleur* in Saint Peter Port.

'What's so funny?'

'I was just thinking about an old friend who could best you in an eating contest.'

This brought a snicker from Thomas.

'Never met the like,' he said. 'We both know there is no such man.'

My stolid friend thumped one fist against his chest and we burst out in tall tales of varying degrees of stupidity or impossibility.

It felt good to laugh again.

Robert Smythe and Simon Beecham were at their usual corner of the coaching inn.

With a wave we shed our coats and shook the dirt from the road before going over to take up our familiar seats.

'Just the two of you?'

My grimace must have betrayed the reason behind our visit.

The two older men listened to my tale with rapt attention. When I had finished they didn't say a word, but, rather than sitting in morose silence, we lifted our flagons in honour of Michael.

Better yet, I got offered a job.

'That's no bother,' Simon said through mouthfuls of bread. 'There's not much to it, Lewis. Up every crossing to fix the mooring, otherwise just keep an eye out for passengers and make ready.'

'It seems… like a waste of coin, when the two of you could just manage it.'

Robert lifted his right hand and flicked a finger against the middle of my forehead.

'What do you think we've been doin' for the last twenty-odd year? This'll save us having to get on and off every bleedin' time we cross, worth every penny.'

'If that's the case, why has it taken you dimwits so long to find someone?'

'Ok, ok… you win,' Simon threw his hands up. 'We're

a charity case, taking you in to pay for your cuts and scrapes, happy?'

I flicked a green pea at the man.

To be honest, I was relieved.

While I had no desire to return to a life at sea, despite my bouts of melancholy over Melior slipping away, the thought of laying around as an invalid had been of grave concern.

Working alongside the ferrymen in Putney, sitting in my little oak-carved toll booth and watching the Thames flow past, was a good deal better than the alternatives. I would need to figure out how my pension tied in with getting a new job and I hoped it wouldn't be an issue, but for the time being the prospect of joining my two friends in their daily tasks was a bright one.

This was to be my new life. A fresh beginning.

My days adopted a routine much like my years of service, but with a quieter and far more relaxed pace.

I would arrive at the ferry crossing on the north bank of the river just before sunrise and take up my position at the small toll booth whilst Rob and Simon got everything ready for the day. The first passengers typically started to trickle in with the morning, although local farmers occasionally demanded earlier crosssings in order to reach the markets before dawn. Much to my relief I was only being paid to work during the day, so I never had to deal with any such hassle.

We usually broke for lunch following the call for Midday Prayer and for supper not long after *Vespers*, or 'evensong' as my two friends called it, and I was sent home after helping with a bit of cleaning on the ferry. Home at the time was a small, single room above the bakery across from Saint Mary's. I was offered a good rate on the place, largely due to the baker's eldest son insistence; the family turned out to be great listeners to my tales. I spent many an evening with them in discussion about all manner of myths about the waters surrounding our island or my own experiences aboard ship.

It was one of the more comfortable periods of my life.

Sure, the ache in my shoulder still flared up with the cold weather, and my thigh would spasm if I put too much weight on it, but for the most part I was perfectly content.

Remember what I said earlier about making God laugh? Well... wait for it.

ॐ

Daniel and his sister Millie were thriving at Cripplegate.

On the days when I was free from work I tended to either visit the Corams or wander up towards my old neighbourhood. I was a much more sensible man when away from the likes of Henry Every or Bill Pritchard. Rather than whoring or drinking until I could barely stand, I found myself preferring to look at the various shoppes' wares or searching for the very best pies in London.

So, I often found myself checking in on the two siblings and paying my respects to Alderman Samuel, who was still the overseer of the poorhouse despite his age. The man must have been getting into his seventies, but he was as fleet-footed and capable as ever. What's more, the death of his son Oliver a few years earlier from the choking sickness had changed the normally stern Samuel.

His welcomes tended to be warmer than they had ever been at seeing me return, and I rarely found him without Daniel and Millie tagging along.

Personally, I think between his advancing years and the loss of his only son, old Samuel realised what an utter bastard he had been and was genuinely trying to make up for it.

The two imps I had salvaged from the gutters were now employed directly under Samuel in caring for the less fortunate, and at the ages of nineteen and eighteen respectively, Daniel and his sister had filled out nicely. Long gone were any signs of mistreatment or hardship. The boy, or rather the *man* I should say, had thick, dark hair and a build which reminded me of the ogre Simon Beecham. Daniel Shepherd, as I had learned their surname years before, was not someone you wanted to piss off over a drink or a woman. To my relief, his temperament matched my friend Simon's as well; laid back and easygoing, Daniel would only really be a danger if someone really set him off.

God, what a danger it would be though. I pity whoever was on the receiving end.

Millie, or Millicent Shepherd as she went by then, was a strange woman. I don't mean that in a bad way, mind you. If anything she was a breath of fresh air from the usual crowds of north London, the less well-to-do ones at any rate.

She pushed boundaries and got a rise from anyone she met. Whether it was on religious topics or which type of cheese was the best, Millicent knew exactly how to poke people to their limits. She spoke her mind and was known to swear like a… well, like a sailor, but she could reel it in and be polite when it suited her. She was thickset, yet not overly-so, and possessed a rather plain face similar to her brother's, but there was a vitality about Millicent that pulled people in. I had come to think of her as a daughter-of-sorts, so she was in no danger from my woeful attempts at flattery, but she didn't lack for company either.

They just had to be very careful to stay on Daniel's good side.

All told, she reminded me a little bit of Alice Dunholm minus the overwhelming looks and free trip to a life in Jamaica. I'd collected my belongings from Samuel years ago and kept them in a new wooden box similar to the one she had taken with her to Port Royal. Every now and then I would read over my father's writings but without any feelings of remorse or anger.

My life was a good one, and I was with friends.

That all shattered one cold April morning after about two years of such bliss.

I was sat with a woolen blanket across my shoulders in my cosy toll booth.

Herons and all manner of waterfowl honked along the banks of the Thames as they sheltered from the rains underneath the dense thickets of trees.

There hadn't been a passenger for the last several hours, and I picked at the bottom of my wooden bench out of boredom. Across the river I could make out Rob and Simon sheltering in the small ferryboat. It was easy to imagine their conversation, having heard it often enough on such dull days.

Breasts, ale, beef and the Church, not necessarily in that order.

Suddenly, I heard a shout and figured it must have been my mind playing tricks out of tedium.

There it was again.

I carefully placed the blanket upon my stool in order to keep it relatively dry and walked out into the mist. It wasn't bucketing down, small blessings, but the usual London drizzle was in the air and it soaked through to the bone.

Coming slowly up the Thames, in a small, rickety wooden punt, was Thomas Coram.

He wasn't alone, and once they came within view I saw my friend Henry Every sitting on the opposite rower's bench. That struck me as odd. The two had met before through mutual acquaintance, but I had never known them to fraternise without me.

Bess was well-maintained after so many years of use. Her wooden hull was free from any sign of damage or rot, and I knew for a fact it was the result of a joint effort between Lucy and Owen spanning the previous summer. The thought of the younger Corams going fishing together made me smile.

'Stop standin' there with yer thumb up it,' Henry yelled. 'Give us a hand.'

Once we had propped the punt next to my rickety old station I beckoned for my two friends to huddle under the meagre shelter.

'I'm still meant to be working,' I grumbled, 'not entertaining the likes of you two wastrels.'

'Good to see you too, prick.'

Henry proceeded to jab me playfully on the shoulder, which brought out a creative string of curses on my part. I didn't even know such words existed.

'Oh fuck, I forgot. Well, I'll get you a drink to make amends.'

'Like I said, still a few hours until supper yet,' I sighed while gently prodding my shoulder.

'We're off to the Swan now, Lewis. You're going to

need a healthy swig of rum when I tell you this juicy bit.'

Coming from the mouth of Henry that put the fear up my back.

Luck was on my side for once.

Rob and Simon decided to call it a day and go home not long after my friends' surprise visit. The rain was no longer just a mist and had begun coming down in a torrent. Anyone who needed crossing in such weather was likely the type of character you didn't want aboard. If some poor unfortunate, innocent soul did need to use the ferry, they could bloody wait.

I was more inclined to go home and out of my wet clothing, but the Swan would have a roaring fire and it didn't take much persuasion. That being said, both Thomas and Henry seemed more awkward than usual in my company, and I grew concerned as to what the story would entail.

Had someone passed away? There was a sombre mood in the air and I was beginning to feel restless.

'We found you-know-who,' Henry gave me a knowing look.

'You don't mean…'

'James Melior, name ring a bell?'

'Where?'

Thomas interrupted with the old gleam in his eye I'd known since childhood.

'One of the slavers we work with talked about a good sale in Port Royal a few months back.'

I bit back a retort about trading with such men. I knew better than to question such things, particularly not with Henry around. The man dreamed of settling on a plantation someday in the Floridas and had no qualms whatsoever about such things. It was hard to explain… I would never begrudge them a chance at making good coin, but after my encounter with Joseph, and having talked with the man on several occasions afterwards, the enterprise made my skin crawl.

My opinions would become even more fierce in the years ahead upon seeing the slave ships' holds below decks, but that will have to wait.

'Turns out one Captain Melior received the shipment for his estate on the outskirts of Spanish Town. He's been a busy boy, building anew in some lush paradise. Turns out his wife was fed up with Port Royal and fancied a change.'

'So much for good, Christian humility,' I muttered. 'Not surprised though. He always did act too pious for his own good, when we all knew he was a flea-bitten dog.'

That brought a laugh from Thomas.

'Weren't sure how you'd react,' he said. 'Glad to see you didn't leap up to throttle us.'

I grinned.

'The night's young.'

He rested his barrel-like forearms on the table and I wisely shifted conversation back to the discovery of Melior's whereabouts.

'Suppose we could have dug it up from the Admiralty, but best to keep a low profile. A merchant, slaver or pensioner poking after a captain's location would have brought trouble, or my name's not Ben Bridgeman.'

'Your name's *not* Benjamin Bridgeman,' I rolled my eyes towards my other friend.

'True, true,' Henry conceded. 'But, old Ben passed years back and I figure it's as good a name as any, should I end up knee-deep in pig shit.'

I'd known my old mentor in sailmaking had died

almost a decade ago, but we drank a long pull of mulled cider in his memory, Thomas joining in despite never having met the man. Then, I sat back against the wall behind my seat at the inn and turned my thoughts to the information.

I finally knew where Melior had slinked off to. Unfortunately, it was on the other side of a very fickle body of water.

We spent the next hour or so in quiet comfort.

The rain was lashing against the thick glass windows of the Swan, and Thomas was on the point of falling asleep when Henry shook us from our lethargy with a clap.

'God, I forgot the best part, Lewis.'
'What?'
'The old codger has himself a tasty thing, from what I gathered. Rules the roost, if you take my meaning.'

Henry's face lit up with a look of pure delight.

'The stupid cuckold prattles on about his faith, meanwhile his missus is probably leaving him wearing the horns. Has every sailor from Port Royal to Hispaniola trailing after her, according to my mate Arthur anyway.'

'Serves him right, hopefully one of them guts h—'
Wait.

A feeling of utter dread wrapped itself around me like a snake.

I won't go into detail since I'm sure it's not what you want to hear, but his name's James and he's a prominent officer in the fleet.

It couldn't be.
It...just fucking *couldn't* be.
'What's his wife's name?'
Henry shrugged.

'Not sure I remember, just that Arthur was sayin' she's a sight and then some, with plenty to spare.'

Thomas clued in as the pieces clicked into place. He'd been to fetch me from Cripplegate often enough.

'You don't think?'

'Did the name Alice come up at all, by any chance?'

'Jesus Christ, her reputation really does get around. Aye, now you mention it that sounds about right. You erm… know her, I take it?'

'A good friend,' I replied. 'I thought she was anyway, instead she just up and pissed off halfway around the world.'

'The workhouse?'

I nodded.

'She ran the kitchens for a few years near the end of my stay.'

We sat and stared at the flickering hearth for a few minutes before anyone spoke.

'So, what's the plan?'

'That's easy,' I snarled.

'First, I kill the bastard. Second, I get some answers.'

Chapter 20

Corunna, Spain, 1694AD

'He said that months ago, and look at how that turned out.'

'Well, what do you suggest, Mister Every?'

The question over pay had become dire. Not a man among us was living in anything close to comfort.

Just last night, during the late-April rains which often passed across the northern coast of Spain, one of the men aboard Flag Captain Charles Gibson's ship had murdered one of his crew over a 'nice coat'. The captain was poorly and abed, and there was barely enough discipline to even carry out the execution.

We hadn't received so much as a shilling in six months.

Come with me, we'll head over to Spanish Town and string him up, Henry had said.

Instead, we were sitting around in Corunna with a chorus of groaning bellies.

For nearly two years my friend had continued to work on ships plying in slaves to the colonies while I stayed in Putney. Finally, last July he had contacted me about a good chance for sailing to Jamaica with a few familiar faces to help with our task, should James Melior put up any form of resistance.

This was all presuming he would be at home or on the island upon our arrival, but it was the best shot we had. Furthermore, once we were across the seas we could hopefully lay in wait to strike if need be.

The King of Spain had commissioned four of our warships to help keep France away from his own lands in the Americas, and, in the hope of plunder and a chance to leave Europe, the crews had been easy to fill. Despite my own wounds at the hands of the French I agreed to enlist as sailmaker aboard *James* alongside several former acquaintances of mine.

What can I say? It seemed like a good omen, the ship being named after the very man I was out to find.

'Lewis, you dickhead, are you listening, or do you have somewhere more important to be?'

I hadn't realised the conversation had shifted in my direction.

'Sorry, sir,' I replied in haste, 'I was thinking about that arsehole Melior again. I heard something about writing to Sir James back in London demanding our pay directly.'

Sir James Houblon was the merchant responsible for this expedition and had yet to cough up any coin. What was worse, rumours of the Spanish not sending the needed approval to leave Corunna and trapping us like sheep were spreading within the ranks.

'Aye, do you think it a worthy enterprise? You've always been good with letters and figures, likely the cleverest of us apart from myself, naturally.'

'To be honest, sir, I think it a waste of time. If the man were in any position to pay us he would have done so by now. No merchant with any sense keeps sailors waiting half the year with no coin. I wager the problem is more to do with King Charles back in Madrid.'

'I've told you to stop calling me sir,' the man looked irritated. 'These days it's *Mister* Williams to you, or better yet, Henry. I'm just along for the ride. A cushy post as negotiator to the French with hardly any work? Yes please.'

Henry Williams, the first captain I had ever sailed under, was as lively as ever at the age of sixty-three. I had been very relieved when I first arrived to see him mingling with the crew and addressing them by name, his usual good humour and acerbic wit still intact.

We'd taken to calling him and Every the *Two Henries*, given they had always been as thick as thieves.

'Old habits are slow to die,' I replied. 'Douglas, what do you suggest? God knows you lot are good at getting coin when it's in short supply.'

My old friend Douglas Fergusson, who had made the move from the docks to fleet service in the early years of the war, picked up on the sarcasm in my voice.

'We tell Houblon tae pay up or else we bade pat, mibbie see whit th' king has tae say,' the Scotsman said. 'We aye dinnae ken who's haudin' back, it cuid be Admiral O'Byrne is tae blame. Th' man's practically Spanish his-sel.'

I gave a bemused grin to the rest of the group. While I'd known the man long enough to get through most of his thick burr, as had the Two Henries, several of the crew sat with blank expressions.

'He said we get Houblon to pay us or take it up with the king, we still don't know where the admiral stands.'

Douglas had a fair point. The Irishman had served in the Spanish Royal Marines for a period of time prior to being put in command of our small expedition.

'Seems reasonable enough,' Henry Every murmured from his corner of the mess. 'I still think it's too light a touch, they have us by the balls and know as much. Where exactly would we go, hmm? Are you going to swim back to England?'

That was the real problem. For all intents and purposes we were stuck in Coronna. Every day wasted was another day spent without hunting down the man who had once tried to have me permanently silenced.

I tried not to think about Alice.

The thought of her laying with Melior was too revolting to contemplate, even with my somewhat mixed feelings about her. There wasn't that spark between us nor the typical lust I experienced with others, but something about them being together gnawed at my mind. The notion of her having dalliances behind his back and making a fool of him would have been a source of great pleasure, had I not been worried about what might happen should he find out. Oh well, problems for another day.

In the end we agreed to raise the matter of pay with Admiral Sir Don Arturo O'Byrne after the merchants back in England refused to loosen their purses. With a level of arrogance to match his long-winded name, the admiral was nevertheless known to be sympathetic to the plight of his crews.

Five of us approached his quarters with the intention of raising the issue directly and trying to gain his support. Henry Every was First Mate aboard *James* and had risen through the ranks due to his own merits, rather than to the usual good fortune of noble birth. The sailors of the expedition were keen for him to voice their grievances.

I intended to do as little speaking as possible, given the failure of my written request to London nearly a week earlier.

'I can see the situation for myself, without your assistance, Mister Every.'

'Of course, sir,' Henry replied. 'But, even with that…

incident over the coat, I'm not sure you grasp just how bad things have gotten. I mean no offence, we know you're a busy man.'

'Oh, drop the loyal toady act,' the admiral waved off the comment. 'We both know you're all thinking of your own pockets, not your duty to England.'

I couldn't resist.

'Well, in all fairness, this *isn't* about duty to the Admiralty, sir. Spain pretty much hired us to do their dirty work, as a private flotilla of four ships.'

'Indeed,' he was swift to reply, 'and who precisely was placed in command of the expedition?'

'You were, sir.'

'Mmmm, and I'm an admiral, funny that.'

'Not an English one,' Henry Williams mumbled, thankfully under his breath.

Whether or not Admiral O'Byrne heard the remark was unclear. He kept his composure and didn't so much as bat an eyelid.

The man's gallant uniform of dark blue and gold embroidery was recently-made, and the bowl of local Spanish fruits and various sundries only highlighted his lack of experience with the ongoing strife. I very much doubted he had skipped so much as one meal in the last six months. At least Captain Gibson aboard *Charles II* had the decency to feign sacrifice and occasionally offer up some of his provisions to the men. Unfortunately, our own Captain Humphreys on the *James* was cut from the same cloth as the admiral, and we were fed up with his lack of care.

'I hear you, *gentlemen*, I truly do,' O'Byrne went on, 'but my hands are tied. Without the proper authority from Madrid I am unable to do anything about such affairs. I recommend the men simply tighten their belts and get on with their jobs, the money will come soon enough.'

What jobs? We'd been at anchor for months. Each of the four ships was in pristine condition, and, apart from the daily tasks of swabbing or checking the stores, we mostly sat around playing cards or dreaming of food other than hard biscuit. A number of my friends had been worried about my weight, as I was thin in the best of times, but I assured them it was no matter for concern. In truth, my shoulder and thigh throbbed endlessly, but as a sort of dull ache rather than any sharp pain.

I could cope.

We bade the admiral a goodnight and returned to our own mess and berths. The ship was no *Lion*, but the girl had sleek lines and a well-crafted body. She was as swift a frigate-built ship as one could hope for. No hope going up side-by-side with the likes of a first rate, but for quick grabs and lesser vessels we were well-prepared.

'Well, so much for that,' I uttered, while collapsing on to my hammock.

Someone's stomach rumbled.

'The fuck are we supposed to do now?'

We sat and mulled over the question for several minutes.

'I say we force our way ashore and demand pay from the local officials,' Henry Williams suggested.

'Ah doubt they'll ken us an' do nowt, although ah cuid hae a gang. '

We conceded Douglas had a point. The various tax collectors or port authorities would likely not act without written orders from the crown.

'How about just refusing to work as we discussed?'

I ventured the question but knew the answer before it came.

'Lewis, there's no work to be done anyhow. They wanted us to leave last week without pay, we've already delayed so far as they're concerned.'

'Funny how the orders to leave came through, but nothing about coin,' I muttered.

'Fuck it.'

We all turned to look as the younger of the Two Henries got to his feet. He cracked his knuckles and proceeded to lean in close. Everyone clustered around to hear what he had in mind.

There are certain moments in life when you feel as though events transpire without any control of your own. The threads of fate weave themselves towards unforeseen ends and all you can do is try to keep up. It can feel like you're being swept along a current, or down a river on the verge of bursting its banks.

Tonight was one of those moments.

⁂

We moved quickly.

Henry Every, along with myself and about twenty other members of our crew, ascended the keel of *Charles II* under the cover of dark.

With the ship's captain abed with some form of bowel rot and the admiral staying with one of his Spanish friends in Corunna the opportunity had been too persuasive to pass up.

Henry was taking us to get coin and food in our bellies, hangman's noose or not. When all is said and done, all-encompassing hunger has a way of overruling any other decisions. I needed a new pair of boots as well.

It was a short-term solution to the matter, but when you back a dog into a corner you can expect a bite.

The other crew didn't even bother to put up a fight.

In fact, a large majority of them were more than happy to throw their lots in with us.

'Alright, that's the first mate and midshipman sorted,' Henry Williams panted.

'They coming along or wanting left behind?'

As our new *captain* Henry Every had no intention of killing any fellows who stayed out of our way, and the policy was a sound one. Shortly after securing the ship's decks and mustering her crew above deck another rowboat from the *James* pulled up along our starboard.

'Is the drunken boatswain aboard?'

Upon hearing the agreed password the men were quickly brought on to the main deck.

It was mutiny, plain and simple.

There was no grey area nor question of pardon. Henry and his conspirators, myself included, were seizing this frigate.

As we went about dividing those men who wished to be taken ashore and those who were coming over to the cause, a loud call was heard from across the water.

'Mister Every, are you hearing this?'

Our rogue captain walked over to the gunwale and shouted back:

'Aye, I hear you well enough, Captain Humpheys.'

'Men are deserting and abandoning their posts, is that not your responsibility as first mate?'

'I know they are deserting well enough, Captain Humphreys.'

Without another word Henry turned to us.

'Raise anchor and ready the sail.'

Several of the men were slow to move and seemed

torn between loyalty to King William and their desire for payment.

'Look lads,' Henry continued, 'I worked the slave routes for years. There's more gold across the seas than in all of Versailles and Windsor combined. These motherless swine have no intention of paying us, I say we go take it for ourselves. Follow me, and you'll be knee-deep in wine and women within the month. That's no idle boast. Now, man your bloody stations!'

That was all they needed to hear.

Within minutes of preparing to leave there was the loud splash of cannon from our starboard side. Captain Humphreys had fire several warning shots in the hope of quelling the rebellion. Instead, with the rising alarms from the night's watchmen in Corunna fading behind our stern, we made our exit under full sail to the middle of the dark, endless ocean.

'India's out best bet, the Mughal has more wealth than he knows what to do with.'

Having dropped off those men wanting no part in our venture shortly after fleeing Corunna, at a small inlet southwest from the port, attention now turned to the captain's promised fortunes. We huddled around the bridge listening to my friend's ideas. To his credit, Captain Every insisted upon voting for any major decisions, even though we all knew he was the one calling the shots now.

Part of me felt a deep guilt at running away from nearly sixteen years' service to the Admiralty. I owed my entire livelihood and many friendships to the navy. But, for all that, I had never felt so *alive* as when I stood on the bridge that day, the rain and wind lashing my skin.

I burst out laughing.

The captain and the entire crew turned at the sound of the interruption.

'I predict a terrible joke in our future, boys,' Henry Williams smirked.

'No, it's nothing like that. Something funny just came to mind, but it can wait until later.'

'Bollocks, you got something good let's hear it. God knows we could do with a laugh.'

After that I couldn't stop the words from flowing out.

'Well, it's just… most of you know of my problems with a certain prick of a captain by now. It was never much of a secret. I've been hoping to find him for years, ever since he tried to have me killed. But, here's the thing… I was trying to expose him as a traitor. Now I'm a fucking *pirate* because of it.'

The sense of irony was not lost on any of them.

After the laughter died down, it was Douglas who spoke next.

'He wis a bas anyhow, ah say we throw his limbs tae th' gulls.'

This broughts a cheer from the men, who, although still ravenous, were emboldened and full of vigour from the events of the last two days. An old quote from Alderman Samuel came to mind, from when he was instructing me in reading Julius Caesar's records from his Gallic campaigns:

Alea iacta est.

For better or worse, we had certainly emptied our entire bags of dice on to the table. Every ship in the fleet would be sure to open fire should we come into range. A good thing *Charles II* was the very definition of speed.

We would certainly need to think about that name though.

'One share of the treasure per man, two for the cap.'

With a strong trade wind at our backs and a decent meal in store for the evening, we all agreed upon the terms for any prize money. Every man stood to gain an equal share in the plunder, with the exception of the captain who received double as was only right.

We were still Englishmen, not a bunch of jumped-up Froglets.

'Just look at what Tew managed, we'll live like the bleedin' Pope.'

A round of cheers went up. Thomas Tew had vanished in recent months, but the tales of his exploits in the Red Sea were exactly what we needed to hear. Silks, spices, gold and every other type of opulence under the Sun had been taken from the Grand Mughal's fleets.

Later in the evening, over a meal of salted beef, bread and ale, the discussions turned to less immediate problems.

'How's bout the ship's name, captain?'

We all nodded our approval of the question. There was no way we would continue to sail under the name of the King of Spain.

'What do you think of the *Alice* then?'

I threw a small slice of meat at the captain. He dodged it, the sly bastard. It's a testament to just how hungry we were that one of the cook's mates didn't even hesitate to pick it up off the deck and wolf it down.

'I'll take that as a no… how about *Bloody Mary*?'

'Too Papist,' yelled a man with terrible, pock-marked cheeks from the back of the mess.

'Hmmm…'

'This is more difficult than I expected,' I said. 'We want something to strike fear into the likes of Melior or his Bible-thumping types. Trouble arrives ahead of us, all that sort of thing.'

'We could name the old girl the *Dagger* or *Sword*?'

'Oh, very creative, Mister Sunderland, did you think of those on your own?'

Guffaws went up as the next name was put forth by sheer accident.

'Jesus wept, but if this beef isn't straight from God's own herds then my name isn't Williams.'

The 'negotiator' washed down the large chunk with a portion of rum.

'Nothin' fancy mind you, but it gets the job done.'

'Wait...that's *it*,' the other Henry's eyes lit up. 'That's it!'

We all looked at one another as if we had missed the punchline to some grand jest.

'The *Fancy*,' he went on. 'We'll paint and dress the wench up worse than any ship on the seas. Cover her in gilding and every type of decoration we can lay our hands on. When we spot a prize, they'll know we're coming to screw them.'

The notion caught on like a house fire. Over the course of the next few days, as we began our long voyage towards the Cape of Good Hope and onward to India, we used whatever was at hand to paint or add a bit of gaudiness to the decks and masts. The name *Fancy* was written near the prow once the original had been covered up, and the sailor had done a fine job.

Make the men rich, bring them fully on our side, then we go after that son of a bitch James Melior.

The sense of Henry's words broke through my impatience to set sail for the Caribbean islands.

He was right.

The grudge was mine alone, albeit with the support of my three close friends, and most of the crew didn't have any direct interest in the matter. Nothing creates bonds like time spent at sea under hardship. A year from now, if things went well, we'd be chomping at the bit to help each other settle any debts. This was particularly true with the relaxation of rank and file. Sure, we still had our jobs to do, and a loose structure was in place, but our common brand as traitors reduced us to the same status.

Or, it perhaps uplifted us. That's a matter of perspective.

As I stood with my hands resting upon the port at midship thoughts of home and the future bounced around my head. Mostly, I hoped John and his family would forgive my choice if I should ever see them again. Thomas probably would, he was always one for getting in trouble. Then again, he had matured since the times we spent fishing on the Thames. Before a fresh wave of melancholy could take hold of my spirit, I ceased scratching at the gunwale and turned to resume my night's watch.

No luxuries for sailmakers on this ship.

As I passed by Douglas and thumped his arm, my anxious thoughts receded into the background. I was with friends and had a full stomach for the first time in what felt like years, which wasn't far off. Once we were laden with riches I was going to make sure our next port of call was the island of Jamaica.

I was going to get answers.

Epilogue

Lisbon, 1720 AD

The Englishman had been pleasantly surprised by the number of sailors awaiting in the yards below.

Once the port wine had run out entirely it had not taken long for him to rise from the small cot and agree to come downstairs. Baltasar das Chagas felt he had discharged his duties befitting a servant of *Santa Casa da Misericórdia* admirably, both in caring for the man's recovery and listening to stories from his younger days. The old shepherd blood still ran through Baltasar's limbs, and he appreciated a good tale on a blistery winter's evening.

Lewis was already talking with the twenty-odd sailors who had responded to the invitation earlier in the morning. His strange intonation and foreign lilt when speaking in Portuguese was easily understood. Indeed, one of the men prompted whether or not it was from spending time in *Brasil* and later Goa on the Indian coast.

All he received in response was a sly grin as Lewis tapped his nose.

The dark of evening had already settled upon Lisbon as they conversed. An alluring and secretive promise of wealth had ensured the men stayed put. Well, that and the excellent quality of stewed fish and white bread on offer from the nearby ovens. Baltasar later discovered his English friend had been generous in his contributions to the cook's own prosperity. Two guineas as if it was nothing.

What perplexed the lay-brother was were exactly Lewis seemed to come upon this endless supply of coin. He didn't carry about his person, that much was clear. All he had was a plain-looking wooden box and the humble clothes on his back. Where on Earth had he acquired the jewel-adorned shirt for Symao de Briho earlier in the day? When Lewis had arrived he had been found washed ashore by tw—

Wait.

Baltasar couldn't actually recall having *seen* the man carried in.

Now that he thought back to their first meeting, Lewis had not been particularly disheveled, save for a wispy beard, wet linen shirt and coarse trousers.

Dragons, corsairs, gifts from the courts of Europe…
It was an act.

Lewis caught his eye and smiled. How would he respond should he learn Baltasar was wise to his ploy? It was not as though he was any threat, if anything the entire situation was deeply intriguing. Did the old menace have some sort of stash or trove hidden away somewhere along the coast? For now Baltasar decided to keep his ideas to himself and see what the future held.

'Sturdy fellows, but then you Portuguese are the second-best mariners in the world, so I'm not surprised.'

'Let me guess who the best are… the French?'

'Now that's a low blow,' Lewis chuckled. 'Probably true though.'

The crew took quickly to his charms and easy manner. The same can be said for pretty much any trade, craft or calling; men, and women for that matter, from similar backgrounds tend to flock together. Familiarity breeds comfort whereas the unknown can be terrifying. Baltasar had known plenty of fisherman, dockyard workers or naval officers, all of whom helped keep the lifeblood of Portugal flowing into its coffers from distant lands. However, he felt out of place and uncomfortable as the Englishman chattered away with his countrymen.

Baltasar couldn't even swim, let alone rig a sail.

It had been a shock to hear such was the case for many sailors. They had told him the best way to avoid drowning is to stay out of the water. He had inquired after what happened should someone go overboard, but only ear-to-ear, devilish grins were given in answer.

'What's the matter?'

Lewis approached after settling a dispute over who had the most scars.

'Nothing, my friend,' replied Baltasar. 'I just feel rather like a painting on the wall.'

'You look more like a strip of leather which has seen better days.'

It was true, both men wore wind-battered faces with the texture of old gloves. Baltasar's features came from years spent on hillsides tending to flocks, but the result was very much the same. He was slightly stockier than the *Inglês* and a few years older, but both wore the signs of time's passage upon their brows.

'I'm sure, is there anything else I can do to assist with your recovery?'

'Oh come, don't be like that. I know you're curious about what I'm up to. No, don't try to deny it.'

Baltasar raised his hands in a gesture of surrender.

'I have a feeling there's more to your recent tale than nearly drowning at sea.'

'Took you long enough, when did you figure it out?'

'When you tossed those two gold pieces to the cook. I

hadn't really thought about it much until that moment, but between the trade to Symao and your treatment of the staff I think you must have some secret lair hereabouts.'

Lewis poked him in the chest.

'You make me sound like some sort of *bucaneiro* or the like.'

'Well, judging from where we left your story, can you blame me?'

'I suppose not. Let me ask you something, Baltasar das Chagas, are you happy here?'

He had been pulled away from the gathering of sailors to one side. A few of them glanced over, but Lewis told them he just needed a moment with the good *friar* to settle his accounts. While reflecting on the seemingly random question they pulled up a couple of chairs across from a cask of port wine.

Was he happy here? It was an easier life than selling fleece in his youth, but…

In his years of working in the capital, Baltasar had never truly considered his own contentment.

෨

'So, there you have it.'

Baltasar's mouth dropped.

'Do the men know?'

'Not as of yet, I was going to wait until I see this galleon from dear Symao first. No point moving on with the plan if it's a bucket of rust.'

As if through divine grace one of the merchant's staff appeared from the small alley leading into the yard. It had not taken much time for Symao to arrange for a galleon to be made ready for his client, but that was hardly surprising given the trader's grand reputation at court.

Now that Baltasar had discovered the purpose behind the request, he just hoped the old crook had been discreet in gathering the requested items.

It was a fair walk to the wharf, and, by the time everyone had finished trailing in at different paces, Baltasar was frozen to the bone. He was wearing his thickest woolen coat and an extra blanket wrapped around his shoulders. Lewis, along with the combination of local fishermen, naval seamen and traders, did their best to feign indifference to the weather. One man's chattering teeth gave him away.

'Thirty-odd guns, yes, this should do nicely.'

The galleon sat with a full compliment of cannon and shot. Symao must have either been feeling uncharacteristically charitable, or he had already received a sum of money from the man now ushering the men to step closer.

'Enough water and victuals for 2 months, judging from the letter.'

Lewis held up a piece of cream-white paper in his hand.

'We must be sure to thank the city guilds for being so forthcoming with supplies.'

It dawned on Baltasar that his friend had been planning this for quite some time on his own terms. The morning's trip across the *Praça do Rossio* had not been urgent or due to any physical weakness.

Lewis just didn't want to get out of bed.

'Two months ago, a dear friend of mine by the name of John was strung up for thievery, his mistress pregnant at the time. He was a good man, well no… he was a bastard, but we got on well. John was always one to share any prizes, and he made many a rich man.'

The mention of wealth had the intended effect.

'My expedition, as it were,' continued Lewis, 'is to set out to rendezvous with three other ships already at sea and raid the waters along the coast of the Americas down to Hispaniola. I have a bone to pick with the man responsible for his death when we stop off in Port Royal.'

A few looks of concern showed on the faces of the potential mates, but he was quick to assuage them.

'Not as pirates, mind, but as *privateers* this time around. Ah, here she comes now.'

Everyone turned to follow Lewis' gaze.

Coming down the wharf was a young man in his early twenties, a heavy-looking satchel thrown over his shoulder. Baltasar watched in confusion as the slender youth huffed and placed the bag upon the dock.

'Pleasure's mine, I'm sure.'

It wasn't a man at all. A young woman stood before them, out of breath and hair hanging unfurled from beneath her woolen cap. Then, her composure restored, she turned quickly on her heel and punched Lewis right in the jaw.

He just shook it off and returned the smack, granted it was to her shoulder.

'Good to see you, Annie,' he said. 'You have everything we'll be needing?'

She pointed a thumb at the heavy sack.

'Well done, girl. I always knew John had a keen sense for getting a crew together. I was just telling these useless dogs about my letter of pardon from Governor Rogers.'

'I'm going to rip his eyes out with my bare hands,' she growled. 'You can't be serious, Frobisher. Tell me you haven't become some soft, pathetic worm of a man.'

'Oh, my dear, you misunderstand. I'm a snake, not a worm. Just because I have a pardon and accompanying letter of marque doesn't mean we can't be... *selective* in our prizes, eh?'

'Thank God,' the red-haired Annie sighed aloud. 'I take it you want to head out within the week? We'd be better waiting for this weather to ease up. Captain Roberts expects us before January.'

'Aye, it's been far too many years since I've settled a score. What say we see to this lot and who's worth having aboard, then go catch up over a hot meal? My friend here Baltasar will be paying, naturally.'

Before the man could object, one of the others interrupted.

'That's all well and good, but what's in it for us?'

'That's an easy question. Good French wine, Spanish gold and whatever else we come across. Double shares to the crew, four to the captain.'

Baltasar tried to suppress a laugh. If any of the assembled crew knew their figures, they kept it to themselves. A clever move by Lewis. A double share always sounded good, but traders had tried to pull similar wool over his eyes at markets in the past.

The guffaw escaped his lips as he realised his own play on words.

'Oh no need to laugh, *Senhor das Chagas*, I was hoping you might come along as Ship's Surgeon.'

'I... I'm need at the hospital, and in any case, I'm no real surgeon, I have just trained enough to feed soup to the starving and change bandages.'

'Men, raise your hand if you're a surgeon.'

No one did.

'That settles it then,' Lewis said, clearly enjoying the

attention and hitting his stride. 'Besides, you know Martim and the rest can manage well-enough without you. The same can't be said for us.'

Baltasar didn't have time to refuse or delay. The promise of coin had won over more than fifteen of the men, and they were already treating him like a respected officer.

'Let me think,' he said without conviction. 'Who's the poor soul you need to *talk* with anyway? In Port Royal, I mean.'

'Oh, about John's hanging? That's the beauty of it, my friend. Woodes Rogers, the governor who gave me these pardons, is the man I intend to pay a visit when we reach the West Indies.'

'We've been over this,' Annie spoke with a cold edge to her voice, belying her youth. After a long breath, she continued her objection.

'When we next see the toad who hanged Jack Rackham, I want him to know it was Anne Bonny who ran him through.'

Author's Note

This book has gone on a voyage of its own, much like Lewis Frobisher and his colourful associates. In my earliest days of planning the storyboard or characters life was fairly easy. We went to work at libraries or any number of public places without so much as a thought. I would spend hours in the libraries of London pouring over other writers' works in historical fiction, while many of my friends would go about their daily affairs in the hope of a pint or game of trivia at the local on Friday night.

Once I felt comfortable with the overall narrative, I began to sit down and put 'pen to paper' in both the literal and metaphorical sense. Several chapters were drawn up in their first drafts. Life was good. I spent time visiting family and friends, with the giddy anticipation of publishing my first work. A sixth chapter was completed, then a seventh.

Unfortunately, the theme of plans going awry for Mister Frobisher also holds true to real life.

In the winter of 2019, the world changed in ways very few people had ever expected. Suddenly and with little warning, libraries were closed. No more could I venture to archives or scenic locations for inspiration. Instead, I was locked away in my room for months at a time. Visiting family or friends began to feel like a distant memory and forlorn hope. My desire to write oscillated between fever pitches and weeks of utter melancholy.

Stress levels reached an all-time high, as family, friends and neighbours tried their best to adapt to the new set of circumstances. (If I ever hear the term 'new normal' again, I will explode with more rage than a broadside from *L'Invincible*). The next two years brought challenges of their own, but I did my utmost to stay the course. Finally, in the late-winter of 2020, the first draft was finished in its entirety. By the spring of 2021 the various phases of editing had completed and *Lion Fangs* was ready for submission. It was as much a journey of discovery for the author as it hopefully is for the reader. My shift from Word to Scrivener proved to be a success, and I could never imagine going back. I engaged with other writers across a number of platforms, many of whom I have to thank for their emotional support during particularly bleak periods, and I developed a network of like-minded friends. On that note, I want to get into some acknowledgements, followed by a few comments regarding my use of artistic license.

First and foremost, I need to thank my family for their continual support throughout the entire process. My Mum (or *Mom*, for my American readers) has always been a bastion of strength and support in my life. I quite literally would not have been able to see this book to completion without her ongoing love and care. I hope she knows I feel the same way about her, and I think she does. If there was ever a woman to wear a 'world's best Mum' t-shirt without it being overly-boastful, it would be her. Just don't ask her to eat porridge or green peas.

My Dad is a very special human being. He's always shown me the same devotion and love, and would give someone the shirt off his back if it meant they wouldn't go cold. He's always been there for trips and time spent together, and I have hundreds of fond photographs from over the many years. His partner in crime Leanne has always been a good laugh as well, and I'm glad the two of them get along so well. That being said, how any man can have such a keen grasp for history, yet lose every single thing he comes into contact with, is beyond me.

Last but certainly not least (these paragraphs could be shuffled in any order) I want to thank my brother Colin, his wife Ashton and their beautiful baby pipsqueak. Angus gets my love as well, with his cheeky face. They have always been there for me to chat with about the latest games, movies, shows or sports back home. I am always glad to hear from them and to catch up. Colin and I share many hobbies and interests in common, so it's one of my great joys in life to discuss such things with him.

Finally, I want to thank my friends, both locals and those who now live around the world, for their ongoing support. I won't mention any names, but you know who you are. I'm pretty sure you will realise which characters are based on you as well. I'd also like to thank the staff at the various museums around Greenwich, the British Museum, British Library, Institute for Historical Research, Museum of London, Putney Library and Scrivener's support team for their never-ending assistance. This first book in a planned trilogy is the culmination of many people and their efforts, not just my own. Osprey Publishing has been a great source of information regarding equipment and gear. Also, Kindle Direct Publishing has been excellent when answering any concerns about formatting or distribution.

With that out of the way, we can turn to some of the potential discrepancies in the work or decisions I made to apply artistic license. I'm sure for some readers they will be interested to hear the thought process behind my choices.

I want to start off by saying right off the bat this is not an academic work.

I spent many years engaging with university conferences across a number of degrees, but this was never intended to be '*A Modern Re-evaluation of Iron Bollard Guilds in the Golden Age of Piracy, c. 1679 to 1720 CE.*' Yes, doctoral theses do have such ridiculous names. Take my word for it.

Rather, I wanted this book to be entertaining. After years spent in dusty archives and being forced to cite dozens of reference per page, I wrote this story with the aim of building interesting characters and events. The overall historical context required a significant amount of research. However, I was not going on flights to conferences around Europe to uncover the most up-to-date academic views on the *minutiae* of seventeenth-century life. Nevertheless, there were a few things I either played around with to enhance the narrative, or elements I added to fill in gaps in the historical or archaeological records. I will try to cover the main ones below (I apologise in advance for any I have let slip through my notes).

My Dad may be sitting scratching his head about the Battle of the Boyne being described as having taken place on the 1st of July, 1690. The ceremonies surrounding 'The Twelfth' are well-known, celebrating (often at the ire of certain other groups) the victory of 'King Billy' over the deposed James II. But, at the time of Lewis' storytelling to Baltasar, England had not adopted the more recent Gregorian calendar. Instead, they were still using the Julian calendar (the 'Old Style' or O.S.) and the dates reflect this point. For example, the

Battle of Beachy Head took place on the 10th of July, 1690, according to modern sources, but under the Old Style it is dated to the 30th of June, 1690, eleven days earlier. I decided to list dates using the calendar system which was in use at the time of Lewis' recollections on his sick bed in Lisbon.

Another area where I filled in some of the gaps was concerning the paint schemes and designs of *HMS Lion* after her various refits. (Also, you may have noticed I avoided using the abbreviation 'HMS' in the book, due to it being anachronistic). We have excellent records concerning the armament and load-outs of the various updates to the *Lion,* but specifics concerning her various colour schemes are less certain. The same goes for her captains. Both Henry Williams and John Torpley were documented with their terms of service on record, but James Melior is a creature entirely of my own making.

Several characteristics from the disgraced Captain Charles Skelton were fused with those of Melior into a single figure. Walter Crouch was based upon one William Crouch who served as a second lieutenant. Another liberty I took was with the length of time the *Lion* spent patrolling and at station in the Narrow Sea/English Channel; the truth is such records are largely non-existent in the late-seventeenth century. I aimed to include Beachy Head and events where her position in the fleet was recorded, but others such as the brief skirmish with 'Ali Reis' were fictional. For those who are perhaps concerned the corsairs felt like a stepping stone to the larger battle, don't worry. You haven't seen the last of the Barbary States.

Many records are sparse prior to the Royal Navy's true

'coming of age' in the eighteenth century, and I tried to keep the overall context accurate with appropriate surnames, towns of origins etc. Henry Every will no doubt be familiar to an fan of swashbuckling tales, and I have tried to maintain the details of his life while filling in the gaps with narratives of my own. The same can be said for Thomas Coram, who is soon to be living in the colonies when our story continues, which is where his historical record starts to become less uncertain. As for the Coram family, they are largely unknown in the records and I tried to create a feasible scenario for his going off to sea while coming from a humble upbringing.

There are also hints of my own family in the Corams, but with a few dashes of other people thrown into the pot. I look forward to hearing them guess. The big reveal at the end of the epilogue needs no introduction; Calico Jack and Anne Bonny were two of the most infamous pirates ever to sail the high seas. The fact she disappeared following her pardon presented a golden opportunity for my own designs. Several others were hinted at throughout the chapters, but all in good time.

Another key point to clarify is the idea of naval ranks and the hierarchy of command. In truth, many of the positions mentioned did not fully come into regular use until the eighteenth century. They were largely applied for clarity of purpose and to help the reader understand the level of complexity behind keeping such massive warships at sail. In the earliest days of the *Navy Royal* under the Stuarts, three ranks were formally used aboard ship: Captain, lieutenant and master. The master was primarily responsible for the sailing and upkeep of the vessel, whereas the two former ranks were of a military heritage.

Of course, with the House of Orange and later House of Hanover the stereotypical image of the navy began to emerge in earnest. Strangely, the early Admiralty seems to have developed many of its layers of rank and command from a relatively early period. My reasoning behind the decision was to distinguish roles aboard ship for the development of characters, and also down to logic; even without formal ranks the crews would have had a 'sailmaker', a 'surgeon' and so on. The role of the midshipman as a sort of officer-in-training emerged in the 1750s, but men performing similar roles while under sail existed in earlier decades.

Lastly, I have used locales such as the Pool of London, Saint Olave's or Cripplegate with the intent to be historically accurate. Any fictional spots (The Swan is a good guess in Putney, but undocumented from what I gathered) have been portrayed with the hope of fitting their surroundings. Guillaume and his inn on Guernsey, *La Belle Fleur*, is a prime example. Pubs, short for public houses, were not common until the nineteenth century in England. As a result, I have tried to build the image of coaching inns, taverns and alehouses in their place.

Grog is another anachronistic term which I chose to include. It is essentially just watered-down rum rations, but the actual term did not become commonplace until its nineteenth-century introduction by Vice-Admiral Edward Vernon. Apparently the name was a shortened form for *Old Grogram* in reference to the type of cloth he tended to wear. Such records are disputed and could very well be unsubstantiated, but it makes for a fun story at any rate.

My final note regarding artistic license is in the naming of Henry Every's famous ship. It is unclear why he chose the name, and I was picturing the scene in my mind. For some reason the idea of meagre rations of beef and 'nothing fancy' came to mind as his source of inspiration. As to whether or not any such decorations occurred, it's unlikely.

Then again, these are pirates we're talking about.

C.A. Fitzroy, 2021.

Printed in Great Britain
by Amazon